SINGLE
SEEKS REVENGE

Tracy Bloom started writing when her cruel, heartless husband ripped her away from her dream job shopping for rollercoasters for the UK's leading theme parks, to live in America with a brand-new baby and no mates. Determined to see it as an opportunity, she turned to her love of words and comedy and started to write *No-One Ever Has Sex on a Tuesday*. It went on to be successfully published internationally and topped the Amazon bestseller list in 2013 as well as being awarded the Best Author Published Read at the Festival of Romance 2013. So now Tracy is chuffed to bits to have a new dream job, making people laugh and sometimes cry through her writing. Back in good old England now with the husband who is forgiven and two children who create mayhem around her, as she cracks on with creating other stories about people who screw up their lives in a hilarious fashion.

TRACY BLOOM

SINGLE WOMAN SEEKS REVENGE

arrow books

Published by Arrow Books 2015

2 4 6 8 10 9 7 5 3 1

First published in Great Britain in 2013 as an ebook

Arrow Books
Random House, 20 Vauxhall Bridge Road,
London SW1V 2SA

www.randomhouse.co.uk

Addresses for companies within The Random House Group Limited can be
found at: www.randomhouse.co.uk/offices.htm

The Random House Group Limited Reg. No. 954009

A CIP catalogue record for this book
is available from the British Library

ISBN 9780099594765

Typeset by SX Composing DTP Ltd, Rayleigh, Essex
Printed and bound by CPI Group (UK) Ltd, Croydon, CR0 4YY

For Mum and Dad
Singing from the same hymn sheet for over forty-five years,
for which I will be forever grateful

Chapter 1

Dear Suzie,

  I have never written to an agony aunt before but there's no-one else I can talk to about this. You see, my husband left six months ago for someone ten years younger than me who he met at a spinning class. Completely devastated, I turned to food for comfort and quickly gained twenty pounds. Then, a couple of weeks ago, he turned up out of the blue on the doorstep saying he was ready to come home on one condition, that I become more adventurous in bed. He left me with a list of what he had in mind, much of which included certain S&M practices that I had to research on the internet to even understand what they were. I love him so much and I'm desperate to have him back, but they don't do the PVC outfit he is suggesting in a size 18. What should I do?

Yours desperately,
Trish

Dear Trish,

Buy the PVC outfit in a size 10 along with some handcuffs and a blowtorch. Call your husband and tell him you will comply with all his demands and you want him to come over straight away. When he arrives, tell him that you have one condition: he must wear the PVC outfit and then you will do whatever he wants. When he's got it on, handcuff him to the bed, then whip out the blowtorch, turn the gas to maximum and ask him what parts of his anatomy he wants burnt off first. Then tell the low-life never, ever to bother you again – you stupid, stupid, stupid . . .

Suzie didn't realise she was banging her head against the computer screen muttering the word 'stupid', over and over again, until Drew gently took hold of her shoulders and pulled her back until she was sitting upright.

'Control, Alt, Delete normally works better than headbutting,' he said as he sat down at his desk next to her and started flicking the switches necessary for him to be able to start his working day.

Suzie was vaguely aware that her breathing was laboured and she was gripping the edge of her desk. Oddly, the office of the *Manchester Herald* newspaper appeared to be humming normally around her despite the fact that she felt anything but normal. She was a Jenga stack on the brink of collapse, just waiting for someone to take out the wrong block.

'You okay?' asked Drew, interrupting the ferocious tapping on his keyboard and peering round to look at her stricken face.

Block extracted. Concern shown by colleague. Collapse imminent.

'Why?' she growled, trying desperately to contain her voice when all she felt like doing was screaming. 'Why am I writing this stupid, bloody agony column?'

'Er, because you suggested it?'

'I know I suggested it,' she said, her face starting to flame up. 'But I was joking – I didn't mean it. If Gareth

3

thinks this is going to bring back our female readers he's an idiot, and he's even more of an idiot for asking me to do it.'

'But you have such experience in relationships,' drawled Drew.

She turned to face him. What on earth made him think that sarcasm would be appropriate in this conversation?

'Really. So that's why at the grand old age of thirty-six I'm alone again, is it?' She grasped one of the several toy trolls lined up on her desk and began pulling violently at its electric-blue hair.

'What's happened this time?' asked Drew with a sigh. He turned towards her and assumed his listening position – a way too familiar sight during the five years that he had occupied the desk next to her, always in the direct firing line of her relationship traumas. Arms crossed, he painted his best *you're-an-idiot-for-putting-up-with-all-this-bullshit* look on his face before glancing down to check his watch. She knew she didn't have long until he pointed out that he had a deadline to meet, so she quickly picked up her phone in order to present him with the facts.

'I got this text from Alex ten minutes after he left

my flat this morning.' She thrust the phone into his hand.

Drew rapidly scanned the message: 'SORRY SUZE BUT THIS ISN'T WORKING OUT FOR ME. LET'S CALL IT A DAY WHILST WE CAN STILL BE FRIENDS AND IT DOESN'T GET AWKWARD AT WORK. ALEX XX'.

'Oh dear,' he said, not looking the slightest bit surprised or sympathetic.

'And . . . and . . .' Suzie continued, fighting off tears, 'we had sex before he left.'

There was an awkward pause as Drew took this in. Finally he muttered under his breath, 'Bastard!' Then he sighed again, unfolded his arms and put his hands on his knees. 'You can do so much better than him,' he offered. 'Just forget about Alex and have patience that someone better will come along.'

'I'm thirty-six, Drew. I don't need patience, I need Botox,' announced Suzie as she pulled a chunk of blue hair out of the troll's head. 'And it's all very well for you to say when you're engaged to the love of your life and not walking around with TWAT MAGNET tattooed on your forehead like I am.' She threw the tortured troll to the floor in fury.

Drew started to speak, but Suzie had things to get off her chest that would wait for no-one.

'I've had enough,' she interrupted, grabbing another troll off her desk, this one dressed in a football kit. 'Look at this – my first ever true love bought me this when we were fifteen, then he dumped me in front of all his mates and told me I was boring.' She let go of the troll and watched it bounce twice on the desk before falling to the floor, next to the partially bald, blue-haired troll loitering by the rubbish bin. 'And as for this one' – she held up yet another troll, this time with bright yellow hair – 'I found him in bed with one of my best friends after we'd been together for ten years.' She dispensed with the desk this time and sent it straight into free fall to join the sorry-looking duo on the floor. 'And this one,' – she brandished a Spanish-guitar-playing troll – 'well, let's just say his life was a lot more complicated than he led me to believe . . .' She trailed off, unable to look Drew in the eye. Amigo troll landed head first on top of footie troll and stayed there as if they were practising position of the fortnight.

'Those trolls are for every boyfriend you've ever had?' asked Drew. 'And I thought you just had terrible taste in executive toys.'

'They're not for every boyfriend I ever had,' she protested.

Drew raised his eyebrows.

'Just the ones I fell in love with.' She bit down hard on her lip, willing her eyes not to spill.

They both stared at her broken-heart graveyard grinning gormlessly back up at them from their bed of dull green nylon carpet.

'Why?' asked Drew, shaking his head in disbelief.

Suzie knew there were no words that could convince the all too rational Drew that her kooky collection was anywhere near sane. She sighed and felt her whole body sag as she resigned herself to the fact that she was about to sound exactly like the desperate middle-aged woman she was fast becoming. 'Because I need something to remind me after twenty long years of dating that there have been at least some moments of love in my life,' she said, bracing herself for an onslaught of meaningless sympathy. She should have known better.

'But Suzie, you just said what twats they all were to you, to quote you in your own words.'

She looked back down at the troll pile-up on the floor. Drew was right. She'd read in some magazine that she should be positive about her past significant relationships, remember the good times and learn from the bad, but maybe it was time to see them for what they really were – a horrifying reminder of the men who'd carved her romantic history into the disaster it was.

Between them they had ruined her one and only love life.

'Bastards,' she said, giving them a half-hearted kick with one of her deadly black stilettos, part of the man-trap uniform she was forced to wear given her ongoing unmarried status.

'Oh for God's sake,' said Drew, his patience all used up. 'You can do better than that. If they were all standing in front of you now, what would you do?'

If they were all actually here, in the flesh? She flinched at the thought. Memories of horrific mourning periods came flooding back. Hours spent trying to work out where it had all gone wrong. Desperate attempts to get them back, usually during lonely taxi rides home at the end of fruitless Saturday nights out when she was powerless to stop her fingers sending drunken, shame-lessly begging texts. All ignored, of course, which stirred up the misery until it escalated into fury, and dreams of retaliation and revenge for what they had put her through. A wave of regret threatened her with either sorrow or anger. She chose anger.

'I'd want to make them suffer like they made me suffer,' she spat out, hands clenched around her chair arms. 'Like I should have done at the time. Too late now.' Everything was too late recently. Ever since she'd decided she was on the fast track to forty, it was too late to get married, too late to have kids and too late to make a career change and extract herself from the slow and painful death of local newspaper journalism. Fatally she'd started to look back and consider how she'd arrived at this point in her life. Unmarried, no kids and writing a ridiculous agony column for a local rag. If only she could go back and do things differently.

'Not too late for Alex, though,' said Drew, interrupting her thoughts. 'I've heard it time and again. You let them get away with treating you like dirt, Suzie. For once just tell him exactly what you think of him and move on. Then ditch this ridiculous troll thing.'

Susie stared at him for a moment before picking up the partially bald blue-haired troll.

'You're right,' she said finally. 'He can't get away with treating me like that. I'm going to give him a piece of my mind.'

'Now that's the first sensible thing you've said all morning.'

'I'll text him.' She picked up her phone. 'What should I put?'

'Don't text him.' Drew grabbed the phone back. 'Confront him. Call him a dickhead to his face, for goodness' sake. It makes you as bad as him, just texting him.'

'Okay,' said Suzie. Icy nerves threatened the bravado she'd built up only moments earlier. 'I'll tell him to his face. Of course I will.'

'Good. As soon as he comes in. No running off to cry in the toilets.'

'Of course not,' said Suzie, trying to sound more confident than she felt. 'As soon as I see him I'll give it to him straight.'

'Excellent.' Drew turned back to face his computer, his hands poised over the keyboard. 'Now I've got to inject some enthusiasm into a story about our rubbish bin service in Manchester. I suggest you find something equally exciting to focus on.' With that he began typing furiously, relationship consultation clearly over.

By three p.m. Alex had still failed to make an appearance, no doubt out schmoozing potential advertisers in an excuse to buy lunch on expenses. Suzie had spent the day nervously glancing at the corridor behind her, see-sawing between desperation to see him and dread at how she would react. She tried to focus on finishing her agony column, due in that afternoon, but couldn't seem to summon up the words to soothe the downhearted when she was in such a state herself. She had just started reading the angry reply she'd written that morning to Trish's problem when Drew tapped her on the shoulder.

'You're on,' he said, nodding over her shoulder.

'What?' she shrieked. She sat frozen, unable to look round, staring nervously at Drew as a familiar jaunty whistle came floating across the office. When Drew nudged her arm she forced herself to turn her head slowly in the direction of the corridor. Wearing an immaculate navy suit, the very expensive shirt and tie she'd bought him for his birthday and wafting an all too familiar smell of heady aftershave, Alex was striding along at a confident speed. He immediately caught Suzie staring at him, flicked her a casual wave, then walked straight past her in the direction of the meeting room.

Suzie's shaking hand hovered in mid-air and her mouth twitched into a weak smile. She stared after him in a daze.

'What was *that*?' cried Drew. 'Go on, go after him now! Tell him – I know you can do it.'

She turned her head to meet his incredulous gaze.

'I can't,' she whispered, shaking her head slowly.

'Why not?'

'Because . . .' She looked away in shame. 'Because . . .' she tried again, knowing she was about to look ridiculous.

'Please don't say what I think you're going to say,' pleaded Drew.

'Because I love him,' she blurted, unable to look up and endure Drew's reaction. What was she supposed to do when she'd been ambushed the minute she'd set eyes on Alex? All the anger and hurt had been kicked into touch by a full-on attack of longing and desire.

At last she lifted her head and saw a look of total bewilderment on Drew's face. How could she make him understand? She couldn't even explain it to herself.

'Sorry,' she muttered, rising unsteadily to her feet and reaching for her coat. She couldn't bear to look at Drew's disbelief any longer. She knew he was right, but the fact was, she loved Alex, and an angry confrontation over an entirely unacceptable, unceremonious dumping was simply beyond her. What she needed was to be alone so she could conduct a moody post-mortem to work out exactly where she had gone wrong and, more importantly, whether she could do anything about it.

Chapter 2

Dear Trish,

I envy you, I really do. Your husband clearly still loves you or else he wouldn't be offering to come home and recreate what you once had by playing out his sexual fantasies, would he?

Of course you shouldn't do anything that makes you feel uncomfortable, but I suggest you sit down and talk to him and agree what you are both happy with. I must also point out that PVC is not flattering to the fuller figure but I can recommend Marks & Spencer's thongs, generally available in a size 18, along with matching large-cup-size bras. I would also recommend

that you attend a spinning class with your husband,
but maybe choose a different gym this time.

Take this chance, Trish, because if you really love
someone they are worth fighting for.

Good luck.

Suzie

Sitting on the bus, desperately mulling over her relationship with Alex, Suzie had suddenly realised that she was about to miss the four o'clock deadline to submit her agony column. She only had to finish the reply to Trish's problem but she now knew how ill-advised her initial response had been. The last thing Trish needed was to be told to take a blowtorch to her husband. The poor woman had a chance at rekindling her love, and you had to make the most of your chances. Trish needed encouragement, not to have her hopes shot down in flames. She tapped out a revised response on her phone and forwarded it to the office just in time, hoping she'd told Trish what she needed to help save her relationship.

No longer distracted by the task in hand, she gazed through the toddler-snot-obscured windows of the bus at the grey, dripping streets of Manchester and wondered what on earth she could do about her own love life.

Gloom engulfed her as they hissed to a stop outside the brightly lit windows of McDonald's and she did what she always did at this point on her journey home. She couldn't help herself. She looked over to the table in the corner of the left-hand window and relived the moment when Alex had first kissed her.

It had been all of six months ago, at the end of one of the happiest days of her life. After all, you don't often get to pull the man at the top of your list, do you? Number five, maybe, if you're really lucky, but a number one – when does that happen? She and her best mate Jackie had started doing TFLPBs (Top Five Lists of Possible Boyfriends) way back in their teens, mostly so that they could laugh hysterically at one another's taste in men (although Jackie never found it funny that Suzie had given Rick Astley a run at number one for eighteen weeks). Jackie no longer needed a list, being happily ensconced in her second marriage, but Suzie still had one, updating in her head almost as regularly as the London Stock Exchange. It was her security blanket, essential to reassure herself that she hadn't yet reached the bottom of the dating pit. Sadly she had been forced to make it more realistic as the years passed by. Famous people had fallen by the wayside in her twenties, highly attractive men were struck off in her early thirties and now, quite frankly, her list mostly consisted of men who were single and didn't repulse her. This was why Alex had been such a revelation. A single man, in his thirties, and absolutely gorgeous. He'd gone straight to the top of her list when he'd arrived at the paper at the beginning of the year to head up the sales and advertising team.

She'd tried not to stalk him like a love-struck teenager, but if she happened to go to lunch at the same time as him, then so be it. She had to talk to him; she couldn't just ignore him. And for some reason she genuinely drank more coffee on the days he worked in the office, which meant she had to make more trips to the kitchen – coincidentally opposite his desk.

In the end she had Gareth the new editor to thank for getting them together. He had gathered them all into a room on his first day and demanded they each come up with at least three ideas to boost sales of the struggling paper. When she'd flippantly suggested an agony column he'd pounced on it.

'Brilliant!' he said, flashing his best thirty-year-old-hotshot-Londoner smile at her. 'Particularly as the dating section on the website currently gets more hits than your entire Lifestyle section,' he'd continued cuttingly. 'I want it in by next week. Liaise with Alex on what advertisers it can bring in – Viagra, Tampax, whatever – just make it pay.'

'You work on the content, baby, I'll bring Durex,' Alex had whispered that night during an extensive and drunken post-mortem of the new editor in the pub with the rest of the team. Later he told her they needed to discuss the new column at length and could they do it in McDonald's, because he was starving.

As she staggered after him through Piccadilly, she told herself sternly that going to a fast food restaurant after a works drink did not constitute a date. However, she couldn't help but feel some excitement at the romantic potential of sitting next to him alone in a restaurant – even if they were surrounded by obese teenagers and anorexic-looking tramps.

She could still taste that first kiss: cheese, with a hint of gherkin.

After he'd satisfied his appetite, to her absolute astonishment, he'd pulled her onto his knee in that very window and snogged her face off.

She could picture them now giggling like naughty schoolchildren, oblivious to their abusive audience.

'I think you're lovely,' he'd said when they finally

came up for breath, and a table of spotty youths had cheered.

She was practically swooning as a chorus of 'Give 'er one for me!' came from the next table.

'I'd like to,' Alex had whispered in her ear and she'd swooned again.

She'd taken him home to bed, of course. She really didn't see why not. She'd been stalking him for a few months, so why waste time? And time was something she didn't have the luxury of anyway. Long courtships were for twenty-somethings. Post thirty, you had to cut corners to find out fast whether he was going to be in it for the long haul. Delaying sex until after they'd dated a while was an indulgence she couldn't afford.

Luckily their post McDonald's consummation marked the start of a beautiful relationship and not a drunken shag between colleagues never to be repeated. It was with great delight that she had rung Jackie to announce that she was dating a number one off her list of possible boyfriends, an absolute first. Nearly twenty years it had taken her to bag a list leader. Now, finally, here she was, convinced it meant that he was the man she had been waiting for all her life to live happily ever after with.

'Calm down,' Jackie had said. 'I know what you're like. You fall in love and you stop seeing sense. You watch way too many of those stupid romantic comedies. As I've told you time and again, stop at the bit where it all goes wrong. They're much more realistic that way.'

But this time she was convinced it was different. She was so happy she almost felt like she could be Meg Ryan. (Before plastic surgery, obviously. And before all the dodgy stuff with Russell Crowe. Really, what was she thinking?) Still, it had felt like they were on a fairy-tale roll. One month in and they were going out together every Friday and Saturday night. Two months in and he was spending every weekend at her flat. Three months in and they had embarrassing pet names for each other. Four months in and there was talk of love as they giggled under the duvet. Five months in and he'd taken her to his mum and dad's ruby wedding party. She'd met his parents, for goodness' sake – surely he knew what that implied? And now six months in and they'd gone from all that to a casual parting text. It didn't make sense. She had to be missing something.

An insistent beep from her phone interrupted her thoughts. She felt her heart leap into her mouth as her head instantly filled with the naked hope that it was

Alex trying to get in touch to tell her it was all a mistake. Her fingers tripped over themselves in the scramble to open the text, then her heart sank painfully as she saw Drew's name at the bottom of the message, a terse reminder that under no circumstances should she attempt any pleading communication with Alex during her post-break-up misery.

She knew that Drew only had her best interests at heart, but he didn't really understand what it was like to be her. He'd had his anchor for so long he didn't remember what it was like to be floating adrift, completely untethered. She had to call Alex. She owed it to herself at least to find out why he'd ended it. After all, it could be something utterly trivial, which could be mended immediately. She couldn't let them fall apart for the sake of one stupid phone call.

For the first time that day she felt a glimmer of hope as the bus pulled up to her stop. She retrieved her umbrella from the mud-soaked floor and made her way to the front. Hope was some relief at least.

Unfortunately, hope took a knock the minute she walked through her front door. As if on autopilot, she glanced down at the shoe rack. Alex had taken to leaving his footie boots there so he didn't have to race home every Sunday morning to pick them up on his way to a match. She'd moved her never-used trainers to be next to them, delighted by the vision of harmony. The boots were gone, a few flecks of mud remaining like ashes on the floor. She dropped her bag and sprinted upstairs to the bathroom. His toothbrush, mini aftershave and deodorant were gone too. He'd cold-bloodedly packed his belongings that morning then shut the door behind him, already knowing it was the last time he was going to be in the flat.

She trudged back downstairs in a daze, desperately trying to make sense of it all. Heading for the kitchen in search of caffeine and something hideously fattening, she was stopped in her tracks at the doorway. She gasped, devastated by the scene that lay before her. Her gaze wandered over the embers of her last evening with Alex, stacked messily on the kitchen counter in front of her.

Two empty bottles of red wine.

The end crust of a French stick.

A congealed cheese-fondue pot.

Half a dozen uneaten mince pies.

Two burnt-down candles erupting down two old wine bottles.

Two dirty glasses. One with lipstick marks. Hers. One with greasy finger marks. His.

One broken coffee mug.

It was the broken coffee mug that made her want to curl up into a ball and weep. Less than twenty-four hours earlier, Alex had knocked it to the ground in a fit of passion, his hands all over her body making her giggle and gasp before she surrendered and allowed herself to be led to the bedroom. They'd had possibly their best sex yet, fuelled by the euphoria of Alex telling her he wanted to spend Christmas with her and her family.

She'd been so nervous about asking him. But as she kept telling herself, all the evidence suggested that she wasn't entering dangerous territory. They spent all their time together, she'd met his entire family and she was on piss-taking terms with his mates. Even so, she'd tried hard to be ultra-casual to avoid putting any pressure on him to say yes.

'So Mum's cooking Christmas dinner this year,' she'd said whilst pouring him some wine. 'D'you fancy coming?'

He'd looked at her for a moment then smiled and declared, 'I'd love to,' before lunging at her and knocking the coffee mug clean to the floor.

Her mind had wandered to a place she hadn't dared

visit for some time: vivid images of roaring fires and twinkling fairy lights and Alex handing over the perfect gifts to all her family before he produced an extra special gift. A small box hidden in the Christmas tree containing a . . .

She groaned and wrapped her arms tightly around herself, realising what an idiot she'd been. She'd gone too quickly for him, it was obvious. She'd asked him for Christmas and scared him off. It was okay for her to meet his family but it was clearly a step too far for him to meet hers. He'd panicked and that's why he'd ended it. She'd made a stupid mistake. Why oh why had she asked him? Why couldn't she have just let it amble along? Let him set the pace rather than her.

She sank to the floor, burying her head in her hands. She felt sick. The prospect of what Christmas now held in store loomed up: her mother asking nervous questions designed to reveal whether or not her ancient, husbandless daughter was actually a lesbian, and her self-satisfied younger sister taunting her with the plans for her imminent hen do.

She would just have to uninvite him, tell him that she didn't mean it. He could do what the hell he wanted for Christmas. It didn't matter, as long as they were together.

Finding a scrap of hope once again, she pulled herself up and grabbed the phone off the kitchen counter. She took a deep breath and dialled his number before raising the phone shakily to her ear and waiting for ten excruciating, heart-thumping rings until he picked up.

'Alex,' he said.

'Hi, it's me,' said Suzie.

'Who?'

'Me, Suzie.'

'Oh. Where are you calling from?'

'Home, why?' she asked.

'Oh, I didn't recognize the number.'

There was an awkward pause.

'Look, Suzie,' said Alex.

'Look, Alex,' said Suzie at the same time. 'You don't have to come to my parents for Christmas,' she rushed on. 'We could go away instead, somewhere warm, anywhere you like.' She stopped. No response. She listened to the silence, hoping it was the sound of his relief.

'Look, Suzie,' he said eventually. 'Time to move on, darlin'. Like I said, it just wasn't working out for me.'

It was her silence this time that hovered momentarily.

'Not working out?' she whimpered. 'Since when?'

'Oh, for a while now, I guess,' he said, offering no further explanation.

'But . . . but I don't understand,' she said, racking her brains to make sense of it all. 'You took me to your parents' ruby wedding.'

'Oh, that was just to get them off my back. They're always nagging me about settling down and I thought if I took you along it might shut them up for a while. To be honest, Suzie, I've been meaning to end it for some time now.'

Suzie slumped back against the worktop. 'But . . . last night you said you wanted to spend Christmas with me?' She felt like a pathetic, clingy, whining child, but she couldn't help it. He'd raised her hopes and now all hope had gone.

'Sweetheart,' he said. 'You caught me a bit unawares. I only said yes because it was late and I was tired and I didn't want an over-emotional chat as to why I was just about to book a week in the Alps with the lads over Christmas.'

She gasped.

'But we had sex,' she whispered. 'Twice.'

'Like I said, I didn't want an over-emotional chat.'

'You had sex with me to shut me up about Christmas?'

26

'No,' he protested. 'I had sex because . . . because . . . well, because I really like having sex.'

She waited for him to finish the sentence.

He didn't.

'*With me!*' she shouted down the phone. 'You are supposed to say you really like having sex *with me*, you tosser.'

She slammed the phone down on the counter, knocking a stray fondue fork to the floor, and surveyed the aftermath of her efforts the previous evening once again.

She'd searched all over Manchester to buy a fondue set after Alex had mentioned that he loved them because they always reminded him of happy times on skiing trips.

She'd made the mince pies herself in the hope that it would get him in the festive mood. A week of practising had finally produced some acceptable offerings and then Alex had told her he didn't like mincemeat.

The lipstick on her glass reminded her she had put on make-up – not to mention washed her hair and even bought a new top.

All that just to dare to ask him if he would spend Christmas with her. All that so he could have sex because he liked it. Not necessarily with her. He just liked it. All that so he could send her an electronic message calling it a day.

Slowly, she sank down the kitchen door until she made contact with the floor again. Wrapping her arms around her knees, she buried her head and waited for the tears. But they didn't come. All she could do was take deep breaths as anger rose up inside her.

How could she have been so stupid as to think that this was going to be her happy ending, to believe that she'd fallen in love with Prince Charming only to discover that she'd been sleeping with the villain all along? Yet again.

A vision of the four trolls reared up inside her head like some pyscho horror movie. Four cartoon faces laughing at her, psychedelic hair licking round their faces like hellfire.

'Bastards!' she cried, kicking out. 'All of you!'

She had no idea how long she sat there curled up in a ball, waves of anger engulfing her as she reflected on her past and speculated on her future. She hated where she was, and right now she blamed them all. Right now it felt like they had not only ruined her one and only love life, they had ruined her one and only life.

Eventually she was disturbed from her misery by the

sound of her mobile ringing somewhere in the hallway. She scrambled up, hoping it might be a sympathetic ear that had tuned in to her distress. It wasn't. It was Gareth. She answered quickly, knowing he bawled out anyone who ignored his phone calls.

'Suzie, it's Gareth,' barked the editor.

'Hi,' she said tersely, not in the mood for one of his infamous stripping-downs.

'I've just looked at your advice column for this week and it's shit,' he said. 'And our audience figures show no uplift in female readership. I want a revised proposal by the team meeting tomorrow. Something that doesn't make me want to puke.'

The line went dead.

Chapter 3

Drew had watched, horrified, as Suzie had staggered out of the office. *Because I love him?* What kind of idiot excuse was that? How Suzie, an attractive, normally intelligent woman, could allow herself to be rendered a complete fool by the likes of someone like Alex he would never understand. Couldn't she see through all the charm and slick, sugary patter? Couldn't she tell that he was about as deep as his fake tan and that he only had genuine feelings for himself? Couldn't she realise that he'd only gone out with her because she had her own flat and he needed somewhere to crash whilst he'd got the builders in at his?

'Because I love him,' he murmured to himself, shaking his head. He had a deep-seated dislike for that particular sentence. It was the *because* that ruined it. The *because* slicked an evil tone over an otherwise perfectly nice few words. The *because* transformed it into a justification rather than a statement. A justification of deficiencies of the *him* in question, which allowed those deficiencies to continue without challenge or recrimination. Drew knew this all too well. He had spent a lot of time considering this very sentence, since it had featured in one of the most significant conversations in his life – the last one with his mother before he had left for university.

'Why don't you leave him, Mum?' he'd asked in a rush of courage as he got into his car. It was the first time he had ever addressed the appalling state of his parents' marriage in public.

Her eyes had welled up and she'd stared at him for a long time before uttering those words: 'Because I love him.'

His father was the landlord of a pub in a rough suburb of Manchester. For years he'd struggled to resist the temptation of the parade of neglected wives who came in to get drunk and pour out their troubles in his ever-willing ear. The first one Drew could remember was a skeletal redhead, when Drew had been about twelve. His mother had found them wrapped around each other in the cellar after closing time. Drew could still picture his mum sitting at the kitchen table, as white as a sheet and trembling, whilst his father begged forgiveness and threw empty promises like confetti. At some point during the angst-ridden few days that followed, his mother cracked and forgave in order to maintain the status quo, but life was never the same. Periods of relative calm prevailed until his dad cocked up again and got discovered, and his mum fell apart. She'd cry for days on end until forgiveness started to wheedle its way in again, just as his father said it would with a sly wink to him one day at breakfast. There was a part of him that was angry with his mother, for being weak and subjecting not only herself, but him, to this lie of a family. And as for using *love* as an excuse, he vowed never to let it affect him like that. Love had no right to force you into a life of hell as it had done his mother. It had no right to manipulate you, fling you from pillar to post and mess with your head. He believed that love was something to be controlled and managed with a firm hand and a clear head. The heart should play second fiddle no matter what, or you could end up like his mother – or Suzie, for that matter.

If Suzie tried using her head a bit more often, rather than listening to her misguided heart, she might be better off. He hoped she'd picked up his stern text message, regarding any contact she might be considering with Alex during her post break-up breakdown. He wouldn't put it past her to call Alex and beg for a second chance. He checked his phone to see if she had replied just as it came alive, heralding the arrival of a very welcome incoming call.

'Not like you to call me at work,' he said.

'I'm sorry, am I disturbing you?' the cool, low voice asked.

'Not at all,' he replied. 'I could do with a dose of sanity.'

'Good. I'm ringing you regarding this insurance policy you wanted me to check over.'

'Great,' he said, relieved to be having a conversation with a woman which didn't involve high drama.

'Well, I've looked at it from a lawyer's perspective and it's certainly all legal,' she said. 'And from a personal point of view I think you're right. It's an entirely sensible idea for us to insure our wedding.'

'I knew you'd agree, Emily.' Drew leaned back in his chair and congratulated himself yet again on his choice of fiancée. This was why Emily was the perfect woman for him – someone who, in the midst of wedding-planning frenzy, could discuss wedding insurance in a sensible manner rather than ringing up tearfully with tales of calamities with carnations or bust-ups with bridesmaids.

'Well, I think it's incredibly nice of you to worry about Dad wasting his money if by any chance a disaster happens,' she said.

'Given that he's refusing to let us pay for anything, then I think it's the least we can do, don't you?'

'Absolutely. And it's good to know that we are covered if any of the suppliers really screws up.'

'Exactly.'

'Or' – Drew could hear her rustling papers at the other end of the phone – 'if you get an unexpected posting overseas as a serving member of the UK armed forces.'

He also liked her sarcastic sense of humour.

'You're right, Emily,' he laughed. 'That would be a disaster.'

'And very unexpected,' she replied. 'I will sleep better, though, knowing that we could still pay for a wedding should either of us sustain an accidental bodily injury that causes death or permanent disablement.'

Drew took a moment to consider this statement.

'So you would still marry me then?' he asked.

'Obviously not if you were dead. As for disability, it depends on the level.' There was a pause as Emily's considerable brain could almost be heard ticking over. 'Brain damage I think would leave me with no choice but to cancel; however, loss of limbs might be acceptable as long as it's not all of them.'

'I see,' he said. 'So exactly which limbs should I avoid losing if I want to stay in with a chance?'

'Well,' she said after a couple of moments' thinking time. 'I think I'd still want you to have arms.'

'Any particular reason why?'

'I don't want to spend my married life wiping your backside, do I?'

'Good point.' Occasionally Emily's rising career as a divorce lawyer gave her an obscenely practical view of marriage.

'So is there anything else I should be avoiding other than the loss of arms?' he asked.

'Well, you'd better check with Toby where he's taking you for your stag do, because there's no cover for death, disablement or injury as a result of participation in any dangerous activity including hang-gliding, scuba-diving,

35

parachuting, motor-racing, rock climbing, mountaineering or horse-riding.'

'I think it's safe to say that Toby is extremely unlikely to have organised horse-riding for my stag do. We can rule that one out.'

'Pity we can't insure against Toby,' sighed Emily. 'I know he's your best friend, but he is the person most likely to cause some kind of disaster at our wedding.'

'No, he's taking it all very seriously,' Drew insisted. 'I've given him a pep talk and said he has to play it straight. No surprises.'

'I'll believe that when I see it,' she said, rustling papers again. 'One last thing then I must go, as I have a client meeting starting in five minutes.'

'Fire away.'

'Well, the policy does state that in the event of either party getting cold feet prior to the day, they do provide cover for professional counselling but no cover for any costs incurred.'

Drew let the silence that followed Emily's comment drag on just a moment too long. He compensated with forced hearty laughter.

'How reassuring,' he said after his outburst. 'We'll have bankrupted your father but be unlikely to slit our wrists.'

'Yes, that's right.' Emily was laughing as well. 'It's a good job there's absolutely no chance of that after all this time. Goodness, if we can't be sure now, when would we be?'

'Yes,' he agreed, 'it would be absolutely ridiculous if one of us got cold feet after sixteen years. What idiots we'd look for wasting all that time.'

'Yes,' said Emily.

'What an earth would everyone say?' he said.

'Mmm,' she responded.

'We'd be a laughing stock,' he added.

Another silence appeared before Emily ushered it away.

'So I'm happy to organise this insurance then,' she said cheerfully.

'Are you sure? You must be so busy organising all the other stuff.'

'It's no trouble, really. Everything else is under control.'

'Well, thank you.'

'Right,' she said briskly, 'must go. See you tonight.'

'Yep, see you later then.'

Drew put his phone down and stared at the professionally taken engagement photograph on his desk, wondering for the umpteenth time if that was really him smiling back as though straight out of a catalogue. After a few minutes he shook himself and decided to check out how his fantasy football team was doing – the truly crucial issue of the day.

Chapter 4

Dear Suzie,

I have been going out with someone from work for over six months now and it's been going really well, so I decided to invite him to spend Christmas with me and my family. As you can imagine, I was absolutely over the moon when he said he'd love to. The following day he sent me a text saying it was all over and he was about to book a Christmas holiday with his mates. He said he didn't tell me the night before because he wanted to have sex. I still really love him and want him back. What should I do?

Yours,

A Hopeless Romantic

She had their undivided attention now. The three men sat motionless, staring at her across the meeting room table, a whole myriad of reactions swarming over their faces as she finished reading out the letter displayed in all its glory on the projector screen behind her.

One look at Gareth, however, sent a wave of panic through her body. He looked confused, on the borderline of angry. Was she making a massive mistake? It had all seemed like such a good idea at three that morning when she was bouncing off the walls after four pints of coffee, three rolls of wine gums and two bars of Galaxy following a late-night garage run. Standing here now on the brink of professional suicide, it seemed like the definition of insanity.

'I've realised that no-one gives the type of advice that would really be useful,' she'd said to her bored-looking editor at the beginning of her presentation. 'No-one actually tells women how to deal with the men who screw up their lives.'

'Suzie,' Gareth had said, holding up his hand. 'When I said sort out the column, what I meant was, give me something to read that doesn't make my skin crawl and that attracts more advertising. What I don't want is some feminist bullshit.'

'It's not bullshit!' she said indignantly. 'What I was writing before was bullshit. Pathetic, run-of-the-mill, send-for-a-leaflet, go-and-waste-your-money-on-counselling bullshit that every other agony aunt churns out. What good does that do? Have you ever heard of anyone who has saved their relationship by filling in awkward silences in a room with a middle-aged woman who asks about your irrelevant childhood?'

Gareth swigged some coffee without taking his eyes off her.

'Continue,' he said putting his mug back down.

She glanced at Drew for some encouragement, but his eyebrows were so far up his forehead they had practically disappeared under his side parting. She'd wanted to run it all past him that morning, but he'd been late in and had come straight to the meeting.

At that point Alex, the third man in the room, was fully absorbed in his BlackBerry and barely listening to anything she was saying. She felt a shot of pure anger which gave her the boost she needed. She was still bristling from where he had touched her earlier after he strode into the room.

'Good morning, people,' he'd declared, as if he didn't have a care in the world. 'Sorry I'm late, Gareth, but it's been bedlam. I've been on the phone all morning trying to pull in a mega-advertiser.'

'Don't tell me,' Gareth said through gritted teeth, 'until it's in writing. I'm sick of your half-baked promises. Now sit down and wait your turn.'

She felt Alex walk behind her, clearly unaffected by Gareth's put-down. She hadn't dared look at him, not entirely sure if her emotions were fully in check yet. But before he came into her eyeline she felt his hand on her right shoulder. She leapt up in her chair with surprise before he gave her a sympathetic squeeze and then sat down right next to her.

How dare he touch her? Sympathy and touching were for yesterday when he broke up with her. She looked at him in shock. He stared back and mouthed a silent 'Are you okay?' before reaching out and giving her hand a squeeze and painting a fake concerned look on his face.

He didn't have that look on his face now. He was all white and wide-eyed and slack-jawed. She'd had to cough to get his attention before she read out the letter displayed on screen, explaining that it was a mock letter used to illustrate her new style of column. Seeing his stunned face hardened her resolve. He deserved this. *She* deserved this. At some point in the dead of night she'd come to the conclusion she had nothing to lose. Her love life was a disaster, and as for her career, well, writing an agony column wasn't exactly fulfilling her dreams of being the next Kate Adie. So screw it. If it all went belly up she'd go and do an *Eat, Pray, Love*. Although knowing her luck it would turn out to be more *Eat, Pray you don't get fat, Love being obese and a spinster.*

There was no going back now. She just had to take a deep breath and go through with it and hope that she came out the other side intact.

'And now I will show you how Dear Suzie will be responding in the future,' she said, leaning over to click onto the next screen without taking her eyes off Alex. She read out the reply letter slowly, allowing every word to sink in.

Dear Hopeless Romantic,
    You are an idiot.
    He doesn't give a toss about you.
    Please read the above sentence repeatedly until you believe it, because it is true.
    My mailbag is full of women like you, writing to me seeking hope. Hope that there is something they

can do to turn their nightmare into a fairy tale so they can live happily ever after. Well, listen to this.

Forget Hope.

Hope is not your friend.

Hope is the devil who will lead you to pointless, desperate measures.

So move on. BUT not before you show this man that he cannot tread all over your soaring heart. Not before you teach him there are consequences to his actions. Not before you make him suffer in the same way as he has made you suffer. And if you can't do it for yourself then do it for every other woman out there, to teach him that he has to treat the next one better.

So, Hopeless Romantic, your cowardly colleague has to learn not one, not two, but three valuable lessons.

Lesson One: Never, ever ruin a woman's Christmas.

Suzie glanced up, her heart beating so loudly she was surprised they couldn't hear it. Drew was still totally wide-eyed; Gareth thankfully was looking vaguely interested; whilst Alex was staring at her as if she was a complete lunatic.

She felt like she was having an out of body experience, watching someone else make a complete fool of herself – or maybe that was wishful thinking. She tried very hard to look in control and confident as she leaned forward to pull the speakerphone from the middle of the table towards her.

'Now for a practical demonstration.' She pressed the redial button and sensed the three men in the room looking at each other in confusion. The phone rang out, filling the silence, until someone could be heard picking up.

'Hello, Pauline speaking,' said a woman's voice.

'Hello, Mrs Collingwood,' Suzie jumped in before Alex could express his astonishment that she was calling his mother in the middle of a team meeting. 'It's Suzie here again and I've got Alex with me.'

'Right, dear. How is he?'

'Oh, he's being very brave, Mrs Collingwood.'

'Is he? That's good. I'm so glad you called me, Suzie. I've been thinking about it all morning. I know it's very hard when you end a relationship, but it's so kind of you to worry about how Alex is going to cope.'

'With parents like you to help, Mrs Collingwood, I'm sure he'll pull through.'

'We're always here for him, he knows that. Do you want to put him on and I'll ask him, shall I?'

'Of course. Here he is.' Suzie elbowed Alex in the ribs.

'What are you doing?' he mouthed to her.

'Just say hello,' she mouthed back.

'Er, hi Mum,' he said, holding his hands up in utter confusion.

'Oh, Alex, I'm so sorry it's not worked out with Suzie. When she called to tell me she'd ended it I could have cried for you, really I could. And she said you were taking it badly and that what you were most worried about was spending Christmas alone. Well, young man, you don't have to worry yourself about that any more. Of course we'd love to have you here with us. It's been so long. And all your little nieces and nephews will love having their favourite Uncle Alex around for a change to play with them. I've already called your sisters and it's all set. A Collingwood family Christmas is just what you need to get yourself out of the doldrums.'

Alex sat opening and closing his mouth.

'But Mum . . .' he finally managed to splutter as he stared red-faced at Suzie. 'I was going to . . .'

'No buts, young man, you're spending Christmas in the bosom of your family and that's that. We'll sort

46

you out, soon have you back to your chipper self. Now I've got to go, because your dad's taking me down to Sainsbury's to get the pick of the crackers. I'll call you later to see if you've had a good day. Chin up, son. Bye.'

The phone went dead and for a moment there was silence in the room. Suzie hadn't really thought forward to this point in the meeting. Her heart was still beating exceptionally fast but she could feel something else, sparked by the look of shock and dismay on Alex's face. Something that felt distinctly like triumph, joy even. What she really wanted to do was stand in Alex's face and let out a highly juvenile 'Waaaaaaaaaah.' She glanced at Drew. His eyebrows were still AWOL but he was nodding and smiling approvingly whilst casting the odd nervous glance at Gareth.

'Continue,' barked Gareth, suddenly breaking the silence.

'What?' shrieked Alex. 'But she's . . .'

'Stop,' said Gareth, holding his hand up to Alex. 'I said you could talk when it was your turn. Now I want to see the rest of what she's got. Carry on, Suzie.'

'Okay,' she said. Not sacked yet, that had to be good. She pressed the button to move on to the next slide.

Lesson Two: Never ever use a text to break bad news.

She reached down and picked up her mobile phone, pressed a few buttons then put it back on the table, folded her arms and smiled straight at Alex. A few seconds later his phone bleeped, causing him to leap up in his chair as if it was a time bomb.

'Aren't you going to pick up your text then?' she asked.

'What, now?' he said.

'Now!' she found herself bellowing.

She'd never seen him so wary of the device that was normally either glued to his ear or his fingers. He picked it up and looked at her nervously before glancing down to read her text. Less than a second later he'd dropped the phone on the floor as though it had burned him.

'You're insane!' he screeched. 'Tell her to stop!' he shouted at Gareth.

Gareth said nothing, just raised his eyebrows questioningly at Suzie.

She bent forward to click on the next slide.

'This is the text that Alex has just received,' she explained to Gareth and Drew as three words appeared on the screen.

ONE WORD – BOBBITT.

That was when Drew lost it. A sound erupted from his mouth like a small explosion, coughing and spluttering mixed with hysterical laughter at the sight of Alex's ashen face. Gareth looked confused, glancing between the three of them in complete bewilderment. Suzie was quick to step in with an explanation.

'For those of us unaware of the plight of Lorena Bobbitt, I shall elaborate.' She changed the screen to show a newspaper clipping with the headline CRIMES BELOW THE BELT: PENILE REMOVAL AND CASTRATION. Gareth gasped as Suzie described the infamous Lorena Bobbitt of Virginia, USA, and her extreme reaction to her husband's misdemeanours back in 1993.

Taking Gareth's subsequent smirk as positive, Suzie decided to press on whilst she appeared to be getting away with it.

'And so finally, lesson three,' she said, clicking on her last slide.

Lesson Three: Sex is a privilege and not a right.

Alex, speechless by now, looked pleadingly at Gareth, who had leaned back in his chair as the smirk grew into a broad smile. Suzie walked around the table towards Alex and he flinched as she brushed past to take an object from the shelf behind him, covered by her best Cath Kidston tea towel. She placed it in front of him before whipping the towel off to reveal a full knife block. Alex whimpered as she removed a large carving knife with a flourish.

All three men were quiet now, a trace of fear flickering in their eyes. It felt as if the whole room was holding its breath until Suzie shrugged and put a reassuring hand on Alex's shoulder, satisfyingly making him flinch again.

'Don't panic, I wouldn't use this on you,' she said, putting it back in the block.

Alex sagged in his chair, emotionally exhausted.

'I think this is more your size, don't you?' She pulled out a small vegetable peeler, made sure everyone had seen it, then slammed it on the desk in front of him before calmly walking back to the front of the room and turning to face her audience.

'And that, gentlemen, concludes my presentation,' she said. 'Any questions?'

A shocked silence hung in the room.

It was Drew who stood up first. Big, hearty man claps

filled the room as he positively beamed at Suzie.

'Brilliant,' he said. 'Just brilliant.'

And to her absolute shock, Gareth stood up too and joined in with the spontaneous applause.

'Not brilliant,' he said. 'Genius. That's what that was. Absolute genius. Look at him. It's every wronged woman's dream to nail a man like that.' Alex was still sitting in his chair as white as a sheet, staring at the knife. A bead of sweat had formed on his forehead. Gareth banged the table with both fists. 'I love it! It's different, it's controversial, it's funny. A revenge column. That's what we need.' He sat down abruptly as he tried to catch up with his racing thoughts. 'It's just so . . . so . . . what is it, Drew?' he asked, snapping his fingers in his direction.

'Tabloid?' offered Drew.

'Yes, that's it! Tabloid!' Gareth leapt up and walked round the table to grasp Suzie's hands. 'Please say you can do the same thing for other losers like you?'

Suzie, reeling from being called a genius and a loser in the same breath by her boss, felt as if she had stepped into a parallel universe. She had quite expected to be sacked by the end of the day.

'I can try,' she managed.

51

'The male tortured masses of Manchester will be forever in your debt,' he told her solemnly before turning and waving his finger at Alex.

'As for you,' he said. 'A list of potential advertisers by lunchtime. Get on the phone to Argos. See if they want to run a promo on kitchen knives.' He left a pause long enough for Alex to turn even whiter. 'Just kidding!' He thumped Alex on the back then turned back to Suzie. 'No knives. Lawyers wouldn't like it.'

'Okay,' she whispered, wondering what on earth she'd started.

'Excellent.' Gareth looked at his watch. 'Let's adjourn, shall we? I need to make some calls. Back here in half an hour.'

He swept out of the room, leaving Drew beaming at Suzie. He walked towards her and put both hands on her shoulders.

'Brilliant,' he said yet again before turning and leaving her alone with Alex.

'Are you okay?' she couldn't help but ask. He looked so weak and pathetic, almost as if he was about to throw up. He dragged his eyes away from the knife and looked at her in a way she had never seen before. She stared back, trying to work out what it was, until finally it dawned on her that he was eyeing her with a sense of total and utter awe.

'Sorry will do,' she said to break the silence.

'Sorry,' he said, biting his lip and nodding his head. 'I am sorry.'

She got up slowly and walked towards him. How good did it feel to see him lean back in his chair, the fear returning to his face. She paused for a moment before squeezing his shoulder to feel him flinch one more time. A grin filled her face and she walked out of the room, her head held high.

'One down, three to go,' she muttered.

Chapter 5

'I can't believe you've never been here before,' Suzie exclaimed.

Drew had been more than happy to accept her invitation to join him in a celebratory drink after work but had been expecting a nice quiet pint, not this lively-looking bar. He felt his body tense as he took in some disturbing signals. Slightly too loud music. A rhythmic guitar sound that reminded him of miserable childhood holidays in Spain. Weird stuff everywhere, including a fake palm tree in the corner and musical instruments hanging from the ceiling. Posters on an exposed brick wall advertising foreign-looking beers next to postcards from faraway places. He jumped as he was almost knocked over by a swirling, whirling couple who were throwing their bodies around what he now recognised as a small dance floor. One look at the male half of the dancing duo confirmed his suspicions. The man's dark Latino looks and lecherous stare down his companion's cleavage told Drew he had indeed entered foreign territory. What on earth was Suzie thinking of bringing him to a salsa bar?

'What on earth are you thinking of bring me to a salsa bar?' he asked, plonking himself on a bar stool next to Suzie. 'Do I look like the kind of man who would enjoy coming to a place like this?'

'Oh, don't be so miserable,' she said, sliding a dirty martini over to him.

He contemplated the dishwater facing him in a glass no man could ever be a man drinking out of. 'Can't I even have a beer?' he asked.

'Nope,' she replied merrily. 'It's happy hour. Two for one.'

He leant forward and took a sip, screwing his face up as the bitter taste hit the back of his throat.

'Can't stay long,' he warned her, looking at his watch. 'Meeting Emily at the wedding venue later.'

'No problem.' Suzie beamed, still riding out her revenge high. 'I just wanted to make sure that you knew how grateful I was, that's all.'

'What for?' He took another tentative sip.

'For telling me to get my own back on Alex,' she said. 'Actually, more than that. For telling me I was *capable* of getting my own back on Alex.'

'Did I?'

'Yes, you did. Yesterday. You said *I know you can do it*. It really spurred me on.'

'Right,' said Drew, a bit nonplussed.

'And,' Suzie took a very large gulp of her drink, 'I wanted to thank you for pointing out that all of my past loves were actually twats.'

Drew mirrored Suzie's large gulp before attempting a response. 'Happy to be of service.' He raised his glass to clink against hers. 'My twat-detection facilities are forever at your disposal.'

'Funny you should mention that,' she said, draining her glass and motioning to the barman for two top-ups. She turned to face him and gripped his arm excitedly. 'I might just need exactly those skills.'

'You got a new bloke already?' he exclaimed. 'Bloody hell, Suzie, that was quick work. Did you bring me here to check him out? Please tell me it's not that pissed bloke over there dancing with a palm tree?'

'No, of course not, give me some credit. What I meant was that I might need you to help me track down my ex-twats.'

'Why?' he asked warily.

'Because,' she said, pumping his arm up and down in excitement, 'I'm going to get my revenge on them too.'

He stared back at her, not sure he'd heard her right. Perhaps the muddied waters of dirty martini might help clear his mind. He finished his first glass and took a confident swipe at his second.

'Did you just say you were going to track down your ex-boyfriends and get your revenge?'

'Yes.'

'Why?'

She released his arm and looked at him so intensely he thought she might combust. 'Because it feels absolutely bloody brilliant for the first time in my entire life to come out on top. Look at me!' she cried, waving her hands around her head. 'I'm so happy and *I've* just been dumped. I'm not a gibbering wreck; Alex is. How amazing is that?'

'Well, yes,' agreed Drew. 'But . . .'

'Imagine,' Suzie interrupted, 'if you went back and did the same with all the others who'd made you suffer. To be able to look back, not with regret and bitterness but with utter pride that those relationships ended how you wanted them to. With them fully understanding how badly they'd behaved. With you having the last say.'

The dirty martinis were not clearing his mind. He felt very confused. He took another large slug.

'Do you really want to drag up the past?'

'No,' she said, 'just rewrite it.'

'I'm not sure I understand, really,' he admitted.

'Of *course* you don't understand!' She sounded a little frustrated. 'Because it's never happened to you, has it? Most normal people get screwed up by a multitude of bad relationships before they meet the one – apart from you, who manages to bag his lady practically coming out of the womb. Of course you don't understand, because your heart is untainted by disappointment and pain. Do you have any idea how rare that is?'

Drew was only half listening. He was trying to work out if it was him moving or the room. He could feel a vague swaying motion that was making him feel slightly nauseous.

'For that matter,' Suzie continued, 'do you have any idea how rare you are – a man who doesn't want to spend his time shagging anything that moves?'

Now that was something he could comment on.

'I never wanted to have to dance to boy band music,' he stated firmly.

'What are you talking about?'

'My mates had to humiliate themselves by dancing to boy band music just to get a shag. Can't be worth it,' he said, shaking his head solemnly.

'Genius!' cried Suzie. 'Take That kept you faithful.'

'Yep,' replied Drew. 'And alcopops. I watched them all having to buy copious amounts of the stuff. Soooo degrading.'

'Drew, you are a legend.' Suzie slapped him on the back. 'I'm sure Emily would be delighted to hear that all it took for you to stay in love with her all these years has been the presence of cheesy music and bright pink alcohol in a bottle.'

She picked up her glass and held it expectantly, forcing him to raise his in a toast.

'To you. The love expert,' she announced.

'Hardly,' he replied. Clink was followed by final gulp was followed by request for a toilet break.

'Going for a slash,' he said, sliding off his stool and walking a little unsteadily across the dance floor to the Gents.

Whilst he was drying his hands, he glimpsed his watch. 'Bollocks!' He was going to be late meeting Emily, and half drunk. He rushed back across the dance floor, trying to dodge the heaving throng of the tipsy post-work crowd. Just as he thought he'd made it, he felt someone grab his hand and haul him backwards.

'It's not boy band music,' he heard Suzie shout in his ear as they were quickly surrounded by gyrating bodies. 'You can't help but want to dance to this.'

He took in her exuberant face and knew he had to disappoint her.

'I don't do dancing,' he shouted.

'Of course you do,' she laughed, grabbing his hands and bouncing them up and down.

'I don't.' He shook his head firmly.

'Emily won't mind.'

'*We* don't do dancing,' he said.

'What, never?'

'No.'

'Time to learn,' she said, pulling his arms so that his feet came unglued from the floor.

He stared at Suzie twirling and whirling in front of him, giggling like a schoolgirl. Sighing, he attempted a half-hearted hip sway, which, to his surprise, grew into a full body sway, such was the power of the now pounding music and the amount of intoxicating lubricant he had consumed.

Suzie clapped with joy at the sight of Drew succumbing to the music. She grabbed his hand, swaying it backwards and forwards as though they were kids in the playground. She threw her head back and laughed with all the joy of someone on top of the world. So infectious was her elation that Drew couldn't help but smile. She leaned into him and shouted in his ear.

'I can't stop thinking about Alex sitting there looking petrified at a veg peeler.'

Drew couldn't resist her glee. Before long they were clutching each other, doubled up as they relived the day's main event over the din of the music. Eventually they calmed down and Suzie coughed in an attempt to pull herself together.

'Best laugh I've had in ages,' she said.

'Me too,' he said. 'Gotta go now.'

'I know. Thanks, Drew. I mean it. Today wouldn't have happened without you.'

'Rubbish. I always knew threatening to cut off a man's penis was in you.'

She smiled. 'Go on, go. Say hi to Emily for me.'

'Will do.' He hugged her awkwardly before turning around and leaving her alone on the dance floor.

Chapter 6

Drew could see Emily standing in the doorway of Ripton Manor when he finally pulled up in a taxi. The light radiating from the hallway behind her looked warm and inviting but Emily's posture was definitely icy. He stumbled slightly as he fell out of the taxi. Hastily stuffing a crumpled note into the driver's hand, he turned and attempted to walk up the ten or so stone steps in what he hoped resembled a sober manner.

A grand old clock was striking seven by the time he made it into the imposing hallway of the manor house. Emily had been replaced by Toby, his best man, who was laughing hysterically at him.

'You are so in the shit you would not believe,' said Toby, almost doubled over with mirth.

'Where did Emily go?' asked Drew as he struggled to take his coat off.

'To inform Tweedledum and Tweedledee that you've finally rolled up. Christ, I'm glad I came now. Seeing you fall from grace has been my lifelong ambition.'

'Thanks,' Drew muttered, putting his coat on an antique chair. He knew he needed to pull himself together or Toby was going to have a field day.

'Don't mention it. It makes a nice change from me screwing up. Where have you been, anyway? Not like you to be late.'

'I've just been for a drink with Suzie. You remember her? She came to our engagement party.'

'I do, as it happens.'

'Well, it's a long story, but she was celebrating something and we went to that new salsa place and I guess I had one too many and lost track of time.'

'Oh, my God, this just gets better,' said Toby, staring at Drew in excitement. 'You're late because you were out drinking with another woman. Bloody hell, Drew, this is awesome. This could be the best night of my life.'

For the first time, Drew realised how it looked. 'Oh Christ. What am I going to say?'

'Just lie, mate, it's easy. Crisis at work or something, job done. I say it all the time.'

'I can't lie,' said Drew. 'In any case, I haven't got anything to lie about.'

Toby stared at him for a moment. 'If that's what you think, mate, then fine. We'll go and test that ludicrous statement now, shall we?'

Toby ushered him into an ornate and imposing ballroom. 'He's here,' Toby announced. 'No need to panic. He only got held up because he was having a drink with a female colleague in a bar where people go after work to get drunk and have a grope on the dance floor.'

There was an audible gasp from the assembled party. A man in a navy suit and gold badge identifying him as Luke the Deputy Manager held his hands over his mouth in horror. A young woman also in a navy suit with a gold badge declaring her to be Tammy the Wedding Coordinator went bright red and dropped her black notebook on the floor. Toby rubbed his hands together in glee as the inhabitants of the room collectively held their breath and awaited Emily's response.

'Suzie?' asked Emily calmly, her only visible sign of reaction a slightly raised eyebrow and a light tapping of the fingers of her left hand.

'How did you guess?' Drew reached over to kiss her on the cheek. 'Remember I told you yesterday that she'd split up with Alex? Well, we went for a quick drink to celebrate because she got her own back by threatening him with a knife today.'

The room gasped again.

'It's a long story,' he said quickly to the navy-suited duo. 'It's not how it sounds.'

'You can tell us later.' Emily extracted a dark blue file from her briefcase. 'But for now shall we get on with what we are here for?'

Drew let out a small sigh of relief. Thank goodness for Emily's unflappable demeanour. He smiled smugly at a disappointed Toby.

'If I came out with a story like that, Chloe would have my nuts for breakfast, I can tell you,' he mumbled.

'Toby,' said Emily, leaning forward and pausing, silently demanding that he listen hard to what she was about to say. 'That is because you are completely unreliable and untrustworthy. Drew can go for a drink with whomever he likes. We have not been together this long without knowing we can totally trust one another.'

Drew stepped forward and shook Tammy's hand vigorously, keen to move the evening away from the danger zone. 'Hi, I'm Drew.'

'This is Tammy, our wedding coordinator,' said Emily. 'And this is Luke, the Deputy Manager.'

'Nice badges,' was all he could think of to say. Both of them stared silently back at him. 'Sorry to keep you waiting, and what Toby said, and the whole knife thing.'

'No need to dwell on it,' said Emily, holding her hand up. Her jawline tightened with a hint of tension. She opened the blue file and took out a sheet of paper. 'So, the objective of this meeting is to agree all entertainment issues. Can I suggest, Toby, that you take us all through your requirements?'

'Of course.' He made an about-turn and strode across the dance floor to stand in the opposite corner with his arms raised, as if he was a gymnast about to start a floor exercise. 'This will be where the magic happens,' he declared, grandly swooping his arms down.

'I hardly call playing a few records magic,' said Drew.

'Drew, how dare you treat my profession with such disdain,' Toby protested. 'I am crucial to the success of the entire affair. I don't see myself merely as a DJ, more a Wizard of Wonderful Times.'

'Failed radio presenter, more like,' said Drew uncharitably, keen to get back at Toby for his part in the bad start to the meeting. Toby had recently set up his mobile disco business after he'd been sacked from his radio job because he talked too much. 'And no chat between the records,' Drew added. 'Some people might actually want to dance, you know, not listen to your drivel.'

'I have an entire day of music planned for you.' Toby strode back across the dance floor. 'I've even brought along my very own mobile disco to talk you through my entertainment choices for the day.' He pulled an iPhone out of his pocket and motioned for them all to gather round.

Emily ticked something off in her file. 'We just want a good mix of music that will satisfy all age groups, Toby.'

'Now you just stop there,' said Toby, looking aghast. 'This is the soundtrack to your wedding. You will remember this music for the rest of your lives. It is crucial that it reflects your personalities perfectly. This is a huge responsibility and I'm taking it very seriously.'

'There's a first,' muttered Drew.

'Shall I continue?' asked Toby. 'Or are you just going to take the piss?'

'Let's hear it then,' said Emily without looking up from her file.

'Right.' Toby pressed a few buttons on his phone. 'Let's start with Emily's arrival for the ceremony.'

He really was taking it seriously. Drew was shocked. A few tunes after dinner was all he'd been expecting, not all this.

'So if you can imagine,' Toby continued, staring straight into Tammy's eyes, 'the huge oak doors swing open to reveal the blushing bride standing in all her splendour next to her proud, resplendent father.'

Tammy stared back at him, a tear teetering on the corner of her eye.

'And what could be better than to gaze at the pair of them and hear the strains of this absolute classic?'

Toby delicately pressed the screen and out came the most hideous racket.

'Bring your daughter to the slaughter!' screamed the members of Iron Maiden as everyone stared at him open-mouthed. Toby grinned back widely before pressing the screen again and filling the air with the glorious sound of the *Jaws* theme tune.

'And so the bride floats down the aisle towards her waiting husband-to-be,' he said over the music. 'And they stand side by side, preparing to be brought together forever in perfect harmony.'

Now 'Don't Stand So Close to Me' by the Police was booming out. Tammy looked from Toby to Drew and Emily in bewildered silence. Toby was so pleased with himself he seemed about to burst, whilst Drew was trying very hard to suppress a smile. Emily had closed her file and had her arms crossed with a somewhat resigned look on her face.

'Finished?' she asked patiently.

'Oh no,' replied Toby. 'We're not even at the reception yet. Now this is what I was thinking for during the reception drinks.'

'We're having a harpist,' said Emily.

'A harpist?' Toby exclaimed.

'Yes, a harpist,' she repeated firmly.

'So you won't want this then.' He switched on 'I Predict a Riot' by the Kaiser Chiefs.

'No.'

'I see.' He switched it off. 'So where's she from then, this harpist?'

'Wales.'

'Have you met her?' he asked Drew.

'No.'

'Is she fit?' he asked Emily.

Emily blinked in disbelief.

'Have we done with this now?' she said eventually. 'You need to discuss your equipment with this gentleman.' She gestured towards the bewildered-looking duty manager.

'I'd rather discuss it with the harpist,' said Toby, eyeing the deputy manager disdainfully.

'Toby!' shouted Emily, clearly having tolerated his fun for long enough.

'Last bit, last bit,' he begged. 'I've nailed it for the speeches, I promise. You're going to love this.' He fiddled around with his phone before looking up with a cheeky grin. 'I hear you're going to be first up, Emily, so I thought this would be perfect.'

Madonna's 'Like a Virgin' filled the room.

'Then for the best man I needed something that really communicated my thoughts and emotions for the day, so here it is.'

'I Want to Kiss the Bride' sang out Elton John and forced a smile onto Emily's thin lips.

'And then for my best mate Drew, at possibly his most

71

nerve-wracking part of the day,' said Toby, 'I've gone for something to really pull at those heart strings.'

The Smiths' 'Heaven Knows I'm Miserable Now' wiped the smile straight off Emily's face again.

'And finally, for that all-important first dance, the song that will define you as a couple to your family and friends for the rest of your lives. The song that everyone will be wishing they had chosen as their first dance at their wedding. Here it is. Please take the floor, Mr and Mrs Carter!'

'I Don't Feel Like Dancin'' was the song that Toby had deemed suitable to serenade them into married life.

'What are you looking at me like that for?' he asked, feigning offence at Emily and Drew's glares. 'I could have gone for this.' The upbeat sound of the Scissor Sisters was replaced by the Divinyls singing 'I Touch Myself'. 'Or even this.' The melancholy voices of 10cc filled the room. The words to 'I'm Not in Love' swirled around them, transporting Drew to a place that he usually only inhabited at three o'clock in the morning when he sometimes woke up in a cold sweat. He was dragged back into the room when Toby pulled him onto the dance floor and twirled him round and round. Drew began to feel sick and disorientated as the cocktails churned inside him.

'I'm not in love,' boomed Toby in his face, until Drew could stand it no more.

'Switch it off!' he shouted. He held his head in his hands, trying to stop the room from spinning around him.

'Switch it off,' he said a little more quietly, as everyone stared at him in silence after Toby had finally found the off switch.

'Hey, calm down,' said Toby. 'It was just a joke, mate. You know me. Thought you'd find it funny. Obviously I went too far.' He tucked his phone back in his pocket and gave it a protective pat.

Drew couldn't speak. He realised he was trembling.

'Look, I'll give you a list,' said Emily, opening up her file and writing something down. 'Stuff we think is appropriate. Oh, and we won't be having a first dance, will we, Drew?' She looked at him in shared under-standing. 'Neither of us likes dancing.'

Drew had a sudden flashback to earlier in the evening when he was swinging his hips and arms and laughing hysterically.

'No, neither of us likes dancing,' he replied.

Chapter 7

Dear Suzie,

I am sixteen years old and my boyfriend wants to have sex with me two weeks on Friday. We are going to a house party and there won't be any parents there, so all the boys have shared out thirty-minute time slots for sole use of one of the bedrooms. My boyfriend wants to know if I'll have sex with him, because if I won't he says he'll ask somebody else as he doesn't want to waste his time slot. I want my first time to be perfect and I am worried that half an hour won't be long enough. Should I ask him to book two time slots?

Please help me.

Sophie

Dear Sophie,

If it takes longer than half an hour please send me your boyfriend's number! I'm just joking. Seriously, I have some very important advice for you.

DON'T HAVE SEX, YOU WON'T ENJOY IT.

Having sex with a sixteen-year-old boy can never be good. Remember, he won't have done it very often, if at all. Consider this. Would you get in a car with him the first time he has to drive? No. He'd be all fingers and thumbs, stops and starts, no idea what knobs and buttons to press, all of which would add up to an extremely uncomfortable ride. And an extremely uncomfortable ride is all you can expect if you have sex with him.

Now let's get to the real problem – the sharing of time slots and his threat of asking someone else. Wake up, Sophie. This is unacceptable behaviour and you are letting these boys take advantage of you. Tell him you will have sex with him and he should book two time slots because you are convinced he is going to be mind-blowing in the sack. When you get him in the room, tell him you have been lusting after his body for ages and you want to see him naked immediately. When he has stripped off, laugh hysterically and run

out of the room to the kitchen where you will have a
pre-prepared chart at the ready for all of you girls to
mark just how small your boyfriends' penises are.
   Good luck.
   Suzie

'Why?' cried Jackie, after she'd read Suzie's latest letter. 'Why weren't you around when I was a teenager? This is exactly what I needed to hear. If you'd been there I might not have got knocked up at eighteen and married that shitbag Carl.'

'I was around, Jackie,' Suzie pointed out. 'We've been best mates since we were five.'

'Then why the bloody hell didn't you say this to me then?' asked Jackie, looking more than offended. 'Look at me. I'm knee-deep in kids. If you'd shown this type of intelligence then, my life might have turned out entirely differently.'

Suzie looked down at Troy, who was bouncing happily on her knee as she sat at Jackie's kitchen table. She knew Jackie didn't really mean it, although she was firm that Troy was the very last of her four kids. The *pre-vasectomy baby*, as she liked to call him. She also had her *teenage pregnancy mistake baby* (Jamie) and her *pretending Jamie wasn't a mistake baby* (Cara). They were both fathered by Carl, her childhood sweetheart, who after ten years together got struck by a chronic case of nostalgia for his teens and ran off with a seventeen-year-old schoolgirl. It had taken Jackie two years to recover and find Dave, and then she'd had her *we must be mad to do this again baby* Lenny, and finally Troy, whose birthday would forever be remembered as the day before his dad had the snip.

'I didn't know then what I know now, did I?' said Suzie.

Jackie hesitated for a moment whilst deep in thought, as if casting her mind back to their early days.

'You're right. You were clueless.'

'I wasn't that bad.'

'Suzie,' said Jackie, putting her hands on her hips, 'Christian Sleaford told you that Appletiser could kill sperm and you should use it after sex, and you believed him.'

'I did not!'

'You did so. You told me . . .' Jackie paused and doubled over, shaking with laughter. 'God, it still makes me laugh today.' She straightened up again and took a deep breath. 'I swear, Suzie, you told me it was a shame it wasn't Orange Tango because you didn't like the taste of Appletiser.'

Suzie could feel herself going bright red. Sometimes having a friend who knew everything about you was both a positive and a negative.

'All I can say, Jackie, is that clearly I was a lot more successful with contraception than you were,' she retorted.

Jackie reached over to relieve Suzie of Troy and sat down to give him a bottle. 'Fair play, Suze,' she said, kissing the top of his head. 'You've got me there. But this is really good.' She handed Suzie's teenage heartbreak letter back to her. 'When I think of all the stupid things I put myself through as a teenager because I knew no better.' She shook her head in dismay.

'Not to mention what we let boys put us through,' said Suzie.

'Exactly.'

'So will you help me find him, then?' asked Suzie.

'Who?'

'Patrick Connolly.'

Jackie screwed her face up. 'You mean your first true love?'

'Yes, my first true love, the one who also broke my

heart, if you remember.' Suzie felt herself blushing again.

'I'm not likely to forget it,' said Jackie. 'You were so upset you turned to the bottle. You forced us to go hardcore and switch from Cinzano to Martini Bianco.'

'Only because Cinzano reminded me too much of him. I couldn't bear to even smell it any more,' Suzie protested.

'But I loved Cinzano,' Jackie declared. 'Bianco got up my nose and made me feel dizzy.'

There was a pause as they stared at each other before Jackie spoke up.

'Never, ever tell Dave that those words came out of my mouth,' she begged.

'What's it worth?' asked Suzie.

'Whatever. You name it. That statement would probably be grounds for divorce if he heard it.'

'Well, help me find Patrick and you might find that I've forgotten all about it,' said Suzie.

'Why on earth do you want to see that toerag again after all this time?'

'Because it's his turn next. I'm going to get my revenge on him for breaking my heart.'

'What, you mean like you did with Alex?' Jackie asked, her eyes wide in amazement.

'Just like Alex,' replied Suzie calmly.

Jackie studied her friend before offering her verdict.

'Well, good for you,' she said, slapping her on the back.

'I'm done with looking back on my life and seeing myself at the mercy of any Tom, Dick or Harry who wanted to take advantage,' said Suzie firmly. 'Time to rewrite history.'

'Wow,' said Jackie. 'I'll have some of whatever you're having, please. You are a woman on a mission.'

'I will be if you can think of anyone who might still be in touch with Patrick.'

'Oh well, that's easy. Me.'

'*What?*'

'We're friends on Facebook.'

'How come?'

'Well, he sent me a friend request.'

'And you accepted?'

'Of course. Why wouldn't I?'

'Why wouldn't you?' exclaimed Suzie. 'He broke your best friend's heart!'

'I take it this means he didn't send you a request then?' asked Jackie, arching her eyebrows.

'No, he didn't,' said Suzie, knowing that her distress at this fact was written all over her face.

'Perhaps it got lost in the post,' said Jackie.

'Very funny,' bit back Suzie. 'So how is he?' she asked, unable to stop herself.

'Well, let's take a look, shall we? Come into my office.' Still holding Troy in her arms, Jackie walked over to the kitchen counter and opened up a laptop.

They were so immersed in a detailed analysis of every aspect of Patrick's Facebook page that they didn't notice Dave, Jackie's husband, walk into the kitchen.

'What *are* you looking at?' he boomed as he stared over their shoulders at a photograph of Patrick clutching some woman's breasts in a nightclub on a mate's stag do in Tenerife.

'Oh, hi, love,' said Jackie without tearing her eyes away from the screen. 'This is Patrick.' She pointed at a very pink face peeping out from behind a mass of boob. 'Suzie's going to do her next Bobbitt on him.'

'What's a Bobbitt, Mummy?' asked Lenny, suddenly appearing at his mother's side. 'Can I have a biscuit?'

Jackie looked down at Lenny, contemplating her response. 'Bobbitt was the name of a lady who cut off her husband's willy because he did something really bad,' she said. 'Do you understand?'

'Ladies!' exclaimed a shocked Dave, covering Lenny's ears. 'What's going on in here?'

'You know I don't believe in lying to the kids,' said Jackie.

Dave stood speechless, glancing from Suzie to Jackie whilst Lenny's ears got coated in the cement dust brought home from whatever building site Dave was working on. He endured being a bricky, not for the love of architecture, but to pay the bills and allow him to indulge in his true vocation, that of lead guitarist and slightly off-key backing vocals in a tribute band named, appropriately, Cheap Purple.

His gaze finally rested on Suzie for an explanation.

'I didn't actually *do* a Bobbitt,' defended Suzie.

'What are you talking about?' demanded Dave.

'Suzie got dumped by Alex and she got her own back by threatening him with a Bobbitt,' said Jackie.

'Good God, Suzie!' Dave exclaimed. 'And I've always considered you to be the wisest and loveliest of my wife's friends.'

'You called her a hysterical old spinster the other week,' shouted Jackie over her shoulder as she walked over to load the dishwasher whilst simultaneously winding Troy.

Suzie looked at him accusingly.

'That was only when you were on the phone crying because you'd just discovered Ben Fogle was married,' said Dave.

'Yeah, well, I've turned over a new leaf,' she said, carefully storing the words hysterical and spinster in the insecure part of her brain. 'I'm off men now. In fact I'm so off men that I've changed my advice column into a revenge column and I'm tracking down ex-boyfriends who broke my heart to get my own back.'

'Isn't it brilliant!' shouted Jackie.

Dave was still standing with his mouth open.

'And this is one of the poor sods, is it?' he said, pointing at the computer.

'Yes, Patrick was my first ever boyfriend when I was fifteen.'

'*Fifteen*,' exclaimed Dave, his voice rising very high. 'You are going to go and find a lad who you haven't been out with in twenty years and threaten to cut off his . . .?' He stopped and manoeuvred Lenny behind him so that he formed a protective shield.

'No, I'm not going to do that again. Old hat now,' said Suzie.

'*Old hat*,' spluttered Dave. 'What about the fact that

you might appear to be some lunatic, vindictive bitch and they could throw you in a mental hospital?'

'Exactly,' said Suzie, undeterred. 'Random violent acts will allow them to be the victim, which totally defeats the object. I have to be a lot cleverer than that, Dave. I've got to make them feel how I felt, or else there's no point in doing it. They have to learn some kind of lesson.'

'Crikey, Suze, I didn't realise you put so much thought into it,' said Jackie, wandering back over. 'And there was me about to suggest suit slashing or something.'

'Way too obvious,' replied Suzie. 'I need to somehow make Patrick feel totally rejected and humiliated.'

'Well, that's easy,' said Jackie. 'His Facebook status says he's single, so you're free to reject and humiliate him at will. All you need to do is pull him, let him fall for you and then drop him from a great height in some spectacular fashion. Job done.'

'I cannot believe I'm hearing this,' Dave interjected. 'It was over twenty years ago, it doesn't matter any more.'

'It does,' said Suzie and Jackie in unison.

'It matters to me,' said Suzie.

'It matters to her,' said Jackie at the same time. 'I'm with you all the way, Suzie,' she said, putting an arm around her. 'Do it for me and for all the things I wish I'd said and done to Carl and never did. You could pull Patrick easily. I know you could.'

Suzie wondered – could she put herself through all that, and would it be worth it? She remembered the broken sixteen-year-old who had cried the whole day of her birthday following their hideous break-up. She looked at the gruesome photograph of Patrick on his Facebook page, groping naked breasts in a nightclub. Yes, she could. Here was a man who needed to be taught a lesson and she knew she was exactly the right woman to do it.

Chapter 8

Drew had been staring at his inbox for the last half hour. He liked to keep it empty. He didn't want loose ends lying around in cyberspace. He dealt religiously with his inbox first thing in the morning and last thing before he went home, ensuring all questions were answered and all correspondence filed, leaving him with a clean slate. He liked his inbox as he liked his life: all ordered and accounted for.

Unfortunately a rogue message had violated his system. The sort of message that hangs around waiting for attention but which you choose to ignore until it becomes absolutely critical. By this time, of course, the amount of effort required to solve the dilemma it contains has grown to epic proportions. Drew normally dealt with such messages swiftly, thereby preventing any possibility of escalation. He hadn't dealt with this one. The probable reason was that it wasn't in his inbox demanding administration; it was loitering somewhere in his head, where it had been buried for a long time. Now it had pushed its way forward to demand an answer.

Did he really love Emily?

Such was his distress that he'd rung his mother that morning. Her shock at a mid-week, mid-morning phone call did not help the flow of what in any case would be a difficult conversation. He'd asked how she was and what she was doing, and then didn't know what to do with the expectant silence that followed. He could hardly come right out with it and ask her what being in love felt like. Asking how she'd felt three months before she got married would have been just as alien, and so he'd made his excuses and asked her over for lunch on Sunday.

He was still staring at his empty inbox when Suzie arrived back with coffee, wanting to show him her first boyfriend's profile on Facebook.

'I actually thought you were joking the other night when you said you were going to find your ex-trolls,' he said, glad for some distraction. The trolls had been reinstated on the desk for the purpose of Suzie's current exercise – except for the Alex troll, who had been dumped in the canal.

'Why would I be joking?' she asked.

'Well, for a start, didn't you say the first one was whilst you were at school? You were only teenagers, weren't you?'

'Don't you start,' she said. 'That is exactly the point. We were only teenagers. The time when falling in love is the most brilliant, exciting, wonderful thing on the planet. And he ruined it. I would have thought you of all people would understand that. You must remember what a rush it was, falling in love when you're so young. It never feels as good as that again, believe me.'

Drew stared at Suzie for a moment, considering how he could use this situation to ask the question he so badly needed the answer to. He winced with his whole body as he forced out the query.

'So how did it feel, then, with this guy?'

'Oh God, I can remember it as if it was yesterday.' She flopped back in her chair. 'My entire world revolved around Patrick and how much I wanted him. He used to go to this monthly disco in the next village and I lived for those nights.' She closed her eyes, as if she was actually picturing it. 'The anticipation of whether he was going to be there and the sheer romantic potential of the evening used to make me feel physically sick.' She opened her eyes and leaned forward. 'And the preparation was epic. My outfit planning, make-up practice and shoe buying would take the whole month to perfect until the night in question arrived.' She stopped and took a sharp intake of breath, staring manically at Drew. 'The entire day would go in slow motion until the two-hour time allocation for getting ready began, and then suddenly it went into fast forward and there I was standing at the door of the hall on the precipice of a new dawn of impending love.'

Drew stared at her, unable to recall any such drama from his own experience. He could remember thinking as he arrived at university, having left the chaos of his parents' marriage, that falling in love was an inconvenience that needed to be got out of the way as quickly as possible. That night he'd put on his best Blur T-shirt and gone down to the student union to check out his fellow freshers.

'Me and Jackie would get there early so we could down a few Cinzano and lemonades,' Suzie continued.

'Not to get drunk, of course, as it's a physical impossibility to get drunk on weak Cinzano out of plastic cups. Believe me, we tried. Then we danced. Oh, did we dance, the only time in your life when you dance just because you want to, not because you're drunk. I thought it was the happiest, most romantic place in the world when I was under that glitter ball dancing around my white patent leather handbag.'

Drew recalled that the student bar was smoky and grimy and he'd been initially unimpressed by the students-in-training, drinking real ale, dancing miserably to music they had never heard of and getting mindlessly drunk before sucking the lips off someone ugly they had barely said two words to.

'I can remember my whole body shook with excitement when Patrick walked into that hall,' said Suzie.

He remembered that on day five he'd spotted Emily sitting calmly in a corner next to a girl in floods of tears. She was nodding patiently, her neat blond ponytail swaying gently.

'Month after month I plotted my toilet trips to coincide with when he went outside for a fag in the hope that we might just bump into one another, and if we bumped into one another then he might just talk to me, and if he talked to me and if I timed it exactly right at the beginning of the slow dances then he might just ask me to dance, and then if we did slow dance, of course we would kiss, because that was the only reason a boy ever asked you to dance, right?' said Suzie breathlessly.

'I guess so,' said Drew, recalling that he'd walked over to Emily straight away. 'Can I borrow you a minute?' had been his killer chat-up line. She'd blinked at him, confused by his familiarity, before realising what he was up to. Then she got up gracefully and told the girl in tears to go and call her boyfriend before following him outside. She explained that her roommate had got off with someone the previous night and now she didn't know what to tell her boyfriend of four years back at home. The next thing she said was music to his ears.

'I don't like crying. Such a waste of energy. If something goes wrong you put your efforts into doing something about it, not weeping hysterically and hoping a solution is going to pop up out of nowhere.' She shook her head and took a very small sip of white wine out of a plastic glass. A woman who didn't like high emotion or crying. A rational woman. He knew instantly that he'd found her. The woman he would fall in love with. He thought it was exactly the sort of love he had been looking for. Not the love he'd grown up with, full of deceit and lies and pathetic, pointless hope. No, he was convinced that it was going to be the right sort of love, which would grow slowly and quietly without pain or any need for female tears.

He was brought out of this reverie by the sound of Suzie singing.

'What on earth is that?' he asked.

'"Never Gonna Give You Up", Rick Astley,' Suzie declared. 'It was playing when we first kissed outside the ladies' loo.'

'How . . . romantic,' said Drew.

'It wasn't, actually,' said Suzie.

'Wasn't it?'

'No. He kissed like a washing machine then took me around the back of the hall and tried to take my bra off.'

'Nice,' said Drew. 'So that was the end of that then?'

'Don't be stupid. I sat at home and waited for him to call, of course. Crap kissing and incessant mauling didn't put me off. And to be fair, he did call and we went out over the school summer holidays. It was total bliss; I thought I was in heaven.' She paused and her face clouded over. 'Then on the first day back at school I went rushing over to him. He was standing in a crowd with his mates. He was acting all weird but I figured it was just because he wanted to chat to his friends, so I told him I'd see him at lunchtime. He turned to me in front of everybody and said that he wouldn't be seeing me at lunchtime because we weren't going out any more. He said he was bored with me now. He'd only gone out with me because his best mate Martin had gone abroad for the entire summer and he needed something to do, but Martin was back now so he didn't need me. It was a week before my sixteenth birthday. I cried the whole day.'

Suzie looked like she was about to cry now, over someone she had loved more than twenty years ago.

'Do you know what the really sad thing is?' she said, sniffing loudly. 'I never felt my heart leap like that again when a man walked in the room. That's why you're so lucky. Your love started with teenage heart leaps – how amazing is that?'

At no time did he ever recall heart leaps – nothing so energetic for him and Emily. They'd merely eased themselves into a comfortable relationship devoid of any of the drama or stress that they self-righteously observed in their friends' relationships. They cruised through university with barely a hiccup and bought a house a week after they graduated, allowing them both to concentrate on their careers. When he got made senior reporter and as Emily fast approached partnership at the law firm it seemed like the logical time to get married. Logical. Just how he liked it. Now, for some reason, as the wedding loomed he was bombarded with illogical thoughts.

'So that's why I'm going to make Patrick fall in love with me,' said Suzie, grabbing football troll off her desk and throwing it in the air. 'Then I'm going to drop him from a great height. Make him feel exactly how I felt.'

What was she saying now? That she was going to make some guy she hadn't seen in years fall in love with her just like that? Was that how it worked? Drew didn't understand any of this.

'Don't you think it's a good idea?' she asked.

'Guess so,' he said, totally bewildered. 'Can you really get Patrick to fall in love just like that?'

She went quiet, blinking rapidly at him.

'You don't think I can get him to fall in love with me, do you?' she said, a slightly accusing tone in her voice.

'No, I didn't say that.'

She looked away, hiding her face.

'Thanks,' she muttered before reaching for a tissue and blowing her nose.

Drew spotted her brimming eyes.

'What? Why are you crying?' he asked.

'I'm not,' she sniffed.

'Don't say that,' he said. 'You're crying. I can see you.'

'No, honestly, it's just . . . you know, you said . . . that it would be impossible for anyone to fall in love with me.'

'No, I didn't.'

'Yes, you did.' She buried her eyes in her tissue.

'When did I say that?'

'Just now.'

'I didn't.'

'You did.'

'I didn't.'

'You did. You said you didn't think I could get Patrick to fall in love with me.' A fresh flow of tears erupted.

How had this happened? This was why he avoided love. You started talking about love and female tears appeared out of nowhere, guaranteed. He didn't know what to do. Emily didn't do crying. If something bothered her she sat him down calmly, explained clearly what he had done wrong, asked him politely to apologise and then laid out how he could avoid the situation arising again. Sometimes it made him feel like a schoolboy who'd been called to the headmaster's office, but he would rather have that than tears any day. Making a girl cry didn't make him feel good. It reminded him too much of waking up in the middle of the night to the sound of his mother sobbing in the next room.

'Please stop crying,' he begged. 'I'm so sorry. I didn't mean to upset you, honestly.'

He looked round, desperate for an escape route. He didn't want to be thinking or talking about love and he didn't want to be sitting next to Suzie crying.

'It shouldn't be that hard,' she mumbled, discarding her tissue and shuffling her mouse until a photograph appeared on her screen. 'Look, he's obviously a lech. I just need to wear a low-cut top.'

Drew looked at the photograph and was distracted from the semi-clad blonde by something dearer to his heart.

'Well, he can't be all that bad.'

'Why?' exclaimed Suzie.

'He supports Man City. Look, he's wearing a home shirt.' Drew grabbed the mouse off Suzie. 'Let's see if he's got anything to say about last night's woeful performance.'

He clicked on Patrick's home page and scanned down for comments on the previous night's game. 'Knows his stuff,' he said, nodding when he found some highly insightful remarks. 'Smart guy.'

'What are you doing?' Suzie looked almost as upset as when he'd allegedly accused her of being unlovable.

'Sorry, sorry,' said Drew, leaping back. He'd forgotten himself for a moment there. Football had led him to a safe place away from his inner turmoil but made him forget why Suzie was looking at Patrick's Facebook page in the first place.

'You can't get between a man and his football,' he said apologetically.

She frowned and he prayed she wouldn't start crying again.

She didn't.

She began to smile instead. A huge smile that he could only respond to by reciprocating.

They sat there grinning at each other. Drew had no idea what he was smiling about.

'You're a genius,' she said, jumping up and hugging him.

What the hell, he thought. He'd never in thirty-four years had a more confusing morning.

'You will help me, won't you?' she begged, pulling back. 'I need to pick your brain on this one.'

'What are you going on about?'

'Football!' she cried. 'I need to know all about football. Come on, I'm buying you lunch and I'll fill you in.'

She beamed at him, looking deliriously happy. Thank God. She'd already put her coat on and was thrusting his at him. He got up. Lunch and football couldn't be turned down. Anything was better than spending any more time alone with love and his mixed-up head.

Chapter 9

Dear Suzie,

Every day when I walk into school the cool boys in my year sit on a wall and call me names like Firecrotch and Gingerbread House. The problem is I'm desperate to have a boyfriend and I really fancy one of them. How do I get him to go out with me?

Lottie

Dear Lottie,

I am afraid you are going to have to face the truth. Being overweight and ginger is not conducive to acquiring a boyfriend whilst at school. My best advice is to go niche. Becoming a Goth, for example, does seem to work for those who are not a perfect size 8 and blonde. Goth boys seem to be able to get past any imperfections as long as they are wrapped in swathes of black or purple along with copious amounts of eyeliner and black lipstick.

Now as for these so-called cool boys calling you names. That is so not cool, and it is so not cool to let them get away with it. So this is what you are going to do. Buy a set of cheap trophies and leave them outside school reception in a box with a note. The note will say that these boys won a Northwest Regional Line Dancing Competition at the weekend but had to leave before they could get their trophies. The Line Dancing Confederation would be very grateful if they could be presented during school assembly to mark this major achievement.

Cool boys no more. Lottie – one cool chick.

Suzie

Suzie sat back and surveyed her work. Writing the agony column had become so much easier now she had been given licence to say exactly what she wanted.

Dreaming up revenge plans was a thousand times more fun than wallowing in the misery of her readers, desperately trying to think of ways to help them force a man who clearly didn't give a toss, to love them. And now, with Drew on board with her next personal revenge, well, she was on fire. Yesterday's lunch had been a riot as their imaginations ran away with them. Talk of football and revenge had intertwined until they had come up with a plan on a scale that blew her away even to think about it. In fact she had to stop herself thinking about it too much, because if she did it made her a tiny bit terrified. But, as she reminded herself, she had a duty to fulfil. She couldn't let her readers down with some trifling payback. A grand scale was the answer and now was the time to set the wheels in motion.

'So, I'm just going to send Patrick a friend request on Facebook,' she said to Drew, who was hard at work beside her.

'What if he just ignores you?' he said, turning to stare at her.

She hadn't thought of that.

Drew sighed and leaned over to tap into her keyboard: '*See you still follow Man City. Can't believe we were so crap the other night! When will we stop buying second-rate Spaniards?'* he read aloud as he typed.

'And that means what exactly?' She stared at the screen, confused.

'That means you will absolutely get a response. No man can ignore a healthy debate about the state of his beloved football team.'

'If you say so.' She watched Drew send the message. 'So what do we do now?'

'We wait.'

'Right,' she said and crossed her arms, staring intently at the screen.

'It might take a few days,' said Drew.

'*Days!*' she exclaimed.

'Yeah. Just forget about it for a while,' Drew said.

She managed all of nineteen minutes before she glanced back at her email to see if she'd had a response. Nothing. Lunchtime – nothing. Post editorial meeting – nothing. Getting up to put her coat on and delaying switching her PC off until the last minute – nothing. This was worse than waiting for the phone to ring.

'Stop looking,' said Drew for the twentieth time that day.

'I'm not. Just checking my meetings for tomorrow

and then it's off and so am I.' She clicked on her calendar then couldn't resist one last look.

And there it was. Patrick's name. In her inbox. Just sitting there innocently. She stared, unable to click it open. The reaction to seeing his name was as physical and real as if he had just walked into the room. Her heart was beating so loudly she was surprised that Drew couldn't hear it. The feeling reminded her so strongly of how she'd felt when he had first called her all those years ago after their dance floor snog that she felt dizzy. He sent me a message, she kept thinking. *He* sent me a message.

'There you go. Told you it'd get a response, didn't I?' said Drew, catching sight of Patrick's name in bold at the top of Suzie's list. 'Open it then.'

She really wanted to open it on her own, savour the moment, but she couldn't explain this to herself, let alone to Drew. So she clicked and held her breath.

Too bloody right. How the devil are you?

'Come on,' cried Drew, pumping his arm. 'You're most definitely in,' he declared, putting his arm around her. 'Can I trust you not to screw up the next bit now? I've got to go.'

'Sure, I'll be fine,' she said, grateful for some time

alone in cyberspace with Patrick. She smiled up at Drew as he shoved some files into his briefcase. 'Thanks,' she said. 'Really.'

'Don't mention it. It's more fun than wedding planning, put it like that. See you tomorrow.'

She sat and stared at the screen for a long time before she tentatively began to tell Patrick her story. The story, of course, that she wanted him to believe: of huge success in all aspects of her life, told with the odd witty turn of phrase, agonised over almost as much as her column.

Over the following days Patrick sent back his story in turn, the one he no doubt wanted her to believe. It struck her that dating was much easier this way. Every move, every comment could be premeditated and fine-tuned until it hit exactly the right note. Not like years ago, when relationships crashed and burned before they'd even begun due to an unplanned case of verbal diarrhoea on an irrelevant subject during that all important first phone call. Maybe if they'd had Facebook when she was younger she would be happily married by now.

When she finally plucked up the courage to call him after days of online posturing, she was surprised to feel her stomach in knots as she waited for him to answer, no longer able to hide behind the written word, making verbal cock-ups highly likely. He picked up the phone with a gruff hello then his tone instantly lightened when he realised who it was. After the obligatory initial awkwardness they laughed and joked quite easily. He sounded more confident than she expected, almost casual, especially as he broke off several times to answer other incoming calls. He apologised for his rudeness: when you operated a global business like he did you had to be at your clients' beck and call whatever the time of day. The word *tosser* sprang to mind and reminded her of the point of her phone call. She had to convince him to go to the match with her the following Saturday. It was an invite to hospitality that did the trick, as recommended by Drew. They were on their way.

Suzie woke up the following Saturday at 4.34 a.m. She sat bolt upright in bed, panicking that she'd missed the alarm. Seeing the time, she felt relieved – an unusual feeling for this hour of the morning. She got up promptly, knowing that the time had come to make the most important decision of the day. What to wear? She had paraded in front of Jackie for what felt like hours the previous evening, fuelled by large glasses of wine. Her initial thoughts had been sophisticated and demure, but

Jackie had other ideas which leaned more towards a tart/ prostitute look. Eventually she decided to hedge her bets. It was only football, after all, so she shouldn't overdress. She laid out her best designer jeans, her knock-off Jimmy Choos, and a fairly clingy sweater that with the right bra looked pretty spectacular, she thought. Outfit sorted by 5.04 a.m. precisely, she mooched into the kitchen and looked inside the fridge at all the food she should avoid eating to ensure the sweater clung rather than bulged.

At two o'clock she met Drew at the stadium. He surveyed her outfit with a look of complete despair as fans swarmed around them outside the doors to hospitality.

'You can't wear that,' he said, shaking his head and staring right at her chest.

'Why not?' she protested. 'It was really expensive.'

'Turn around,' he said gruffly.

'Why?'

'Just turn around a minute,' he repeated.

She rotated slowly and sullenly like a schoolchild showing her new uniform to Granny.

'You'll have to take it off,' he declared.

'But I love this jumper.'

'I'm sure you do, but we'll have nowhere to hide the wires. He'll spot them a mile off.'

She stared at him. Bugger. He was right. The whole plan relied on her being miked up so Drew could talk to her secretly whilst she was with Patrick. If they couldn't do that then it all fell apart.

'We'll just have to improvise.' Drew looked around for inspiration. 'You really need something with a collar, to hide the wires going up to your earpiece. Got it,' he said, starting to unbutton his powder-blue shirt.

'What *are* you doing?' she exclaimed.

'It's alright. I've got my lucky match shirt on underneath,' he said. 'You don't get to see me naked.'

'Do you really think I'm going to wear your shirt to meet an ex-boyfriend? I want him to think he made a mistake all those years ago when he dumped me, not that he had a lucky escape from a transvestite.'

He stopped mid-unbuttoning. 'Okay, we'll not do it then, shall we? I'm quite happy just to watch the match.'

'No,' cried Suzie, putting her hand on his arm to stop him walking off in a huff. She needed Drew. Not only was he crucial to the entire plan, she also felt a distinct sense of confidence when he was around.

'Please don't go,' she said. 'I'm sorry. I'm just so nervous, that's all.'

Drew reached over to drape his shirt around Suzie's

shoulders then bent over so their eyes were level. 'There's no need to be nervous,' he said gently. 'I know you can do this. Do you hear me?'

She gulped and looked away before she got mes-merised by his pale blue eyes. 'Okay,' she said with a weak smile.

Suzie headed for the Ladies and scrutinised herself in the mirror. It took some adjustment to make Drew's shirt look sexy. In the end she decided on tucked in, as luckily she had worn a rather funky rhinestone belt, and she left enough buttons undone to show a decent amount of cleavage. The bizarre thing was that the shirt did make her feel sexy. It reminded her of all those romantic films where girl sleeps with boy and then gets up in the morning and makes him breakfast wearing nothing but the shirt that was ripped from his body in a frenzy of passion the night before. Sadly she'd never got to act out that fantasy. She found that mornings after the night before usually consisted of her and whoever taking a trip to McDonald's to sort out their hangovers. Actually she had attempted it once, many years ago, but when she went to pick up said shirt it stank of booze and cigarettes and made her want to retch.

She found Drew in the unused commentary box that

he'd managed to blag through the sports writer on the paper.

'It looks better on you than me,' said Drew, looking at her chest again.

'It's all in the styling,' she said as she heaved up the picnic basket she'd painstakingly put together and dumped it on the ledge that ran along the front of the small room. She turned back to face Drew and put her hands on her hips. 'Now mike me up, Scotty,' she grinned.

After they'd had a few awkward moments fiddling around inside her shirt trying to get the minute microphone system to work, Drew left Suzie to it, retreating to a room a bit further down the corridor. Having established they could hear each other by singing 'Twinkle, Twinkle Little Star', she set about laying out her sumptuous feast.

'This is not just food, this is revenge food,' Suzie hummed to herself as she carefully laid out the flaky sausage rolls and sumptuous double chocolate fudge cake. Then she ceremoniously popped the cork on a bottle of champagne, poured herself a glass and downed it in one.

'Ready and waiting,' she declared softly just as there came a knock at the door.

'Fucking hell, he's gorgeous,' she muttered as Patrick strode confidently into the room in a cloud of designer aftershave.

She gazed up at him dizzily, just as she'd done every time he'd walked into a room all those years ago. Somehow he looked even better than he had then. His strawberry blond hair had lost the threat of ginger that had always lingered around the roots. It had also been skilfully waxed and tweaked into a stylish peak at the front, hardly reminiscent of his mum's do-it-yourself job he had been forced to endure in his youth. There was a subtle hint of stubble, a personal favourite of hers as it always seemed so damned masculine. And there it was. The smile that had made her weak at the knees all those years ago through a haze of weak Cinzano was making her quite giddy now in the aftermath of champagne on an empty stomach.

'Focus, Suzie, focus,' Drew said sternly in her ear just as she felt herself swoon as his delicious aftershave captivated her nostrils.

'Suzie,' said Patrick, enveloping her in a hug that almost caused her knees to give way. 'You haven't changed one bit,' he continued, holding her at arm's length and giving her a good look up and down.

Suzie had a sudden flashback to the Eighties when it was considered cool to wear your dad's shirt pulled in by a huge white belt. And here she was in Drew's shirt, looking like she was still stuck in the previous century's worst fashion decade. She surveyed Patrick's outfit. It was clear that each item was a highly priced designer piece, thrown together to complement his club shirt in that casual way that Manchester men do best. Liam and Noel Gallagher had a lot to answer for. She was embarrassed that he looked infinitely cooler than she did.

'And look at you,' she said, ruffling his hair and struggling to know exactly what to say. 'All grown up,' she finally managed.

She was sure she heard Drew groan in her ear.

'So I nearly couldn't find you,' said Patrick. 'I asked and they said this is actually a commentary box.'

'Oh yeah, well, I thought you've probably been in loads of executive boxes here, and this would be just a bit different for you. And this commentator I know managed to swing it for me.'

'Oh right,' he said, looking around. 'Who's that then?'

'Oh, erm, it's er . . .' she stalled, waiting for Drew to

say his mate's name but nothing came. 'Oh, you wouldn't know him. He doesn't commentate here; he just knows people who do. Champagne?'

'Wow, don't mind if I do,' he said, nodding appreciatively. 'Here, let me.' He took the bottle and filled two glasses.

'So,' he said, looking her up and down and lingering maybe a little too long at cleavage level. 'To old friends,' he continued, raising his glass to toast her.

'To old friends,' she replied, unable to stop herself beaming right back at his broad smile.

'So, Suzie Miller, a hotshot journo, hey? I have to say I'm very impressed.' He reached round her shoulders and gave her a chummy squeeze. His stubble brushed against her and she thought she might collapse. 'Imagine, my old mate Suzie in the media. Awesome.'

'Well, er, you know, I worked really hard to get where I am.' She could hear a mocking guffaw from Drew.

'Now don't be modest, Suzie. I always knew you would go far.'

'Really?' she exclaimed.

'Oh yeah,' he said, reaching over to top up her glass. 'You were always one of the brainy kids at school, weren't you? I tell you, when I pulled you I couldn't believe my luck. Thought I'd hit the jackpot. Brains and beauty. What a combo.'

'Really?' she exclaimed again.

'Really,' he said nodding vigorously. 'I never thought you'd look twice at me, to be honest. And then when you did, I remember thinking all my Christmases had come at once.'

'You did?' She took a long gulp from her glass. Had she got the right Patrick, or was this a case of mistaken identity?

'Such a shame we met when we were teenagers. We were just too young to make a go of it, weren't we?' he said, running his fingers carefully through his waxed-up hair.

'Yeah, I guess so,' she muttered. Maybe she had got it all wrong. Maybe it hadn't happened how she remembered it.

'But hey,' he said, throwing his arms open. 'We're here now, aren't we, and I have to say it's really good to see you.'

'Well, Patrick. That's . . . that's a lovely thing to say. Thank you.'

Patrick took a long gulp of champagne and looked her up and down again. She hoped he noticed that she was only one size bigger than she had been as a teenager.

'It's true, Suzie,' he continued, shaking his head. 'I've had some crazy women in my life, believe me, including my ex-wife – but don't get me started on her. That's a whole other story. But you turning up like this. A lovely, sane woman who earns her own money and likes football. Suzie, I think all my Christmases might have come again.' He gave her a suggestive smile.

She hoped Drew had heard every word of that. Too risky to rely on him falling in love with her – that's what Drew had said. Christ, he was practically proposing. She watched, mesmerised, as he sat down and stretched his long body out on a chair before putting his hands behind his head and throwing her a contented smile. His apparent satisfaction was contagious. She couldn't help but wonder what this would feel like if Patrick really was her boyfriend again. Clearly they would be a champagne picnics type of couple. The scene popped into her head so clearly that she didn't want to lose it. She saw herself and Patrick in a summer meadow on a checked blanket idly feeding each other strawberries and champagne before he made tender love to her right there in the sunshine. Maybe fate was taking a hand. Perhaps her whole revenge mission was just a way of making her find

Patrick again, rediscovering the first man who had made her heart beat faster and who had certainly raised her temperature the minute he had swaggered in. It was just possible that they were meant to be together all along.

'Why don't you bring over those sausage rolls and another bottle of that bubbly and come and sit next to me,' he purred.

'Okay,' she giggled, tripping over her own feet in her haste to be near him.

She put the bottle down on the shelf in front of them and sat down, her heart beating very fast indeed. She couldn't help but notice the soft hairs on the back of his hands, something he definitely hadn't had when he was fifteen. He'd been a boy when they were last together, but he was a man now – all man, by the looks of it, and probably entirely different to how he'd been back then. He'd had time to mature and realise what he really wanted in life. He wasn't the fickle teenager he used to be. She was still staring at him intently, thinking all this through, when he took her hand and raised it to his lips, looking deep into her eyes.

'Oh Patrick,' she couldn't help murmuring as he moved forward.

'I don't usually move this fast, but you're different,

Suzie.' He started to kiss her, and all thoughts of her mission were instantly obliterated by the feel of his lips on hers.

'Suzie, I need to talk to you NOW,' came an urgent whisper in her ear.

She pulled away sharply, worried that Patrick would hear Drew through her earpiece.

'What?' asked Patrick, surprised. 'There's no need to be scared, Suzie. It's just me,' he said gently.

'*Now!*' Drew screamed, making Suzie jump.

'I just . . . I've got to go to the Ladies,' she gasped. 'I'll be back in a minute. Don't go anywhere.'

Suzie stormed down the corridor. What the hell did Drew think he was doing interrupting like that?

'What the hell are you doing?' said Drew when she entered the room. 'Were you kissing him?'

Suzie looked down at the floor.

'I can't believe you're letting him kiss you,' said Drew, exasperated.

'And I can't believe you are shouting down my ear and telling me to stop,' she replied crossly. 'I'm a grown woman, you know. You can't do that.'

'Have you forgotten why we're here or have you just taken leave of your senses?'

'No, I haven't forgotten, Drew, but . . . Didn't you hear him? He wanted me back then. He said so. It was just because we were teenagers, that's why we split up. I got it wrong, don't you see? And he likes me, I can tell. This could be it, Drew. He could be the one. I think we need to forget the revenge plan and see where this goes.'

Drew stared at her. 'I did hear him, Suzie,' he said gently. 'I don't think he really remembers going out with you. He's making it all up. He's coming on to you because he thinks you're minted because you work in the media and can get him into a box at the football.'

'No, that's not true,' she said, shocked at Drew's attitude. 'He said he thought he was lucky to go out with me. You heard him. He said he thought all his Christmases had come at once.'

'Oh Suzie, anyone could say that. Look, I'm not trying to ruin this for you, honestly; I just don't want you to get hurt, that's all. I don't trust this guy. All that stuff about when you went out together as teenagers, he's making it up.'

'No, he's not.'

'Okay,' said Drew, starting to look a bit annoyed, 'I'll

tell you what. Why don't you ask him about how you got together or how you split up? If you meant that much to him he'll remember, right?'

'Of course he'll remember.'

'Well, if he does, great. I'll turn off the mike and watch the match in peace. But if he doesn't, then I want you to tell me that we're going to go ahead as planned.'

'Okay,' she agreed sulkily.

'We'll have a password so you won't have to leave the room again.'

'If we must,' she said with a sigh, eager to get back to Patrick.

'Good, so the password is, let's see . . . What about . . .'

'Screw you,' interrupted Suzie. 'Because that's what I'd like to say to you when he remembers everything about our relationship.'

'Fine,' said Drew. 'Screw you it is.'

'Come and sit down, lovely lady,' purred Patrick when she got back to the room. 'It's nearly kick-off time. I've got to tell you, this is the best view I've ever had at a match. I've been sending all my mates who are sitting in the North Stand photos on my phone. They hate me, how good is that?'

'That's great,' said Suzie, deep in thought as she reached for her champagne. 'So, do you still see much of Martin?' she asked.

'Martin who?'

'Your best pal at school, Martin Holmes.'

'Oh him, nah. No idea what happened to him. We lost touch after school, you know how it is. He was a bit of a tosser actually. Glad to get rid of him.'

'Right,' she said, nodding. She paused to consider what to say next. 'I still feel bad about the way we split up, you know,' she said, as casually as possible.

Patrick looked at her quizzically. She looked back expectantly.

'Oh Suzie, I had no idea,' he said, taking her hand and stroking it. 'You really don't have to feel bad any more. I know how it is. Teenage girls are picky. One minute you're in, the next you're not. I only cried for a week, I promise.'

Suzie stared back, speechless. He actually thought that she'd dumped him.

'Tell you what?' he continued. 'Consider this your apology. I'll forget the fact that you heartlessly dumped me when I was a poor, defenceless boy if you can keep getting me into gigs like this. How about that? Would that make you feel better?' He glanced down at his watch then looked out of the window.

'Come on, you Blues!' he screamed at the top of his voice, leaping up to cheer his team onto the pitch.

Suzie's heart was beating fast again, but not through joy. Not even through disappointment. It was the realisation that yet again, having promised herself faithfully she would not let it happen, she had teetered on the edge of hope. For a moment she had thought she was looking at her happily ever after, but he was just a fraud, feeding her whatever lines he thought necessary to get what he wanted. She was a fool.

She bit her lip and muttered, 'Screw you, Patrick Connolly. Screw you.'

Chapter 10

Drew sat back and heaved a huge sigh of relief. What was it with this girl? She must have something missing in her brain to be this stupid when it came to men. Actually it wasn't her, he remembered; it was the love thing that made her stupid. Thank goodness he'd finally come to his senses and decided to dismiss his sudden angst over love. He'd weighed it all up carefully and just couldn't find any evidence to show that love was the essential ingredient to ensure a long and happy marriage. Most divorced couples had declared they were passionately in love when they got married, and what good did that do them? He was best just to forget about it. Focus on the fact that there were a million logical reasons to marry Emily, even if he wasn't absolutely certain that love was one of them. Compatibility, shared interests, similar intellectual capacity, the same sense of humour – good, solid reasons that had seen them through sixteen years. Longer than most couples stay married.

Throwing himself into helping Suzie with her latest scheme had successfully occupied his brain, thus avoiding any further thinking time. The scale of it and his vital role had kept him awake at night, but that was a fine reason to be staring at the ceiling at three in the morning. Much better than his previous topic of internal debate during the small hours.

He picked up his mobile phone to make the call that would put the next stage of the plan into place. Now that he had met Patrick, if indeed only via Suzie's wire, his initial nervousness about what they were about to do to a fellow fan had disappeared. Once he'd called his mate in the announcers' box, he sat back to enjoy the football.

As the last few minutes of the first half arrived, Drew tuned back in to see what was going on with Suzie and Patrick. There was absolute silence other than the

122

occasional comment on the football from Patrick. Suzie must be bored stiff. Then Drew heard several loud bangs and the sound of the door opening.

'Sorry to bother you,' he heard his mate say. 'I'm Steve Bromley, the half-time compere. My assistant has screwed up on getting contestants for the half-time City's Biggest Fan Quiz. Anyone interested?'

'Oh yeah,' said Patrick, jumping up out of his chair. 'I've always wanted to do that. I always get more questions right than the losers you normally get up there.'

'Fantastic. You don't fancy it, do you?' Steve asked Suzie. 'I still need someone else.'

'Okay,' she said.

'Er, Suzie, I don't think . . .' started Patrick.

'No, I'll do it. I'm game. It'll be fun,' she said.

'Okay,' said Steve. 'Brilliant. We can have boys v. girls. Spice it up a bit. I'll see you both downstairs in the foyer in five.'

'They ask really hard questions, Suzie. I'll beat you easily,' said Patrick as soon as Steve had left the room.

'Patronising bastard,' muttered Drew.

'I don't know,' said Suzie. 'I'm a pretty big fan, you know.'

Drew heard Patrick laugh a little too hard.

'If you say so, Suze. If you say so. But I'm warning you, no-one beats me when it comes to Man City. Especially not a girl.'

Drew looked out to the centre of the pitch at Suzie's tiny figure standing on a podium next to Patrick, who was busy taking photos with his mobile phone and waving merrily at the enormous crowd.

'Ladies and gentlemen,' boomed Steve into his microphone. 'It's boys v. girls today in our quest to find Manchester City's Biggest Fan. Can the girls prove it's not just a man's game or will the boys claim their territory?'

A massive roar went up in the stands and Drew watched as Patrick strutted around the podium, arms held high as if he'd already won.

'You can do this,' whispered Drew. 'You have nothing to worry about. You are playing it exactly right. Let him think he's going to win.'

'I'm crapping my pants,' came the whispered response from Suzie. 'There are like a million people out here all looking at me.'

'Focus, Suzie, focus,' said Drew. 'Five minutes and you're done. The end is in sight now. I know you can do this.' He didn't tell her that his stomach was also doing somersaults with nerves.

'So, can you tell me your name and how long you've been a City fan?' said Steve, shoving the microphone in Patrick's face.

'I'm Patrick and I've followed the Blues since my dad started bringing me when I was three years old. He's over there in the North Stand. Hi, Dad!' Patrick stepped to the front of the podium and shouted at the top of his voice, 'I'm City till I die,' waving his arms frantically until the entire stadium took up the chant.

I'm City till I die,
I'm City till I die,
You know I am,
I'm sure I am,
I'm City till I die.'

The sound was deafening and Drew watched as Suzie stared around her, looking petrified.

'And what about you?' Steve asked Suzie after the din had died down.

'Er, I'm Suzie Miller and I've been a fan for, like, ever,' she said before punching the air half-heartedly and muttering a rather feeble, 'City forever.'

Drew cringed in his seat. This had better work or

he'd never be able to be seen with Suzie in public again.

It was amazing how such a large crowd could make such a noise one minute and be so devastatingly quiet the next.

'Right, so let's just go over the rules, shall we?' said Steve. 'I will ask you two questions each. Whoever gets the most right wins; however, if it's a draw then we go to a sudden death question. You got it, guys?'

'Bring it on!' Patrick shouted back.

'Yeah, okay,' breathed Suzie.

'Okay then, here we go. We'll start with you, Patrick. Your first question is, in which year did City win their first ever league title?'

'1937,' said Patrick without even pausing to think.

'Correct,' shouted Steve as Patrick sprang in the air and did a victory lap around the podium. The crowd roared in appreciation.

'OK then, Suzie,' said Steve gently. 'This is your question. What did they do the following season that no other club has ever achieved?'

There was almost silence in the packed stadium as Suzie stared blankly at Steve.

'Would you like me to repeat the question?' asked Steve.

Suzie nodded her head in silence and a mocking ripple started to ebb around the crowd.

'The season after City won their first ever league title, what did they achieve that no other club ever has?'

Suzie was now staring at Steve desperately.

'I'm pretty sure they got relegated,' Drew said into the mike. He was feeling sick; maybe this hadn't been such a good idea. He may have been devoted to City all his life but answering questions under pressure was hard. Even if he wasn't the one under the spotlight.

He watched as Suzie leaned to talk into the microphone. Drew held his breath.

'Did they get relegated, Steve?' she said, a slight quiver in her voice.

There was the faint sound of respectful clapping in the crowd before Steve responded.

'Yes, they did,' he roared, slapping her on the back. Suzie grinned from ear to ear, finally looking like she belonged on the podium. Patrick nonchalantly shrugged his shoulders as if he thought her answer had been a lucky guess.

'Okay, Patrick. Pressure's on now. Can you keep it up for the lads?' asked Steve.

'I can keep it up for anyone,' he replied with a wink.

'Right then, your second question. Who did City beat to win their only European trophy, the Cup Winners' Cup?'

'Górnik Zabrze from Poland,' he replied instantly, then jumped up and down in victory even before Steve had confirmed it was the right answer.

'Well done, Patrick. The right answer. Now, Suzie, you need to get this question right to stay in the game. In which city did Manchester City win the Cup Winners' Cup?'

'Vienna,' said Drew down the mike. Thank God for that. They might just pull this off.

He looked down at Suzie, who was standing frozen on the podium, not saying anything.

'Vienna,' he repeated. 'Vienna.'

Suzie was looking desperately up at the stand where he was sitting.

'What the fuck's she doing?' he said, jumping up in frustration. The wire attached to his headset sprang to life, dancing merrily around him. 'Fuck, fuck, fuck,' he cried as he realised he'd become disconnected and she couldn't hear him. He jammed the connector back into its socket and screamed, '*VIENNA*,' just as Steve was asking her for the final time.

'Warsaw,' he heard Suzie suggest desperately the split second before he was reconnected.

'*NOOOOOO, VIENNA,*' he screamed as Suzie's hand flew to her left ear, a shocked look on her face.

He watched through his fingers as Suzie laughed hysterically and punched Steve playfully on the shoulder.

'Just kidding, Steve. Of course the city where they beat them was Vienna,' she said with a triumphant wave of her arm.

'That's not fair,' Patrick declared. 'She heard them shouting from the crowd.'

'Now, come on, Patrick, I'm sure Suzie didn't hear anything, did you?'

'No, of course not,' said Suzie.

'Yeah, right,' retorted Patrick. 'Can you just tell them to stop shouting out the answers?' he continued, waving a derisory hand in the direction of the North Stand.

Suddenly the sound of booing echoed around the ground. They're turning against the cocky git, thought Drew. Perfect.

'Now let's be sportsmanlike, shall we?' said Steve. 'Or can't you take being beaten by a girl?' A wicked grin appeared on his face. Patrick stared stonily back at Steve as the booing subsided into gentle laughter.

'So now it's sudden death,' said Steve. 'I'm going to ask you both the same question and the one who gets closest to the right answer wins the title, Manchester City's Biggest Fan. Are you both ready?'

'Yes,' said Suzie and Patrick in unison.

'Since records began in the late 1800s, how many players have played for Manchester City Football Club?' asked Steve.

A gasp went up around the crowd. That was a really hard question. Drew thought he might throw up. It was a really, really hard question.

'So, Patrick, what's it going to be?' pressed Steve after giving them a few moments to think it through.

Patrick had his eyes screwed shut in concentration. He opened them and said, 'I reckon it's about eight and a half thousand.'

'And what do you think, Suzie?' asked Steve.

'I think he's gone too high,' whispered Drew. 'I've got a feeling they didn't play during the war. Just go a bit lower.'

'Er, I think I'm going to go with eight thousand,' said Suzie, the wobble back in her voice.

Shit, thought Drew. She went too low.

'Is that your final answer?' asked Steve.

Suzie nodded silently.

'Well, I can tell you that you are both very close,' said Steve. 'Will Suzie bring it home for the ladies or is Patrick going to carry it home for the boys? Let's have a bit of hush, shall we, while I reveal the final answer.'

The crowd quietened whilst Drew prayed way up in his little box room.

'The answer to the question, how many players have played for Manchester City is . . . eight thousand two hundred and fourteen.'

There was a pause as everyone tried to work out who had won. Suzie and Patrick stood glued to their spots, unsure what the answer meant.

'So that means that this week, Manchester City's Biggest Fan is . . . *Suzie*, by a whisker. So sorry, Patrick, but today *you* have been beaten by a girl.'

It was Suzie's turn to do victory runs around the podium as Patrick looked on in horror. He stood stock-still, clearly in shock as a chant began to rise from the crowd.

'Beaten by a girl
Beaten by a girl
Beaten by a girl
Beaten by a girl!'

He gazed wide-eyed up at the North Stand where the chant had begun. Thousands of his beloved fellow fans were pointing an accusing finger in the air and mocking him in the worst way possible. He went pale and appeared to shrivel as all the arrogance and cockiness was sucked out of him in the face of such disgrace. Suzie caught sight of him and couldn't help but laugh out loud. The scale of Patrick's humiliation was beyond even her wildest dreams.

'Does Manchester City's Biggest Fan have anything she'd like to say?' asked Steve as he shoved the microphone in her grinning face.

'I certainly do,' she said as she turned to face the jeering North Stand and raised her hands in the air. 'I would just like to thank this truly magnificent crowd.'

A massive cheer went up in response to her appreciation.

'What the fuck,' screamed Patrick, grabbing the microphone.

'No swearing, please,' interjected Steve. 'There are children present.'

'I'm Manchester City's Biggest Fan,' he roared. 'There's no way she's a real fan.' His deathly pallor had been replaced by pure beetroot red as the shock subsided into anger. 'When I went out with her she didn't even know who Francis Lee was, for Christ's sake. She's Rick Astley's biggest fan, not Man City's. She used to bore me to death about him, so I dumped her.'

Suzie gasped.

Drew gasped.

'So you do remember,' she breathed.

He gave her a look of complete contempt.

'Yes, I do,' he replied defiantly.

Suzie couldn't believe it. Everything he'd said upstairs was a lie, and not only that, he'd labelled her boring yet again in public. She'd thought beating him in front of his fellow fans would be enough to teach him a lesson but clearly she needed to go further. This wasn't over. She hadn't intended to go this far but he'd asked for it. She took a step forward and prodded the club emblem proudly displayed on his chest.

'Call yourself a fan,' she hissed. 'I remember what you did that summer we went out.' She grabbed the microphone back off him. 'Let's share your guilty secret with everyone, shall we?'

It was Patrick's turn to gasp as the colour drained from his face for the second time that afternoon.

'Don't you dare!' he screamed, making a lunge for

her. Fortunately Steve decided it was time to intervene.

'Easy, boy,' he said, laying a firm hand on Patrick's shoulder. 'That's no way to behave, is it?'

Suzie cleared her throat as she prepared to make an announcement.

'Nooooooooooooooooo,' Patrick screeched, dropping to his knees in front of her. 'Don't do it,' he begged, clasping his hands together. 'Anything but that, please.'

He looked pathetic, so different from the arrogant façade he'd presented earlier.

'Not here,' he whined. 'You can't say it here, I'm begging you. I'll be crucified.'

She savoured his terrified face for a moment longer before she bent forward and whispered in his ear.

'Not nice, is it?' she breathed. 'Being humiliated in front of the last people in the world you would want to be. This is exactly how it felt when you dumped me and now it's your turn.'

Patrick sank back and stared at her as she stood up and lifted the microphone to address the crowd.

'In the summer of 1988 Manchester City suffered a crushing defeat of 4–1 to Oldham Athletic, leaving them languishing at the bottom of Division Two,' she announced clearly and confidently. A knowing mutter rippled around the stadium. 'Patrick was at that match and as he left he made an unforgivable decision.'

The mutter rose to a rumble.

'He decided to defect from supporting Manchester City.'

The rumble grew louder.

'Noooooo,' shouted Patrick, his hands now covering his ears.

'That's not the worst of it,' she continued. 'He shunned Manchester City in their hour of need to support . . .' She paused for effect. 'Manchester United, for five whole days,' she finished triumphantly.

The rumble grew to a roar as the stadium took on the guise of a gladiator's pit. Menace oozed from every corner as Patrick's fellow City fans booed and jeered with all their might, rejecting him with all the vocal energy they could muster. His relationship with them, with football, with Manchester City was changed forever. There was no greater sin than supporting a rival team from the same city.

'Do you have anything to say for yourself?' asked Steve solemnly as he hauled Patrick to his feet to face the wrath of his fellow fans.

'I was young,' he bleated. 'I thought United stood a

better chance of winning something.' He hid his face in his hands, unable to face the thousands of angry faces. 'It was only five days,' he muttered.

When the missiles of plastic bottles and polystyrene cartons started landing on the pitch Steve realised it might be wise to conclude the half-time activities.

'Let this be a lesson to you,' he said, grimly shaking his head. 'And as for you,' he turned to Suzie. 'You are what this team is all about. A shining example of commitment and loyalty. Ladies and gentlemen, please give it up for today's winner of Manchester City's Greatest Fan, the one and only Suzie Miller!'

The crowd roared their appreciation. Patrick looked on in bewilderment as Suzie strutted around the podium with all the confidence and joy he had displayed minutes earlier. He flinched as she paused right next to him and leaned over to whisper in his ear once more.

'Make the most of this moment, Patrick,' she said. 'I suspect it's the last time you'll ever be able to set foot in this stadium. Enjoy.' And with that she skipped off the podium and ran across the pitch.

As Drew watched Suzie bounce off the podium he realised he had to go and find her right now. He ran out of the room and down three flights of stairs before going up another set of steps to enter the stand. He could see Suzie below him being ushered through a barrier at the side of the pitch by security staff. She was just about to disappear.

'Suzie!' he bellowed. She didn't turn. She hadn't heard him.

'Wait, Suzie!' He hurtled down the steps towards the pitch, oblivious to the weird looks he was getting.

He shouted again, and finally she turned round. Realising who it was, she fought her way past the two security guards who were trying to get her safely through the crowd with her prize – a coveted signed shirt.

'Drew!' she screamed, running up the steps towards him. 'I did it, I did it!'

They met halfway up the steps of Stand 104 and embraced, jumping up and down for joy.

'I did it,' she kept saying. She pulled away. 'Did you see his face? He could not believe what was happening. It was brilliant, Drew.' Tears were now rolling down her face, but Drew didn't mind this time; he knew they were happy tears. She moved forward to hug him again and he hugged her right back.

Suddenly he realised that he wasn't sure when to stop hugging her and if indeed he wanted to. There was something very heart-warming about having a woman cry with joy on your shoulder. He sprang back as if she had just caught fire.

'So,' he said, needing to destroy the moment. 'One last question.'

'What's that?'

'Can I have the shirt?' He nodded at the collector's item clutched in her hand.

'Of course! I never would have got it without you.' She thrust it into his hand.

At that point a middle-aged man in the seat next to where they were standing leaned over.

'You must be the luckiest man alive,' he said to Drew. 'Not only does your wife like football but she gets you a signed shirt as well. Can't even get my wife to let me have Sky Sports,' he grumbled.

'She's not my wife,' said Drew.

'I'm not his wife,' said Suzie simultaneously.

The man looked at the two of them, confused, before a look of enlightenment crossed his face.

'I see,' he said slowly. 'Then you're not just lucky, you're a lucky bastard,' he said, shaking his head in awe.

'No, you don't understand,' protested Drew. The man raised his eyebrows as if he understood perfectly.

'Come on,' said Suzie, tugging at his sleeve. 'We have to go and celebrate.'

'No, I can't,' he said firmly. 'I promised Emily I'd take her to the Loft tonight. I can't turn up drunk again. Not after last time.'

The man coughed behind them.

'Of course,' she conceded. 'I've borrowed you enough for one day. How am I ever going to repay you?'

The man coughed again.

Drew decided to ignore him. 'You already have,' he said, holding the shirt up.

She laughed. 'Well, I'll see you on Monday.' She leaned forward for one last embrace. They held each other a second too long.

He was the first to pull back. As he walked away up the steps, it took all his willpower not to turn back to see if she was watching him.

Chapter 11

'You should have seen him, Em,' said Drew that night, as they sat in one of Manchester's finest restaurants. 'He was absolutely floored. I've never seen anything like it. The whole crowd was chanting at him like he had just given a penalty away in the last few minutes of the FA Cup.'

'Mmmmm, that's great,' nodded Emily, studying a small black notebook she had pulled out of her handbag.

'What are you looking at?' snapped Drew, just a little upset that Emily was clearly only half listening. He'd gone to great pains to make sure she was aware of what he'd been up to with Suzie to ensure there could be no misunderstanding, but she was about as interested as she ever was with anything related to football.

'Invitation wording,' she mumbled, not looking up. 'We still have to agree the wording for our invites.' She wrote something in her notebook.

Drew sighed. He'd been on a high ever since he'd left the stadium and he wanted to share it with Emily, but she was clearly having none of it.

'We don't have to do it now, do we?' he asked.

'No, of course not. I just wanted to have a quick look through our checklist for the wedding whilst we're together, make sure we're on track.'

'Great, good idea,' sighed Drew. Bloody hell. He was after a good time, not a debate on whether *request the pleasure of your company* was a better way of saying *come to our party*. He sat quietly, hoping that Emily would come to the conclusion that they were on track without his input.

'By the way,' she said, looking up.

Here it comes, he thought. Fruit cake or sponge?

'I've been asking around and I've managed to get hold of what is deemed in the industry to be the fairest prenup agreement. It's in my briefcase at home. We should really sign it as soon as.' She looked down at her book again and crossed something off.

He put his drink down quickly. He hadn't been expecting that particular pre-wedding dilemma.

'Is that really necessary?' he asked.

'What do you mean?' she said, snapping her book shut and putting it back in her bag.

'Well, I wouldn't have thought we'd need one of those, would you?'

Emily laughed. 'If you gave me a pound for every couple who walked through my door and said that, I'd be a millionaire by now. No-one thinks it's necessary, Drew. *I* don't think it's necessary but I do think it's sensible. More sensible than wasting thousands of pounds on expensive divorce lawyers like me if the worst happens. It's better to agree what you will do in a calm, lucid manner before you get married rather than in an over-emotional, irrational way at the point when you hate each other.'

Drew looked at Emily. He knew he shouldn't be surprised at her suggestion. She had a unique ability to be totally rational about what could be very emotional issues.

'So what does this prenup say, then?'

'Basically, we both retain any assets that we had before the marriage and split the proceeds from the house and the joint account in half. It's very simple. Nothing to worry about.'

'But what if we have kids?' he asked.

'Joint custody. The savings account we've set up would be used for education and other exceptional items to be agreed upon between the two of us. I'll show it to you later if you want. I'm sure you'll be fine with it.' She took a large bite out of her bread roll.

He watched her chew methodically. It was as if she had just announced that she was having the goat's cheese as a starter, not that she had already planned what to do with their non-existent children should they ever decide to write off their wedding vows. He didn't know what to say.

When he didn't respond she finished eating and then reached across the table and took his hand in both of hers.

'Don't look so worried,' she said. 'I know we'll never need it, but it just seems stupid not to have one. I see too many couples behaving appallingly to each other ever to want to see that happen to us.'

'Okay,' he said weakly after a long pause.

'Shall I tell you about my dress fitting today?' she asked, rubbing his hand with vigour as if trying to shake him out of his current mode of thought.

'Yes,' he said, still a little dazed but eager to grab hold of a positive aspect of their impending marriage. 'Good idea.' He attempted a smile.

She smiled back and squeezed his hand before launching into a detailed account of her discussion with the dressmaker. Soon enough he was enjoying letting Emily tease him with hints about her wedding dress, and the awkwardness of the prenup issue slowly became a distant memory.

Emily had just launched into the hazards of wedding shoe shopping when Drew's features froze as he caught sight of something over her shoulder. As the two figures advanced rapidly towards them he was overwhelmed by a desire to run away and hide.

'Hey, there you are,' cried Suzie as she reached their table. A woman stumbled up behind her, clutching her shoulder as if to steady herself.

'What are you doing here?' asked Drew, struggling to take his eyes off Suzie's friend's enormous boobs which were threatening to burst over the top of her lace bustier and poke him in the eye.

'Well, I was telling Jackie – oh, this is Jackie, by the

way. Sorry, I'm so rude not introducing you. Jackie, this is Drew and Emily.'

'Drew, you are a legend,' said Jackie, looking slightly the worse for wear. 'Suzie's told me all about what you did this afternoon and I don't mind telling you, you are a god.'

Emily coughed and looked around her, clearly concerned as to who might be able to overhear the conversation.

'Jackie wanted to come and meet you,' Suzie explained. 'And you said you were coming here so I thought we'd just pop in and buy you both a drink to say thank you.' She was looking so pleased with herself that it was hard not to smile back. 'Especially you, Emily, for lending me Drew all afternoon.' She gave Emily a squeeze on the shoulder.

'Er, thanks,' clipped Emily. 'Good to see you, Suzie, but we were just about to order, so maybe another time, eh?' She picked up her menu and gave Drew a pointed look.

'Why don't you come to our party?' shrieked Jackie, right in Emily's ear.

'Excuse me,' said Emily, leaning so far away from Jackie it looked as if she was about to fall off her chair.

'Come to our New Year's Eve party,' Jackie elaborated, swaying towards Drew this time. 'You can meet Dave, my other half. I've already told him all about you, Drew. You are the man,' she said, stabbing her finger in Drew's shoulder, 'who told her to go and chop their penises off.' Instantly there was a hush at the surrounding tables that even Jackie sensed. She looked around and proudly pointed at Drew to ensure everyone who was staring had no doubt who she was talking about.

'I didn't,' said Drew, shaking his head vigorously at Emily and the surrounding diners. Suzie's smile had disappeared as she realised that perhaps Jackie's exuberant drunkenness was misplaced in the stylish and calm surroundings.

Emily stepped in to take control. 'That's a very kind invitation,' she said to Jackie, slowly, as though talking to a small child. 'But I'm afraid we always go to my parents to bring in the new year.'

Jackie stared back at Emily as if she hadn't understood a word she had said.

Emily tried again.

'We always go to my parents,' she said, even more slowly.

'I heard you the first time,' said Jackie. 'You don't

have to go to your parents, you know. What are you – nearly forty? A bit past being stuck in like bad teenagers, aren't you?'

Emily pulled down the hem of her smart jacket and squared her shoulders as if preparing to take down a rogue witness.

'Besides, our party will be way better,' Jackie ploughed on. 'Because Dave's brother works at the cash 'n' carry.'

No-one said anything as Jackie looked around expectantly.

Suzie tugged hopefully at Jackie's arm.

'Come on, Jackie,' she said. 'We're disturbing their meal. Let's go and get something to eat, eh?'

'What about you, Drew?' asked Jackie, undeterred. 'You're up for it, aren't you? Last year we told our Jamie that he could have a shandy if he did the Macarena dance for thirty minutes solid whilst wearing a Margaret Thatcher mask. We're thinking of putting him up for *Britain's Got Talent* next year.'

Drew glanced towards Emily and thought of the pianist that her parents hired most years as entertainment.

'Like I said, we always go to my parents,' repeated Emily, giving a false apologetic smile.

'But it wouldn't hurt to have a change, would it, just

for this year?' said Drew, surprised to hear himself even suggesting it.

Confusion crossed Emily's face for a moment. 'You know we always go there. We always have and we always will,' she said brusquely, picking up her menu again and pretending to study it. 'Besides, I've already told them we're going.'

'Tell them you've had a better offer,' said Jackie, getting dangerously close to Emily's personal space again. 'Better still, bring them with you. The more the merrier.'

'I'm not sure it would be their cup of tea,' said Emily, holding her ground.

'What's that supposed to mean?'

'Come on, Jackie,' begged Suzie, tugging again at her arm. 'Leave it, eh? We'll miss Dave's gig at this rate.'

'Put it this way,' said Emily, ignoring Suzie in her effort not to be intimidated by Jackie. 'I doubt they've ever heard of *Britain's Got Talent*, never mind watched it.'

Jackie was undeterred. 'Are they Deep Purple fans then? Dave's in the tribute band, Cheap Purple. You might have heard of them. They're in the middle of a tour at the moment.'

'Where of?' asked Emily. 'Strangeways?'

Jackie gasped and stepped back quickly, then

stumbled. She pulled herself up to her full height and pointed at Emily.

'Stuck-up cow,' she said before grabbing Suzie by the arm and turning to leave.

'It was a joke,' said Emily unconvincingly as Jackie staggered towards the exit, pulling Suzie behind her.

Drew stared after the pair, horrified. Suzie looked over her shoulder and mouthed a sorry to him.

'I'd better check they're okay,' he said, and got up before Emily had a chance to stop him.

He found them outside on the pavement trying to hail a taxi. Jackie saw him first and walked straight over, flinging her arms around him. 'Sorry I called her a cow,' she said, leaning her head on his shoulder.

'Let's just forget about it, shall we?' said Drew, trying to extract himself from her abundant exposed flesh.

'I'm so sorry, Drew.' Suzie looked flustered and tearful. 'We shouldn't have come.'

'It's fine, really,' he said.

'*You* could still come to our New Year's party,' said Jackie, flinging her arms over him again.

'I don't think that would be appropriate, do you?' said Drew. 'Thanks for the invite, though.'

'Fair enough.' She released him and wandered aimlessly towards a taxi that had just pulled up.

Drew and Suzie hovered awkwardly together, neither knowing what to say.

'I hope we haven't ruined your night,' she said eventually, her voice trembling. 'After all you've done for me today.'

'We'll be fine,' Drew reassured her. 'Go on, off you go,' he urged as Jackie shouted to Suzie from the waiting cab. 'I'd better go back inside to Emily.'

He watched them as they drew off, Jackie waving cheerily through the back window and Suzie looking downcast, clearly concerned over the impact her friend had made. He walked back into the restaurant and decided to take a detour to the Gents and gather himself before he returned to the table.

He locked himself in a cubicle and put his head in his hands. He felt physically sick as he wondered how he was going to handle Emily. He knew she would be condescending and critical of both Jackie and Suzie for the rest of the night, and he really wasn't sure how he was going to cope with it.

But that wasn't the real reason why his insides were churning. There was something no-one else had seen during the incident. An occurrence that was far more upsetting than anything that had happened during the last few minutes. Something he knew he'd never experienced before in his life.

He'd sat there in the middle of the restaurant and felt his heart leap, his breathing quicken and a feeling of joy rush through his body. He hadn't moved. Nothing had changed. All that had happened was that Suzie had walked into the room.

Chapter 12

Dear Suzie,

I met my soulmate in a bar a few weeks ago. It felt like we were made for each other. We liked all the same things, even rum and raisin ice cream – and I've never met anyone who likes rum and raisin ice cream. We talked all night, until eventually my mates got fed up of me looking googly-eyed at Peter (he has the same name as my first pet rabbit!) so they left me to it. I ended up going home with him and he was the perfect gentleman, even offering to make up the spare bed. But it felt so right that I ended up sleeping with him. Afterwards we both said that we had never felt like *this before about anyone. The next day he had to work so I left early. He took my number and promised to call but that was three weeks ago. I've been to the bar that we met in nine times but he's never there. I've driven past his house every night on my way home from work but he's never in. I have even been to his local supermarket and loitered in the ice-cream section, but still no sign. Now I think something bad must have happened to him. Do you think I should call the police?*

Desperately Worried of Didsbury

Dear Dim of Didsbury,

To coin a phrase, 'He's just not that into you.' Nothing bad has happened to him, he just never wants to see you again.

Now the crucial thing here is how you deal with this. No tears and no feeling sorry for yourself. Most importantly what you must NOT do is walk away quietly. An entire book was devoted to giving this advice, and guess what? It was written by a man. How convenient and how devious to make women think that this route would actually give them the upper hand. What rubbish. The thing to do is make the biggest fuss possible to ensure he thinks twice before he does it again to another woman.

You are going to post a note through Peter's letter box telling him you need to meet him secretly later that night because your boyfriend has found out that you slept together and you are very concerned for his safety.

When you meet you should tell him your boyfriend is a bouncer and you are engaged to be married. One of his bouncer mates saw you leaving the bar together and snitched on you. He has pulled a photo off the closed-circuit television which has been circulated to all the bouncers in Manchester, and there's a reward on Peter's — preferably very bruised — head. Suggest he doesn't go out at all for at least three months, when maybe it will have died down. Finally, apologise for using him just for sex and wish him luck in finding a nice girl.

Let me know how you get on.

Suzie

Suzie hit *Save* on her laptop and leaned back on her kitchen chair. She let out a long sigh as the early Sunday afternoon silence enveloped her and she wondered what she should do with the rest of the day. She had already been through her usual Sunday ritual. After lying in bed until she was bored, she had eventually mooched downstairs for strong coffee before throwing her full-length winter coat over her pyjamas to wander to the corner shop. There she had purchased two newspapers, one trashy and one serious, just in case she bumped into someone she knew. She'd also scanned the shelves for some kind of delicious treat that contained no calories. After a fruitless search she'd settled for her usual box of Mr Kipling's apple pies, then rushed home to munch her way through most of them by the time she made it to the tabloid gossip section. The TV had muttered gently in the background with its so-called hangover programming that was really just an excuse for it being crap.

By one o'clock, the papers had been read, pies eaten, coffee drunk and crap hangover TV shows replaced by serious political debate or John Craven wittering on about badgers. The dreaded Sunday afternoon had arrived – a social desert for any single person. Hangover cured, there was a sudden desire to socialise, to get out into the real world, to feel part of the human race again. But as everyone knows, that is exactly the time when the rest of the world chooses to retreat into their nests. Couples snuggle up on sofas and watch Sky Sports or *EastEnders*, depending on who wears the trousers in the relationship. Families gather around the table and tuck into Sunday lunch, leaving singles to flounder through the long hours of a Sunday afternoon with nothing to do and nowhere to go and, most importantly, no-one to share it with.

Starting her column for the week had provided some relief, but now Suzie needed another distraction to get her past the endless alone time looming in front of her.

At 1.56 p.m. exactly she crumbled. With a deep sigh she pulled out the drawer underneath the TV and surveyed her collection of romantic comedy DVDs – or relationship porn, as Jackie called it. She decided to close her eyes and just pick one. She couldn't bear to sit there for the next twenty minutes and analyse each storyline to decide which would cheer her up most or depress her least. Her blind selection produced *When Harry Met Sally*, which she was pleased with. A quality romcom if ever there was one, produced long before Sandra Bullock got in on the act and reduced chick flicks to pointless pap. (*While You Were Sleeping* excepted, of course. A truly excellent piece of pointless pap.)

She slid the disc into the DVD player and staggered back to the sofa on all fours. Once there, she fluffed a cushion under her head and prayed sleep would come before Sally realised she was alone and nearly forty.

She felt a satisfied glow as she heard the first few familiar lines. Then, as Harry began his farewell to his college sweetheart full of 'I love yous,' and promises to be in constant touch, she started to feel uneasy. By the time he had uttered the words 'I miss you already', she was plunged into nostalgic despair over her long-dead college romance.

His name was Antony. They had met during freshers' week on the steps of the student union bar. They both had a rabbit-in-the-headlights look on their faces, the hallmark of any new student who'd not had a gap year. Neither of them had the back catalogue of egotistical stories set in exotic landscapes like Brazil or Guatemala that gave the gappers their confident swagger. They bonded over their lack of world travel and body piercings, choosing to reminisce over the brushed-cotton sheets and real gravy they had left behind along with their doting mothers.

It wasn't long before Antony had as good as moved into her room in halls where they lived virtually as man and wife. They collected mutual friends along the way, mainly couples, of course, who shared their love of cosy dinner parties with copious amounts of chilli and cheap red wine.

Suzie thought she had it made. She had no doubt that sometime in the future she would become one of those women who say, 'My husband and I met at college.'

As she watched an elderly couple appear on screen and tell the story of their romance, she felt deeply sad that her own story had not turned out as she had expected. She hit the *Pause* button. Wandering upstairs into her bedroom, she opened the wardrobe and pulled down a large cardboard box, coughing as disturbed dust rose up. She held it in her arms for a moment, considering whether to put it straight back, then trudged her way downstairs.

She laid the box on the rug in the sitting room and hit *Play* on the DVD to reveal Sally blissfully kissing a man in an airport.

'Sucker,' she said to the screen quietly.

What she found at the top of the box caused her heart to sink even lower. She yanked the large Jiffy bag out, causing a puff of dirty grey confetti to flutter over the carpet like ashes as the padding oozed out of a ripped corner. How fitting. Slowly, she extracted a clutch of envelopes and spread them on the floor. Each one bore her name and one of a selection of addresses that charted her progression around the dodgy suburbs of Manchester during her twenties. She spotted one addressed to the halls of residence she lived in during her first year of college and pulled out some flimsy sheets of writing paper that matched the envelope. The sight of fountain pen ink made her want to run back to the early Nineties and beg someone to stop developing the computer there and then. It seemed so quaint and old-fashioned, and so utterly romantic. Antony's signature at the bottom of the page revealed itself like a long-lost friend. Three kisses falling perfectly over the tail of the last letter of his name. She had to read quickly; the force of his early love for her somehow blasted right off the page, making it hard to breathe. She deduced it had been written during a rare weekend home to see his parents during term time. He had been gone for just two nights and still felt the need to write to her. How utterly amazing. And how unbelievably archaic it now seemed. Was it conceivable that today's electronically enhanced man would even consider sitting down with pen and paper, writing a letter, going to the post office to buy a stamp and then posting it?

She flicked through the forty or so envelopes that were now scattered on the floor to see if she could spot one that would have been written towards the end of the relationship. Eventually she found a large, pale green envelope with her last address on it. She pulled out a birthday card and for a moment was confused. It wasn't the type of card you would get from a boyfriend. It was a stupid, funny card with badly drawn cartoon animals on the front making some pathetic joke about age. She opened it up and was amazed to see that it was from Antony. *Love Antony*, it said. No kisses this time on the Y. No kisses at all. No message of undying love. Just a scribbled *Love Antony* in green biro of all things, inside a birthday card with joke-telling old badgers on the front. If ever there was a signal that a relationship was dead and buried, there it was in cartoon colours sitting in her lap.

She surveyed the bookends of her relationship with Antony, clasped in her hands. How had they descended from the giddy heights of matching stationery and fountain pen fervour to the depths of petrol station card patheticness? She held the birthday card up and shredded it into tiny pieces, throwing each individual scrap at the TV screen as she did so.

Her sport was interrupted by the shrill ring of the doorbell. Sunday afternoon hell interrupted by a visitor. Her prayers had been answered – as long as it wasn't Jehovah's Witnesses. She was desperate, but not that desperate. She flung open the front door and there stood Drew in his Sunday afternoon casuals, hands deep in pockets, looking as though he was just about to take off again. She smiled with relief. A good long chat with her old mate Drew would be the perfect way to while away an hour or so. Then it would be nearly teatime and another Sunday afternoon knocked on the head.

'Come in, come in,' she said, tugging on his arm before he could run away.

'Can't stop,' he said too quickly, looking awkward.

'No,' she cried. 'Just come in for a minute.' She panicked as the hour she had mentally just deleted, loomed large again.

'No, honestly, stuff to do,' he protested.

'Just come in, will you?' She virtually pulled him through the doorway. 'You can't make me talk to you on the doorstep in my dressing gown.'

'Only for five minutes then,' he said as she slammed the door behind him.

'Make yourself at home,' she beamed, pointing towards

the lounge door. 'I'll just go and make myself decent.'

'Er, yeah,' he said. 'Good idea.'

She ran up the stairs at breakneck speed and threw on some clothes. Her sweatshirt had a coffee stain down the front but she knew Drew wasn't the type to hold that against her. She ran back down and screeched to a halt inside the lounge doorway. 'Tea?' she breathlessly shrieked.

There was no reply from Drew, who was perched nervously on the edge of her sofa surrounded by the sea of love letters sprinkled with torn-up pieces of birthday card and grey Jiffy bag fluff. To make matters worse, Meg Ryan was happily gasping away in the background, having a fake orgasm.

'I think I'd better go,' he said, getting up. 'I'm not sure I need to be a part of whatever is going on here.'

'No!' she cried, grasping his shoulders and forcing him to sit back down. 'You have to stay. I was just looking at some old love letters, that's all. I need to start thinking about my next revenge, actually, so it's great that you're here. You can help me work out how I can give Antony a taste of his own medicine.'

'No, Suzie,' said Drew, shaking his head. 'I've come here to say that I cannot be a part of this any more. It's just . . .'

'But I need you,' she cried out.

Their eyes locked for a moment as she felt panic swirl around her body. Drew gave her confidence. Without him, she wasn't sure she could be the fearless woman who was capable of standing up for herself in such dramatic ways.

It was Drew who looked away first. He stared at his shoes and muttered, 'I can't, Suzie. I'm really sorry, but it's time for me to leave you to it.'

'But why?' she pleaded. 'We made such a great team yesterday. We were awesome. You said so.'

'I know,' said Drew. He cleared his throat. 'But after last night with Jackie and Emily, I just feel that I need to step back.'

Suzie stared at him, surprised by the tears threatening to make a fool of her. For goodness' sake, she thought. It wasn't like they were splitting up or anything.

'I'm really sorry about Jackie,' she said. 'She shouldn't have acted the way she did. She'd had too much to drink and Emily wound her up. She's sorry too, you know. Maybe if she apologised to Emily she'd let you still help me.'

'This is nothing to do with Emily,' Drew said sharply. 'You don't need me.'

Suzie racked her brain for something that might convince him still to help her. They worked so well together. But he did look really stressed, which was unusual for Drew. Perhaps she'd better leave it for now.

'Okay,' she said finally. 'I understand. You'll stay for a cuppa, though, won't you?' she asked hopefully.

He gave a huge sigh – of relief or resignation, she wasn't sure.

'Just the one,' he said. 'Then I really have to get going.'

'Brilliant,' she grinned and dived through the door to the kitchen before he could change his mind.

When she re-entered the sitting room with two steaming mugs of tea she was surprised to see Drew rifling through the box on the floor.

'Why on earth do you keep all this crap?' he asked, holding up a pale pink T-shirt with a large T on it which had obviously been the victim of an unfortunate washing incident.

'Oh my God, I can't believe I still have that,' she said, putting the tea down. 'I wore it to go and see Take That years ago. There were eight of us and we all had a letter on our shirts so we could spell Take That when we stood together.'

Drew stared at her, completely bewildered.

'Gary Barlow waved at us. We went crazy. It was brilliant.'

'And what about this?' Drew had tossed the T-shirt on the sofa and was now brandishing a large piece of card featuring a line graph drawn in felt-tip pen.

'That's the cool chart.'

'The cool chart?'

'Yep. One of my friends thought she was really cool until she started going out with a bloke who wore Gola trainers, so the rest of us decided she had lost her cool and drew her a chart to show her how much. She got her own back by adding the rest of us. This is me when I was drunk and I snogged a guy who was wearing a peach shirt and white jeans and this is . . .'

'And you spent time doing this?' he interrupted.

'Well, that's the kind of stuff you do in your twenties, isn't it? You carry on behaving like a student whilst having the advantage of being in full-time paid employment. You only stop being a student when you finally take a step up the career ladder, which means that being hungover all day at work is no longer an option.'

'I guess,' he said, putting the chart back in the box and pulling out a photograph album with a white cover.

'Wow!' shrieked Suzie, wrenching it out of his hands.

'The wedding album! I haven't looked at this in forever.'
She turned to the first page.

'So who got married?' asked Drew, peering over
her shoulder.

'Oh, no-one,' she replied. 'It was a pretend wedding.'

'You're not serious.'

'Oh yeah,' she said. 'A crowd of us were moaning that
we hadn't been to a wedding in ages. I think Angie was
trying to get Antony to propose to me as we'd been
going out for so long. Anyway, he didn't take the bait,
but someone said why don't we have a pretend wedding
so we can have all the fun without any of the commitment.
So we did.'

'You staged a wedding?'

'It was just an excuse for a party, really, but it kind of
grew and grew until by the time we actually did it we
even had pretend hen and stag dos the night before. And
then on the day we set it all up in our back garden. Look,
see?' She pointed at the picture. 'Brian dressed as the
vicar. The guys wore suits and went to the pub before the
ceremony and got free drinks because the landlord
thought it was a real wedding. Richard was the groom
and he thought he was going to pretend to marry Emma,
who was Brian's girlfriend, but we managed to convince

Guy to come down from Edinburgh where he lived and be a shotgun bride. He wore a thick veil so no-one knew who he was until the end of the ceremony. Then look, we even had a real wedding cake that my mum made.'

'You were all mental,' said Drew, shaking his head. 'I was busy acting as though I was forty in my twenties. Me and Emily left college and got straight on the property ladder. I guess we didn't go out much because Emily was busy studying for her law exams and we had no money because we were paying a mortgage.'

'But it was all worth it, though, wasn't it? Look at you now. You have a lovely house and you're about to marry a very successful career woman. Whereas loser me is in a poky flat, buoying up the single-inhabitant statistics. Perhaps I should have done a little more planning for my future back then rather than running around in a stupid peach bridesmaid dress at a fake wedding.'

'You look like you were having a great time, though,' he said quietly.

'We were,' she agreed, looking down again at a picture of the entire wedding party. 'They were good times. I hardly see any of them now. We were so close and then without warning we all zoomed off in different directions. Either up the career ladder and moving away, or down the wedding snake to disappear into the black hole people go to when they have children.'

'So which one is Antony?' asked Drew, scrutinising the picture.

'Oh, he's only in the later pictures,' she said, flicking through the rest of the album. 'He was heavily into local politics by then and he was out campaigning for some election or other that afternoon. To be honest, I think he thought it was all a bit silly, so he stayed away until the evening. There we go,' she said finally, stopping at a page near the back of the album. 'Don't we look the perfect couple?' She laughed bitterly.

Drew looked down at the photo before snapping his head back up to stare at Suzie.

'That's not who I think it is, is it?' he asked.

'Depends on who you think it is.'

'Is that Antony Barwood?'

'Er, yeah.'

'*The* Antony Barwood?'

'Guess so,' she shrugged.

'Oh my God,' he said, leaning back against the sofa in amazement. 'Antony Barwood, Liberal Democrat MP for West Keeling, is your troll with bright yellow hair?'

'Correct,' she replied.

'Bloody hell,' whispered Drew.

'What's that supposed to mean? No, don't tell me. You're amazed that I could possibly have the mental capacity to have gone out with someone who ended up being an MP. That's it, isn't it?'

'No. I just can't believe you never told me that you used to go out with Antony Barwood.'

'Why would I? Have you told me the names of all your ex-girlfriends?'

'Er, no, but she wasn't famous or anything.'

'She?'

'Yeah, what?'

'You only had one girlfriend before Emily?'

Drew blushed deeply and looked away. 'I was shy when I was younger, okay?'

Suzie looked at him for a few moments then decided she had to ask the question.

'So have you only slept with two women in your whole life?'

'No,' he said defensively.

'You've had a few one-night stands then?'

'No!' he said, outraged.

'Sooooo . . .' she said, looking at him expectantly.

'So, I have only ever slept with Emily, okay? We were still at school when I went out with the other girl and then I met Emily at college. What am I supposed to do? Sleep around just to get my sex average up?'

'No, no,' said Suzie. 'You're just so unusual.' She gazed at him.

Drew decided the interrogation had gone on long enough. 'Anyway, this is not about me, it's about you and the fact you hid from me that you went out with an MP.'

'That's because I partly blame politics for splitting us up.' Suzie began flicking through the wedding album again. She stopped and jabbed her finger at a rather plain-looking girl dressed in an unflattering Laura Ashley floral number.

'Charlotte Campbell-Wright,' she declared. 'Or Charlie to her mates when she still had mates. Her grandfather was in the House of Lords, a fact that made her very attractive to Antony. She was really shy around men and then suddenly she seemed to blossom, overnight really. Little did I know that a few flattering words from Antony were the cause. Next thing I knew she was spending every weekend with my boyfriend on the campaign trail whilst he was getting invited around for tea with Lord Campbell-Wright to discuss party politics. Eventually I came home early from work one day and found them shagging in our bed amongst a sea of yellow rosettes.'

'Weird,' said Drew, wincing. 'What happened?'

'Antony looked relieved to be discovered, to be honest. I told him to pack his bags and leave. Three hours later every trace of him was gone and I've never seen him since. Ten years we were together,' she marvelled, shaking her head. 'And in the space of a few hours it was as if those ten years had been erased. All memories completely worthless. My future up in smoke.'

'What about Charlotte?' Drew asked.

'Oh, she did apologise at least. She stood on my doorstep in floods of tears saying how sorry she was. She said she loved him and couldn't help herself and she hoped that one day I might forgive her.'

'I guess sometimes you just have to follow your heart,' said Drew, staring at the floor.

'Bollocks,' said Suzie, coming out of her minor gloom. 'Heart's got nothing to do with it. Men cheat because they're cowards.'

'That's a bit harsh, isn't it?'

'It's the truth. Most men cheat because they're too

pathetic to be honest and tell their other halves it's over. Heaven forbid they should be brave enough to tell their poor girlfriends and wives to their faces that they don't love them.'

Drew looked at her, stunned. He got up quickly as if to go.

'Oh my God!' Suzie shrieked, grabbing the remote control and Drew's arm. 'Just wait one second and watch this. This is my favourite bit.' She turned up the volume. Harry and Sally were now in the final scene at a New Year's Eve party, balloons and streamers tumbling around them.

'Just listen to what Harry says to Sally,' said Suzie, jabbing Drew in the ribs. 'This is what women want.'

'*And I love that you're the last person I want to talk to before I go to sleep at night,*' muttered Suzie under her breath as Harry spilled his true feelings. '*And it's not because I'm lonely. And it's not because it's New Year's Eve. I came here tonight because when you realise you want to spend the rest of your life with somebody, you want the rest of your life to start as soon as possible.*'

Drew was motionless, staring at the screen until the final credits started to roll.

'More tea?' asked Suzie, making him jump.

He looked as if he was about to say something then changed his mind and glanced at his watch.

'I'm a dead man!' he cried and made a break for the door without so much as a goodbye.

Chapter 13

Drew stared in through the store window, still panting heavily from his run halfway across Manchester. The headless mannequins looked oddly comfortable in their morning suits and puffed-up pastel-coloured cravats. Maybe it was the casual dangling of the formally clad arms, or the relaxed foot resting on a large prop present festooned with wide white ribbon. They looked as though they didn't have a care in the world. Maybe that's what having no head did for you – stopped you from thinking. Drew nodded thoughtfully. Yes, he could see how not thinking could lead to a really carefree existence. From where he was standing, being headless was exactly what he needed. It would stop these thoughts from popping up, coming out of nowhere like tiny missiles and wreaking absolute havoc. He would rather go and try on corsets for a period drama than these suits just now. In fact, corsets would make him feel less trapped in his own body than the suit that would seal the rest of his life.

He shouldn't have gone in. If he hadn't entered her house then he would not now have the mental image of Suzie in her pyjamas. Bad move number one. If he hadn't gone in he wouldn't have known what it was to feel at home in the mild chaos of Suzie's life, where stuff was dropped rather than carefully placed in its pre-assigned location. Where there was real, fluffy carpet rather than characterless floorboard. Where random photographs in mismatched frames of random happy moments were hung jauntily in random locations rather than overpriced modern art in overpriced brushed steel frames, interior designed into the perfect position.

When he had first sat down on Suzie's sofa he had instinctively fallen back on its copious cushions and put his feet up before he leapt in the air and sat up straight again. He never put his feet on the couch in his sleek, clean, modern house. Ever. This realisation made his heart pound so strongly that it was as if he had done something terrible. But all he had done was put his feet up on another woman's couch, he had to remind himself.

It was whilst he was taking a few deep breaths to try and restore calm that he had cast his eye over the box that lay open on the floor in front of him. The debris of Suzie's life was random and crazy and absolutely glowed with her personality. Seeing this box made him wish that he had one like it. He couldn't think of one thing that would come anywhere close to summing up his twenties. He struggled to think of any big moments he had wanted to preserve for posterity. What on earth had he been doing with his life? Seeing Suzie's memory box had been bad move number two.

But worst of all had to be hearing the story of her relationship with Antony: a budding college relationship that should have bloomed into a lifetime partnership, only to be thwarted by the intervention of a third party. Her words swarmed around his head like a shoal of disorientated fish.

'Stop,' he said aloud in an effort to halt his swirling thoughts. He took a long, hard look at his reflection in the window. 'Enough,' he whispered as he took a deep breath, opened the door and crossed the threshold.

*

'Look at me,' cried Toby the minute he saw Drew arrive. 'This is exactly the gear we need to set this wedding on fire.' He made a small bow. 'Hot or what?'

'You look like a ponce,' said Drew, surveying his best man dressed in a white tuxedo teamed with a candy-pink striped shirt and deep purple tie standing in the middle of Moss Bros. 'If you think we're wearing that you're an idiot. They'll think it's us two getting married, not me and Emily.'

'Aw, come on, man, just try it – you might be surprised. Don't you want to wear white just like the bride?'

'Er, no. You know me and white clothes are not friends. Unless, of course, there is a coordinating bib to go with it. Anyway, Emily has armed me with strict instructions on exactly what to wear. I have it all written down here.'

'Fan-bloody-tastic,' said Toby with a sigh. 'Undertaker with an uplifting hint of burgundy it is, then,' he said as he took off the pristine jacket.

'You never know,' said Drew. 'She may have chosen something a little daring to fit with your oh-so-cool image.'

'Emily? Oh-so-classic Emily? Cummerbund probably amounts to swearing in her fashion world.'

'She just wants it right, that's all,' said Drew, feeling defensive. 'She is the star of the day, after all, not you.'

'Really? Then why am I attending, remind me?'

'Because despite the fact you are a complete tosser, you are my best mate and I'd really quite like you to be there.'

'Oh yeah. And I get to insult you in front of an audience; I remember how you sold it to me now.'

'No, you get to be all emotional when you tell everyone what a good mate I've been for the past twenty years.'

'Fuck off. You're getting the works, man. Including a public airing of the story of when you wet your pants in the reptile house at London Zoo on that school trip.'

'I did not wet my pants, I sat in something – how many more times do I have to tell you?'

'Did you really? That will make the stag do easier then.'

'What has it got to do with the stag do?'

'Well, I was thinking of having a wet clothing theme. I thought we could tell attractive girls they can throw beer in your crotch because you're fond of wet pants. In return you get to wet their tops, you know, like a wet T-shirt type thing.'

'You are disgusting.'

'Aw, come on. Don't you want to see some girls' tits through a see-through top before you commit yourself to a life of celibacy? I know there's no way we're going to get Mr Morality into a strip club.'

'No, I don't. Can't we just go for a curry?'

'A curry! I have a reputation to maintain. Would I ever be able to hold my head high if I organised a stag do that was *just* going for a curry?'

Drew stared at Toby for a moment. He was thinking again. Why couldn't he stop this damned thinking? 'Why is there such a bloody fuss around weddings?' he finally asked, exasperated with himself. 'Why can't you simply just get married and then get on with the rest of your life?'

'Can I help you, sir?' asked a shop assistant, suddenly appearing at Drew's side.

'Yes,' snapped Drew. 'I'd like to dress up as an idiot, please, on the most important day of my life. Can you help me with that?'

'Certainly, sir,' replied the elderly man without missing a beat. 'What particular sort of idiot would you like to dress as?'

'This one,' said Drew, thrusting Emily's list into the man's hand.

The man studied the piece of paper for a few moments whilst Drew stared at Toby defiantly.

'I would like to compliment your future wife on her choice. There is no doubt *she* will be the star of the show. If you would like to wait here a moment I will gather together your costumes.' The man gave Drew a reassuring smile and a squeeze on the shoulder

'Thank you.' Drew sat down heavily on a worn leather armchair and put his head in his hands.

'That was funny. You're not normally that funny. Are you ill?' asked Toby.

'No,' said Drew from behind his hands.

'So what's with you then, sunshine?' Toby asked. 'Is this a touch of cold feet, or have you had a personality transplant?'

Drew contemplated what on earth he should tell his best mate. He didn't know what to tell himself, never mind articulate it for someone else.

'I don't know,' he finally said despairingly. 'All this fuss and bother, I guess it's just getting to me a bit.'

'Well, pull it back a bit then. You don't have to be Prince bloody Charles, you know.'

'But this is what Em wants. I can't deny her that.'

'It's your wedding as well. What you want matters too.'

Drew stared at Toby for a long moment. 'But what if I don't know what I want?' he said finally.

'Mmmmm, I see.' Toby walked over and plonked himself down on a footstool. 'Are you saying you don't know what you want in terms of red or white wine at the reception, or are you talking on a much deeper level? Like maybe on a blonde or brunette level?'

Drew stared at his shoes before replying.

'I'm perhaps at the blonde or brunette level,' he said. He felt like crying.

'Fucking spiders,' said Toby, leaping off his stool. 'The man is not a saint after all. Who is she? Have you shagged her yet?'

'I haven't shagged anyone. It's just that someone's making me think twice a bit, that's all. There is absolutely no chance that anything would ever happen between us, but the fact that I'm thinking about it is kind of confusing me.'

'Shag her, get it out of your system, and get married. Simple. Crikey, this best man malarkey comes to me naturally, don't you think?' said Toby, grinning his head off to the shop assistant who had now returned with their suits.

'Sorry, what was that, sir?' he asked politely.

'The groom here has cold feet brought about by some warm breasts that don't belong to the bride-to-be having caught his eye. I am advising him in my role as best man to shag her.'

'And in what way will that help the gentleman with his dilemma, may I ask?'

'Get it out of his system. Last-chance workout, as it were. Leaving him free to marry. Job done.'

The man glanced from Toby to Drew, who was sitting with his chin in his hands staring gloomily in front of him.

'Shag her,' he said. 'Now, do you want to try on these clown suits or shall I put them back pending any major decisions here?'

Drew stood up without saying anything, grabbed the hangers from the man and disappeared behind a curtain.

'I'm not shagging anyone,' came his voice from behind the curtain.

'Clearly,' replied Toby.

'What's that supposed to mean?'

'Just that I've never seen you so tense, that's all, buddy.'

'What do you expect?'

'Well, to be honest I was expecting my mate. Cool, calm, comfortable Drew. Or Mr Sensible, as I like to call him. Only through a curtain, of course, never to his face. And instead I have super-stud himself. It's taking some getting my head around. You are encroaching on my territory. I thought I was the balls in this relationship.'

'I am not a super-stud. I haven't done anything.'

'Well, maybe that's just it, my friend. You haven't done anything. You've been an absolute saint in like forever. Shit, you've only ever slept with Emily. Who does that these days? The Pope, that's who.'

'I don't think the Pope slept with Emily,' interjected the shop assistant.

'You're right. They've never met. Thank you for pointing that out,' said Toby.

'You're welcome. All part of the service,' he replied and wandered off again.

'Look, who could blame you for sowing a few wild oats before you get committed, hey? Better to do it now than after you're married. I've never told you this, but if it helps, that's what I did.'

'Did what?'

'Had a bit of a fling before I got hitched to Chloe.'

'You're kidding me! That's disgusting.' Drew flung the curtain aside and glared at Toby.

'See, this is why I didn't tell you. You're so bloody

moral sometimes. And well, it was kind of awkward. But that's not the point. The point is I had a fling, I got it out of my system and now I'm a happily married man. No harm done.'

'Does Chloe know?'

'Shit, no. She'd slice my balls off. You know the temper she's got.'

'Precisely,' said Drew. 'Imagine how she'd feel. You can't do that to the people you're supposed to love. You just can't do it.' He turned to inspect himself in the mirror. He didn't look like a clown. He didn't look like an idiot. He actually appeared quite handsome. Emily had chosen a style that suited his broad shoulders and slim waist and he was relieved she had gone for a tie rather than a ridiculous cravat. And thankfully no waistcoat inspired by Fifties flock wallpaper.

The shop assistant appeared by his side and nodded approvingly.

'You look good,' he said. 'You look ready. Are you ready?' he asked.

Drew turned to look at him but didn't reply.

'She obviously knows you well,' the man continued. 'Don't you think she has chosen well?'

'I do,' he muttered finally. 'I do.'

Chapter 14

Dear Suzie,

I have been living with my boyfriend for five years now and I thought he was planning to propose on my birthday. He's been acting very secretively for ages – disappearing for hours on end, hiding room tariffs for the swankiest hotel in Manchester in his washbag, dropping phone calls on his mobile as soon as I enter the room and generally acting kind of nervous all the time. Anyway, my twenty-ninth birthday came and went and he didn't propose. Nor did we stay at the posh hotel. I think he bottled it because he's nervous about whether I would say yes.

I do want to marry him, so should I ask him to marry me?

   Kerry

Dear Kerry,

   He's never going to marry you. The reason I know this is because he is having an affair. Mysterious disappearances, dropped phone calls and hotels only ever add up to one thing with men and it's not a proposal. You are at that critical age when men face two choices if they have a girlfriend. Get married or have sex with someone else. Note this does not include facing up to the fact that you no longer love your girlfriend and that you should tell her. That would be far too brave.

   So he has obviously taken the sex route. Now you hold the power, because you know but he doesn't know you know. So dump him. But dump him in style.

   Find out when he is next having a rendezvous at this posh hotel by calling them and telling them you are his wife and you want to surprise him with something. I will arrange to be there waiting for him with a photographer. When they both arrive I will leap out and congratulate him on being the winner of

*Manchester's Most Romantic Couple as nominated by
his girlfriend Kerry. The room will be paid for by us
and their photo will appear in the paper. He will wish
he had been honest with you when he has to squirm
his way out of that one, and when he sees his photo in
this column under the headline, Manchester's Biggest
Love Rat.*

Suzie

Suzie particularly liked writing responses to letters about
cheating, the very worst crime committed by man as far
as she was concerned. Tortured was the only way she
could describe how she'd felt following Antony's defec-
tion. Sure, she'd suspected for some time that something
was going on, but she'd successfully managed to shove
all the warning signals into a box marked IN DENIAL.
She simply couldn't comprehend that Antony would
ever think so little of her as to cheat on her, and with
Charlie, of all people. Certainly she was pleasant enough,
but her mousy looks and shy disposition didn't scream
man-stealer. Suzie was clear in her own mind that
Antony was entirely the guilty party. Charlotte's only
crime was being weak and easily charmed.

Nonetheless, as she approached the charity shop

where Charlie now worked, she couldn't help but feel a trickle of long-buried anger. She thought that approaching Charlie first would be easier than squaring up to Antony cold. She also hoped that information gleaned from Charlie could help her formulate a fitting revenge plan for Antony.

However, as she looked up at the neglected façade, meeting the woman she'd last seen in bed with her boyfriend didn't feel easy at all. It was terrifying. She opened the door and slid in as discreetly as possible, wanting a good look at Charlotte before she was spotted. After all this time, she needed to deal with the shock unobserved, not under Charlotte's scrutiny. She ducked and dived behind a number of shelving units and packed hanging rails, pretending to check out a lavender plastic mac, before she dared to look up at the counter. She's not here, she thought as she looked straight past the rather ample lady writing something on a notepad. Wasted visit. She rammed the raincoat back onto the rail and took one last glance at the desk as she prepared to leave. Her jaw dropped and she looked more closely. The chubby, drab-looking woman now serving a customer couldn't possibly be Charlie, could it? She studied her face. She certainly had her eyes. Then she heard her laugh gently and she was sure. She was barely recognisable, but she was Charlie. Suzie felt the makings of a grin slowly form on her face. Charlie got fat, she thought to herself. How absolutely brilliant. There is nothing more satisfying than clapping eyes on someone who you haven't seen in ages who has let themselves go more than you have. Especially when this particular person happens to have stolen your future husband.

Armed with the carrier bag of old clothes she had brought along as an excuse to be visiting the Cats' Protection League charity shop, she strode towards the counter with a renewed spring in her step.

'Charlie?' she said as she approached the desk. 'Is that you?'

Charlie didn't look up from the book she was writing in.

'Charlie,' Suzie repeated, more loudly.

'Oh, sorry,' Charlie said, looking up quickly. 'No-one calls me Charlie any more . . .' She trailed off as her mouth dropped open.

'Suzie,' she said in a tone that suggested neither a statement nor a question.

'Fancy seeing you in here,' Suzie ploughed on. 'I never thought I'd see you working in a place like this.'

Charlie appeared to scan the room as if searching for an escape route, or possibly a large hole to swallow her up.

'I volunteer twice a week.'

'Really? I suppose that's what every good politician's wife does,' said Suzie.

A small bead of sweat appeared on Charlie's top lip and Suzie felt as though she could almost smell the fear.

'Did you bring something in for us?' Charlie asked finally, grabbing at the bag clutched in Suzie's hand.

'Oh yes, of course. Just a few old bits I was throwing out, you know. All in size 12.'

'That's, er, really good of you,' muttered a now rather flushed-looking Charlie. 'The cats will be very grateful.'

'Crikey, I didn't realise that you give the clothes to the cats to wear. I don't think I'll have anything in their colour.' Suzie peeled into hysterical laughter at her own wit, fuelled by the mind-blowing high that she looked so much better than Charlie.

Charlie cracked a very small smile whilst awkwardly running the corner of one of Suzie's old T-shirts through her fingers.

'So how are you?' she asked. Suzie could have sworn she saw a small tear in the corner of her left eye.

'Oh, fantastic,' replied Suzie. 'I work at the *Herald*. Yeah, it was hard work, but I got to be a reporter just like I said I would.'

'That's great,' nodded Charlie. 'I'm really pleased for you.'

'Thanks. I really love it. I'm doing this great column at the moment that's all about how women should handle men who behave badly. It's incredibly popular.' Suzie paused before she continued. 'So, how's Antony?'

Charlie froze then looked away. 'He's fine,' she muttered.

'Good, good, that's great. Well, I have to say being the politician's wife obviously agrees with you, you look fantastic.'

Charlie whipped her gaze back towards Suzie before frantically tugging at her cardigan sleeve and sniffing violently. Suzie watched in amazement as Charlie finally managed to tug a damp-looking tissue out and hold it firmly to her eyes.

'I'm sorry,' she muttered from behind her soggy mask. 'I think you'd better leave. I don't want you to see me like this.'

'Are you crying?' Suzie was incredulous. This wasn't how she had expected this to go at all.

'You've not gained that much weight really,' she said, at a loss as to what to say. 'In fact I didn't even notice till I got up close. You can hardly tell from a distance.'

'Please, just go,' Charlie sniffed back, still hiding behind a now very damp tissue.

The bell above the shop door gave a loud ding-a-ling and an old lady shuffled in dragging a basket on wheels from which a loud mewing could be heard. She looked across at the counter and was about to open her mouth when she noticed Charlie's distressed state.

'Oooh,' she uttered. 'What's up wiv her then?'

Charlie sniffed loudly but offered no explanation.

'Cat died,' said Suzie. 'Going to have to shut the shop actually,' she continued, going over to hustle the lady out. 'Cat undertaker is on its way.'

'I'll call Connie on Bridge Street,' the woman shouted over. 'Dolly has just had a big litter. I'll tell her to bring one over tomorrow, shall I?'

'Great idea,' said Suzie as she shut the door in the woman's face and turned the sign around to Closed.

By now Charlie's shoulders were heaving methodically as she attempted to press the very damp tissue right into her eye sockets.

What was she supposed to do now? Suzie wondered.

Put an arm over her shoulder and ask her what the matter was? She couldn't do it. Sympathy wouldn't come just yet.

'Tea?' was all she could spit out. Yes, tea was good. Get Charlie doing something and then perhaps she should leave so she could try and work out what the hell had happened during this bizarre reunion.

Charlie sniffed loudly then squeezed her backside past the end of the counter, knocking an entire stack of paper bags to the floor. She waddled towards a door at the back of the shop without even looking at Suzie.

Should she leave or stay? Suzie had no idea what to do. Her curiosity got the better of her and she wandered after Charlie, who was now in a tiny back room putting teabags into two cat-adorned, chipped mugs. Suzie shuffled past her to get to a high stool whilst Charlie drooped into a saggy old armchair and wrestled with the lid of a Quality Street tin. Once she had opened it she reached inside and offered Suzie a Penguin biscuit. Suzie looked at it but couldn't resist one more jibe.

'No, thank you,' she said primly.

Charlie stared at her with the look of a broken woman. She then looked at the Penguin biscuit for a moment before she crumbled. Ripping open the wrapping, she took a large bite as the tears began to stream down her cheeks yet again.

Words of compassion still wouldn't surface for Suzie. All she could feel was an overwhelming relief that she didn't want Charlie's life. She had spent all these years thinking that she should be living the life that Charlie must be, only to find that it had made her fat and sad. But she had to say something, as clearly Charlie was incapable of starting any conversation.

'So . . .' she began. 'What's happening?'

After grabbing a clean tissue from a box housed in a knitted blue and white cat and blowing her nose loudly, Charlie collected herself enough to respond.

'It's nothing,' she said eventually.

Suzie raised her eyebrows.

'How bloody ironic,' Charlie continued, shaking her head sadly and staring at the floor.

'What is?' asked Suzie, unable to stop Alanis Morissette beaming instantly into her brain and for the millionth time pondering the true definition of ironic.

'Nothing,' replied Charlie flatly.

'Aw, come on,' said Suzie. 'If it's not really ironic I won't tell anyone. Hardly anyone gets the real definition of irony right, and I should know – I'm a journalist.'

Charlie gave Suzie a confused look.

'If Alanis can get it wrong so can you. It's okay.'

'Alanis?'

'Alanis Morissette. "Isn't it ironic?" Don't you remember we played it to death in the summer of '95? Ten thousand spoons when all you need is a knife? What was she thinking? Someone buy that woman a dictionary.'

Charlie had stopped crying now and had a furrowed brow. Finally she spoke.

'I've missed you,' she whispered.

'You're right. Bloody ironic, that,' said Suzie, forcing a smile.

Charlie didn't reply. She just ripped shreds off her tissue and scrutinised it closely.

'Why are you crying?' Suzie asked. She had to know. She realised she was starting to feel for her. No-one should feel this low.

Another loud sniff before she looked up at Suzie.

'I think Antony might be having an affair,' she said before hiding her face in her hands and starting the whole heaving, crying thing again.

'Fuck me,' breathed Suzie. 'Alanis eat your heart out.' The irony of ironies. She meets the woman who had an affair with her boyfriend after ten years only to find he is now cheating on her too.

'I'm not absolutely sure. He might not be, but . . .' mumbled Charlie.

'Charlie,' said Suzie sharply. 'I can absolutely guarantee he is.'

'But I don't really know for definite, I could be wrong.'

'Listen to me,' said Suzie, leaning forward enthusiastically on her stool. They were on her territory now. 'He is. And do you know why? Because we are programmed to think the best in this situation. We see all the signs as clear as day and still we think we must be wrong because the alternative is too hard to bear.'

'But how can you be so sure?' asked Charlie.

'Answer me these questions,' said Suzie, warming up. 'Do you find him in odd rooms in the house, behind shut doors, talking on the telephone?' she asked.

'Er, yes.'

'Does he suddenly end calls when you enter a room?'

'Occasionally, yes.'

'And does he go away for the night and claim that you can't call him because there is no phone reception?'

'Yes, he does.'

'When he talks about a certain woman does his tone change or does he pause slightly before he mentions her name?'

Charlie bit her lip and nodded, allowing fresh tears to spill.

'Has he suddenly started deleting all his text messages as soon as he's read them?'

Charlie nodded silently.

'And do you know this because you sneak down in the middle of the night to check the messages on his phone, because you're so desperate to find out for certain if he is playing away?'

'Yes,' she sobbed. 'How do you know that?'

Suzie paused, wondering if the clearly distraught Charlie needed to know the answer to that question.

'Because it's what I used to do when I suspected he was sleeping with you,' she said quietly. 'I think it's what every woman does when they're trying desperately to find the evidence to prove their suspicions wrong.'

'I'm so sorry,' sobbed Charlie. 'I'm so sorry we did that to you.'

Suzie said nothing.

'You must think I'm getting everything I deserve,' said Charlie.

'No, actually, I don't,' said Suzie eventually. 'Antony is the one who's at fault, not you.'

'What am I going to do?' said Charlie.

Suzie remembered why she was there. To make Antony feel how she had all those years ago, when the future she had banked on had been ripped from under her. What better way to do that than through Charlie? This was her time. Rather than walking away quietly and licking her wounds for months on end, Charlie could do what needed to be done and teach Antony a lesson. This could be fantastic.

'Charlie,' she said tentatively, worried that she might not let her get involved. 'If you let me I will help you stop feeling like this and get back in control. I told you about my column, didn't I? This is what I do. I help women who have problems with their men.'

'But why would you want to help me?' asked Charlie, looking completely pathetic with a very red and blotchy face. 'Surely you must hate me?'

'Because,' sighed Suzie. 'To be totally honest, helping you will help me. There are so many things I didn't do or say when I found out about you and Antony and I've regretted it ever since. If I can help you treat him the way he deserves then I can't tell you how good that will make me feel.'

Charlie stared at Suzie for a long time.

'I really have missed you,' she said finally. 'I'm so sorry.'

Suzie smiled back. 'Right,' she said. 'First things first. Let's get the facts. When did you first suspect there was something going on?'

Chapter 15

Drew hadn't gone into the office that day. The incessant thinking was stopping him achieving anything approaching his normal routine. He had left Moss Bros with renewed resolve that his life was indeed on course. He was following the right path. All in the world was well. That had lasted until 11.04 p.m., when he reached over to check that his alarm was set for the morning having just had an altercation with Emily concerning carnations. Drew's mum's pride and joy were the carnations she grew in her tiny back garden in the summer. Given her love for this particular flower, she had asked if Drew would wear one as his buttonhole for the wedding. Emily's and her mother's dead bodies had been used in opposition to this proposal and Drew had been asked to break the news to his mother. Having tentatively taken the 'it would really please my mum' route he was under no illusions that having carnations amongst the blush-pink anthuriums would ruin the entire wedding. Not having the energy to push it further, he had switched off his bedside light and laid his head on his pillow, at which point the thinking had renewed its relentless pursuit of his peace of mind. By three in the morning he had been reduced to trying to remember the score of every away match for Manchester City over the last five years in the hope that it would divert his overactive brain. Fitful sleep arrived but by morning he was exhausted.

Unable to face Suzie in his muddled, exhausted state, he had set up base in a local café with Wi-Fi and called in to say he was working off-site. The article he was attempting to write on a domestic violence case involving a wife who had fed her husband crushed maggots baked into lasagne because she was so sick of his fishing obsession was doing nothing to settle his mind or his churning stomach.

At around lunchtime he heard the door open and a familiar giggle reverberate around the room. He ducked down behind his laptop as Suzie bounced into the room. He peered over the top of his screen just in time to see Gareth throw a casual arm over her shoulder as they both gazed up at the blackboard to make their selection from the day's specials.

He stared at their easy proximity feeling confused, horrified, relieved, angry, you name it, every emotion available to a man entirely unsure of his heart.

He watched, mesmerised, as they took a table at the far side of the room. At least they hadn't spotted him. They chatted and laughed merrily through the entire meal. Suzie looked mightily pleased with herself and Gareth appeared to be laying the charm on with a spoon – something he usually reserved for his best-paying advertisers.

Every time Suzie's laughter pealed through the room he felt a sharp pain somewhere in his chest. She clearly fancied Gareth – and there he'd been thinking that she'd totally given up on men. He idly tapped Gareth's full name into Google to see what came up, hoping he'd uncover the fact that he was a convicted murderer in Kansas on the run from Death Row. Just as Drew was unearthing Gareth's glittering background during his time at Cambridge, a pair of sparkling eyes peeped at him over his screen.

'Peep-bo,' chimed Suzie. 'What are you doing hiding in here?' She plonked herself down in the seat opposite. 'I've been waiting for you to turn up all morning. I have sooooo much to tell you it's untrue.'

'I . . . I just needed some quiet to get this done,' he stuttered, waving at Gareth's graduation photo on his parents' blog which fortunately Suzie could not see.

'This,' she said, slamming his screen down, 'is much more exciting. I've just had lunch with our esteemed editor, and Drew, guess what? He loves me.'

'He *what*?' exclaimed Drew. This was worse than he thought. How long had this been going on?

'He thinks I'm the best thing since sliced bread because advertising revenues have doubled off the back of the success of my new column. *Doubled*, Drew. Can you believe that? I knew I was getting loads more letters and emails, but who would have thought this could happen? And guess what?' She didn't wait for an answer. 'Apparently, ever since I suggested that woman should threaten to burn her husband's private parts off with a blowtorch, sales of them have tripled. Homebase want to take out a full-page ad. Awesome. That's what Gareth said. *Awesome*.' She reached over and finished the last bit of donut that Drew had been saving.

'That's really great,' said Drew, wallowing in the relief that Gareth and Suzie were not having a passionate affair.

'And,' she said, munching away, 'that's not the most important thing I have to tell you.'

Drew felt himself tense again. They were in love. Now that Suzie was single-handedly saving the paper, Gareth had fallen for her.

'Yesterday I went to see Charlie.'

Bloody hell, he thought. Where's this guy come from? Who the hell was Charlie?

'You know, Antony's wife,' she said, spotting the troubled look on his face. 'The best news actually is that she's fat. Made me so happy, I cannot tell you.' She paused as she noticed he was still looking confused.

'It's a girl thing,' she said. 'Anyway, guess what?'

'What?' he muttered.

'He's only bloody at it again.' She dropped her tone to an excited whisper. 'He's having an affair.'

'Oh my God,' said Drew, the news sweeping his previous worries clean out of his head.

'And you will not believe who with,' she whispered into his ear so he could feel her breath on his cheek, sparking off a whole new wave of thinking.

Chapter 16

Dear Suzie,

I am twenty-eight years old and I recently got in touch with my first ever boyfriend Michael, via Facebook. After emailing each other a few times we got together and it was just like old times. We got on so well and this time I even got to have sex with him. He said he didn't want to be in a relationship because he'd just had his fingers burnt by his ex-girlfriend, but he thought he could manage on a 'friends with benefits' basis. This has been going fine for the last few months, but now he's started asking me if I'm still in touch with any of the really pretty girls from school and if I'll bring them along next time we meet. I don't want to because then we won't be able to have sex. I don't think he realises this. Do you think I should point it out to him or would that be too forward?

Yours sincerely,

Lisa

Dear Lisa,

Please don't get me started on the whole 'friends with benefits' thing. You may as well hang a sign around your neck saying 'FREE SEX – NO QUESTIONS ASKED'. Also the fact that you assume he's a friend just kills me. That's not called a friend, it's called a client. Get real, Lisa, he's taking advantage of you and it's time to turn the tables. Tell him that you are still in touch with the most gorgeous person from school and that they are absolutely dying to see him again. Say you should all meet at his house because this person likes your 'friends with benefits' status and is interested in a threesome. Arrive early and tell him that you think you should turn the heating up and strip down to your underwear to set the right mood. When he has stripped down to his boxers and five minutes after your guest is due to arrive, get out your phone and check for messages. Tell Michael that Gary is two minutes away and he's absolutely gagging for it. Tell him he's a great friend of yours and has got one very, very big benefit.

Have fun.

Suzie

'Stuck-up, over-ambitious bitch,' muttered Jackie to Suzie as they settled themselves on a line of chairs somewhere deep in the bowels of Keeling Library.

'Shush, she might hear you,' Suzie muttered back.

'Don't give a damn,' said Jackie, a little louder this time. 'I mean, look at her in her oh-so-prissy little polyester suit. As if butter wouldn't melt in her mouth. Not that I even want to think about what has been in her mouth if she's been screwing that shit Antony.'

'Thanks for that mental picture, Jackie.'

Antony had practically handed Suzie a revenge plan on a plate. If it worked the result could be spectacular, although it had taken a little time to persuade Charlie of her role. Several visits to Ben & Jerry's in the Trafford Centre had been required while they plotted in secret, consuming large tubs of Chunky Monkey for inspirational purposes. Charlie now appeared to be fully on board with the Dear Suzie philosophy of how to deal with errant men. At this moment, however, Suzie was feeling a little unsure as she sat waiting her turn to see Antony for the first time in nearly ten years during his constituency surgery.

'Here she comes,' said Jackie, jabbing Suzie in the ribs. 'Troy, you got that lollipop ready, mate? You just make sure you stick it on the nice lady's A-line, okay?'

Troy beamed up at them both as they were approached by the navy-suited young lady.

'Hello, ladies, I'm Megan,' beamed the excruciatingly tidy and shiny woman. 'What a beautiful baby,' she gushed, bending over to stroke Troy's cheek. Sensing possible food, Troy grabbed at her finger and stuffed it in his mouth before biting down hard. 'Oooh,' she squealed in surprise.

'No, Troy,' said Jackie sternly. 'You don't know where that's been.'

Megan and Jackie exchanged fleeting glances, both noting that this meeting was unlikely to flourish into a wonderful relationship.

Megan coughed, adjusted her rimless glasses and stared down at her clipboard.

'Antony's just in with another constituent at the moment, but if you could give me some details of what you wish to discuss with him it will save time later,' she said, looking up and smiling condescendingly.

'So you're like the elf before we get to see Santa?' asked Jackie.

Megan stared back at her before bursting into peals of laughter.

'Oh yes, very funny. Actually, I'm an intern,' she said, giving Jackie a fake smile.

'Well, it's lovely to meet you, Monica,' said Jackie, reciprocating with a false grin.

'Actually, it's Megan.' The fake smile faded and a pink glow rose up from her stiff, school-uniform-sharp white collar.

'If you say so,' said Jackie.

Suzie couldn't help but smile to herself.

'So,' said Megan, gathering herself. 'Can I check that you are a constituent of Antony's? Can you tell me where you live?'

'On the Fairlawns Estate, sweetheart.'

'Excellent,' she replied, nodding.

'I know, I'm a genius,' replied Jackie. 'I know my own address.'

'And what do you wish to discuss with your MP?' asked Megan, starting to look slightly nervous.

'I should like to discuss the disgusting lack of breast-feeding facilities in the area,' Jackie began. 'If my Troy gets a thirst on whilst we're out and about then I quite often have no option but to bare all in public. It's shocking, I tell you.'

'Er, yes, I imagine that must be most uncomfortable for you.'

'Too right. It's not an easy task being discreet with these nellies,' Jackie told her.

Megan was unable to resist the urge to stare at Jackie's chest.

'Do you see what I mean?' urged Jackie.

'Yes, er, no, er . . . ' Megan stuttered.

'So anyway, I was thinking that it would be a really good use of taxpayers' money to provide some facilities for women who need to feed their young.'

'Yes, yes, of course. And do you have any proposals as to where these facilities should be located? It always helps when you can go in with a solution rather than a problem. That's what Antony . . . er, Mr Barwood always says.'

'I'm thinking there's a smoking room at the White Hart that can't be used for smoking any more so maybe that could be used for breastfeeding,' said Jackie. 'Handy for refreshments, you see. You can't afford to be dehydrated when you're breastfeeding.'

Megan looked over to Suzie for some kind of validation that what Jackie was saying was as stupid as she suspected it was.

'Such a genius idea, Jacks,' nodded Suzie. 'And guess what. They've just reinstalled Pac-Man.'

'No way?'

'Yes way.'

'How cool is that?' exclaimed Jackie, addressing Megan. 'What a gift to the community, for the White Hart smoking room to become a haven for all breast-feeding mothers. I think your Antony is going to love this idea, don't you?'

Megan was still staring at them both when the door to the room behind her opened and out staggered a man with a walking stick.

'Good day, dear,' he said, lifting his trilby slightly in salute to Megan. 'He's all yours,' he grinned.

'Er, I won't be a moment,' muttered Megan. She scuttled through the open door and closed it firmly behind her.

'How did I do?' asked Jackie.

'You were brilliant,' Suzie told her. 'Just hope he doesn't smell a rat and refuse to see us or else the plan is down the swanny.'

'He'll see us, he has to; he's my MP.'

'Mmmm, I hope so,' said Suzie, chewing her nails.

'You okay?' asked Jackie.

'Just feel a bit weird, that's all. You know I haven't seen him in years. I don't quite know how it's going to feel.'

'Just you remember who you are and why you're here. You are in control, remember? That's what you keep telling your readers. By the way, I'm loving the free chocs I got for signing up for your newsletter on the website.'

'You got them, did you?' asked a chuffed Suzie. 'Can't believe we've got a sponsor already. We only set the site up last week. Apparently we're signing an STD clinic as chief sponsor next month.'

'What would I get for that? A free dose of the clap?' snorted Jackie.

At that moment the door opened again and out walked Megan, looking a little flushed, Suzie noticed. Antony really was a shit.

'He'll see you now,' said Megan, addressing Jackie.

'Sorry, darling. A small emergency has arisen and I have to go. Troy needs feeding, actually. But due to the insane lack of breastfeeding facilities I'll be forced to expose myself in the reference section,' she said very loudly, to allow the maximum number of Greater Manchester's inhabitants to hear. 'However, my good friend Suzie here will take my issue up with Mr MP in there. So bye, bye. Lovely to meet you, Monica.'

'It's Megan,' said Megan firmly.

'Whatever you say, darling,' said Jackie as she bustled past, Troy slung under one arm, kicking and screaming.

The young intern forced a smile as she stood aside to allow Suzie through the door before closing it behind her.

Antony was looking down as Suzie entered, writing something on a form. She noted a slight bald patch on the top of his head and instantly felt her confidence rise.

'Come in, sit down,' he said, not looking up. 'Won't be a moment, Mrs, er, Mrs . . .' He scanned the form wildly.

'Ms Miller, actually,' she said. 'Ms Suzie Miller.'

'What?' Antony's head shot up. 'Suzie, what are you doing here?'

She found that she couldn't speak. She was too busy watching her relationship with Antony flash before her eyes as his face prompted a million memories that had previously been wallowing in the deep recesses of her mind. First kisses, last dances, summer picnics, winter walks, dinners out, breakfasts in bed, big celebrations, tender commiserations, they all flooded her mind in fast forward. He looked the same apart from the fact that he'd been MP-ified. His shirt shouted boring and middle-aged. His tie was neatly knotted at the top rather than pulled loose as it always used to be, and his hairline was receding to meet his bald patch. But apart from that he looked exactly the same. Oh, and he was wearing a wedding ring. That was new since she'd last seen him.

'Suzie,' he repeated. 'So . . . how are you? This is such a surprise.' He tapped a pen nervously on the table.

'Well . . . I'm fine,' she faltered. The video player in her head had just about reached the end of their relationship and was starting to replay the moment she'd found Antony in their bed with Charlie. She could see his pale buttocks pumping up and down and she remembered how her first thought had been that she'd never seen that view of him before.

Antony looked away, unable to hold her gaze, and started nervously organising paper clips in a blue plastic desk tidy. Eventually, when she didn't speak, he looked up and furrowed his brow. He gave her a good look up and down.

'You look great,' he said finally.

She had tried so hard not to dress for the occasion. She desperately wanted not to care what Antony thought of how she looked, but pride had won the battle and her best business suit teamed with sexy killer heels had been dusted off and deemed necessary in order to boost her confidence. It was also necessary, she thought, to cast herself in the role of hotshot reporter and all-round success story. Today she wasn't Suzie Miller, Agony Aunt for the *Manchester Herald*. Today she was Kate Adie, minus the bulletproof vest, on a serious quest for the truth. Feeling nervous as Antony continued to look her up and down, she wondered what Kate would do next. Take no shit and wade right in, she thought. Act as if she owned the place. Ignore the battle, just get to the truth. Kate Adie had been Suzie's idol when she was young. She hadn't quite made it to the battlefields of the Middle East, but people's relationships was where she was obviously destined to fight for the truth.

She sat down on a plastic chair in front of Antony's desk and pulled her notepad from her bag. Clicking her pen, she looked squarely into Antony's eyes and asked her first question.

'Antony Barwood, I have reason to believe you are

having an affair. Would you like to confirm that?' Bollocks, she thought immediately. Kate wouldn't ask such a closed question – what was she playing at?

'What the . . .' He threw his pen down on the desk, scattering paper clips everywhere. 'What the hell is this? What do you think you're doing coming in here and asking a question like that?'

'Antony, I'm a reporter for the *Manchester Herald*. I have evidence that you're having an affair and I would like your comment . . . please?' she added. Damn, she thought. Kate would never say please.

'Suzie, I don't know what the hell is going on here but I think you'd better leave. No-one comes in here accusing me of having an affair.'

'I do,' said Suzie in a low voice.

'Oh no you don't. I am not having a fucking affair. Now get out,' he said, getting up from his chair.

Suzie calmly wrote on her pad while she considered her next move.

'What are you writing down?' he shouted, walking around to her side of the desk.

'"I am not having a fucking affair,"' said the Member of Parliament for West Keeling,' said Suzie as she continued to write.

'Give that here,' he said, snatching the pad away from her and throwing it on the desk. 'You do not come in here with these lies. What is this? Some kind of weird revenge for what happened to us? After what, nearly ten years? You're sick, is what you are – go and get some therapy and never come here again.'

'I am getting therapy,' replied Suzie, still sitting firmly in her chair.

Antony stopped in his tracks en route to opening the door.

'Good, good,' he said more quietly but with a distinct look of fear on his face. 'That's really good, Suzie. Now off you pop. I'm sure your psychiatrist would not be advising you to be here now, would they?'

'Oh yes they would,' she said in a sing-song voice. 'This therapy is self-administered and it really is doing me the power of good.'

'Self-administered?' he questioned. 'What the hell is that supposed to mean?'

'Well, you're entirely correct. This is revenge. You're still such a clever chap, aren't you?' She spotted dark patches peeking out from his underarms.

'Revenge?' he asked, swallowing audibly.

'Yes.'

'For how we broke up?'

'Yes.'

'But it was years ago,' he said, his hands flying up in exasperation.

'Oh, I know. But, you see, you didn't give me a chance to do it then so I'm doing it now.'

'By accusing me of having an affair? You have to be joking. I married Charlotte, didn't you hear? I would never cheat on my wife.'

'She thinks you are,' said Suzie calmly.

'What?' squealed Antony.

'Cheating on her.'

'You've seen Charlotte? What is this? I'm going to get someone to call security.' He made a dive for the door again.

'Why don't you ask Megan?' said Suzie, studying her nails nonchalantly. 'I'm sure she'd be happy to oblige in any way.'

Antony froze with the door open just a fraction.

'What is that supposed to mean?'

'Just that she seems like a very obliging young girl, that's all. You must be very pleased to have her around to cater for your every need.'

Antony closed the door again.

'I am not having an affair,' he said through gritted teeth.

'Let's ask Ms Lewinsky out there, shall we?' said Suzie.

She thought Antony might explode right in front of her before he managed to calm himself enough to reply.

'You have no proof, now get out of my office!' He flung the door open and stepped aside to let her out.

'Excuse me,' a high-pitched voice suddenly piped up, followed by the impeccably groomed ponytail bouncing jauntily over Megan's head.

'Sorry to bother you, Antony, but the Mayor has called and would like you to call him urgently,' gushed Megan. She turned to give Suzie an apologetic smile.

'Suzie . . . er, Ms Miller was just leaving,' stated Antony.

Shit, thought Suzie. What now? She knew that Antony was right. She didn't have any proof. All she had was Charlie's suspicions – and suspicions regarding adultery were usually proved to be correct. 'Kate Adie, Kate Adie, Kate Adie,' she muttered to herself.

'So you're the one who's sleeping with Antony then?' she blurted out to Megan.

There was silence as the world adjusted to the public airing of the fact.

Megan's hand flew to her mouth and she looked at

219

Antony's horrified face. His mouth was making motions to speak but nothing was coming out.

'I'm an old friend and we've had a good chat,' said Suzie, smiling at Antony.

'But I thought we weren't going to tell anyone,' interrupted Megan. 'I thought we were going to wait until after we were re-elected?'

'*We* were re-elected?' cried Suzie, unable to contain her anger. 'You already think you're a *we*? You've shagged a few times behind his wife's back. You don't get to say *we*.'

Antony grabbed Megan's arm and pulled her into the room, slamming the door behind her.

'Keep your mouth shut,' he hissed. 'She's a reporter and a maniac so let me do the talking.'

Megan staggered back as the situation dawned on her. 'Oh God,' she kept saying, over and over again, as Antony pulled himself up to his full five foot seven inches and squared up to Suzie.

'It's your word against mine,' he said. 'No-one is going to touch this on your say-so alone.'

Suzie slapped her forehead in mock surprise. 'You're right,' she said. 'Of course you're right. Your word against mine. Actually, technically it will be Megan's word,' she continued as she reached into a pocket and pulled out a small Dictaphone, allowing Antony to glimpse it for a brief moment before she placed it in her jacket pocket, leaving her hand protectively over it.

'How dare you!' he ranted. 'Hand it over.'

'No,' she said, stepping forward so her face was barely inches from his. 'Do you know what I hold in my hand? Your future. On that tiny little machine is your future and it's in my hands. Just like you held my future in your hands all those years ago. You told me we had one. I was counting on that future and you took it away. Now I can do the same to you. How does that feel, Antony?'

Antony's bottom lip was visibly trembling now and the smell of his sweat – or maybe it was his fear – had unpleasantly reached her nostrils. She stood firm, holding his gaze, ignoring Megan simpering somewhere behind him.

'Okay, so you've had your fun,' said Antony slowly. 'I'm sorry for what I did, I really am. But let's call it quits now, shall we? You hand that thing over and you can rest easy that you got your revenge.'

'You want your future back, do you?' Suzie asked.

'Yes. Like I said, I'm sorry. Just give it to me, please,' he begged.

221

'No,' she said abruptly. 'You can't have it because I have to give it to someone else.'

Megan was now sobbing in a heap in a corner, her impossible tidiness in ruins.

'No, Suzie, please, you can't do that. I'll do whatever you want. You know that if you print that I'm finished.'

Suzie stared at him for a long time, wondering what she'd ever seen in him.

'I might have known it would be your precious career that would be your first concern,' she spat out finally. 'What about your wife, Antony?'

He didn't answer. Megan was suddenly silent.

'You're right, I've had my fun,' said Suzie. 'I don't need to take this any further.'

'Oh Suzie, thank you,' said Antony, visibly sagging with relief. 'You will not regret this, I promise you.' He held his hand out for the Dictaphone.

'Not so fast,' said Suzie, taking a step back away from him. 'I've had my fun. But now it's Charlie's turn. She's the one who'll be getting this.' She tapped her pocket. 'I think it should be up to her to decide your future, don't you?' She turned and left the room before Megan could start sobbing again and before Antony could drop to the floor and join her.

222

Chapter 17

Dear Suzie,

I am fast approaching forty and I thought I'd lost my chance at finding love, but everything changed when I met the perfect man six months ago. It's like a dream come true. We get on like a house on fire and the sex is out of this world. There is just one thing getting in the way of us living happily ever after. His wife. He doesn't want to leave her because he says it will destroy her life, but I don't want to spend the rest of my life only being able to grab a few hours here and there with the man I love. I just want to do what normal couples do. Go on a date, wake up in his arms, do the grocery shopping together. Is that too much to ask?

    Yours sincerely,
    Katherine

Dear Katherine,

    Yes, it is too much to ask. Give me one good reason why he would throw away your sex-with-no-ties relationship. Is it really appealing to him to spend hours making small talk whilst wasting money in a fancy restaurant? Does he really want to have to hold you all night when he can have his way with you then get up and leave and go home to his own bed for a decent night's sleep? Does he really want to discuss with you what brand of toilet cleaner to buy? No. This set-up is perfect for him because he gets sex from you which allows him not to face up to the fact that there is clearly a major problem with his marriage which he needs to deal with.

    So I am calling on you and all women who currently find themselves playing the role of 'the other woman' to STOP NOW. I hereby declare next Friday to be official BUNNY BOILER DAY. I ask you all to celebrate your liberation from a compromised

relationship by mailing your cheating man a stuffed
bunny with a note attached saying next time it will be
a real one if they don't leave you alone and start being
honest with their wives.

    Be strong.
    Suzie

'Bunnies?' mumbled Drew into his scarf as he stomped his feet in the freezing December early-morning air.

'You don't have to tell me what a good idea it is,' responded Suzie, staring around her at the throng of journalists gathered outside the gate of Antony Barwood's Manchester residence. She allowed herself a small smile. Bunny Boiler Day was a great idea but her revenge plan for Antony was a stroke of genius. She glanced at her phone to see whether Charlie had sent her any messages. Nothing. She hoped this was a good sign.

'So are you going to tell me what's going on here?' asked Drew. 'I still don't get why you gave away Antony's confession.' He reduced his voice to a whisper to avoid being overheard. 'Do you have any idea what you could have done with that? Talk about giving away the opportunity for an exclusive *and* revenge. What were you thinking?'

TRACY BLOOM

'You'll see,' she muttered as she watched the front door of the house open to reveal Antony doing his best to look like a casual Saturday MP in his badly fitting jeans and a skiing jacket that had clearly been nowhere near a slope. Charlie inched out from behind him wearing sunglasses and a very large three-quarter-length black raincoat.

'Oooh, bad choice,' winced Suzie. 'She looks like a gas barbecue with its cover on. I can see the headlines now: MP's Wife Gets a Good Grilling.'

'She's probably not overly interested in looking her best at the moment,' said Drew. 'She must have a lot on her mind.'

'But I told her to go glamorous,' muttered Suzie, kicking the ground. 'Fuck, what if she's not listened to a word I said?'

Antony and Charlie were nearly at the gate now. They were holding hands but walking in silence. Antony looked grim but determined. Charlie was impossible to read, given the sunglasses. Suzie hoped they weren't hiding red eyes. Cheerful and upbeat had been her advice, not funeral in a downpour.

Antony stopped just the other side of the gate at the end of the leafy drive and nodded his acknowledgement

226

of the twenty or so reporters and photographers from all the major nationals gathered on the other side. He reached inside his jacket and pulled out a piece of paper before clearing his throat and squeezing Charlie's hand.

'Thank you for coming,' he said gravely. 'I stand here before you today in the name of honesty and openness, characteristics I believe you should expect in a Member of Parliament. And as such I feel I must tell you that I have made a very grave mistake. Recently I have had an inappropriate relationship with a woman other than my wife. The relationship is now over. I have had the chance to be honest with Charlotte and express my extreme regret at having made this mistake.' He looked up at his wife and nodded seriously before returning to his speech. 'As a public servant it is now my duty to be honest with my constituents and the great British Public. I realise that I have let everyone down and apologise profusely for that. I cannot tell you how much it grieves me to be standing here today having to make this statement. I have devoted my whole life to being a public servant, and this is not something I ever envisaged would happen. My intention was always to serve others and to make a difference in their lives.'

He paused for a moment and looked up from his

statement. The flash bulbs went wild, bathing the awkward couple in a fluorescent glow. What sounded like a million voices suddenly crowded the air as the waiting hacks took their opportunity to go in for the kill.

'Simon Andrews, the *Mirror*. Who was the lucky lady then, Tony?'

'Richard Bartholomew, the *Telegraph*. Will you be resigning?'

'Phillip Barker, the *Sun*. Now you've joined the Super-Stud MPs' club will you be appearing in *Hello!* magazine with semi-clad women in their twenties?'

Antony blinked in the haze of light for a moment, looking startled, before he managed to regain his composure. He continued with his statement, without referring to his piece of paper.

'I was momentarily distracted and displayed a weakness that I am not proud of. But as I said, I became a public servant in order to make a difference to people's lives, and with my wife's support I hope to continue to do so for a very long time.' Antony was now pointing into a TV camera to accentuate what he was saying to the public watching at home.

'He thinks he's bloody Bill Clinton,' said Suzie to

Drew, horrified. 'All that finger pointing. He thinks he's going to do a Clinton and walk away unscathed.' She looked around at the crowd who were now silent, appearing to hang off his every word. She stared back at Antony, unable to believe her eyes. 'Look at him,' she continued to no-one in particular. 'He thinks this actually might be good for his career. Hitting the headlines with a sex scandal will make him famous rather than just being some idiot MP no-one's ever heard of.' She looked at Charlie who was staring at the ground. 'Oh come on, Charlie. What the hell are you playing at? This is not what's supposed to happen.'

'What are you talking about?' muttered Drew, scribbling furiously in his notebook, trying to get the statement down word for word.

'She's just standing there. Standing by him. Which is exactly what she said she wouldn't do. I said I'd get her the proof and then she would do the decent thing and most certainly not stand by her man and would destroy that stupid song for good. Free up every woman on this planet to do the right thing and walk away. No man would stand there and be humiliated like that. For Christ's sake, the suffragettes will be turning in their graves. They didn't fight for the vote just to have women allow members of parliament to get away with shagging who the hell they like.'

Drew looked up from his scribbling. 'So you did a deal that you'd get proof if she then publicly humiliated Antony during his garden-gate, *I'm-oh-so-sorry* speech? Antony's future in tatters, revenge complete. Only now she's doing a great Tammy Wynette impression.'

'Bloody well looks like it.' Suzie stared down at the pavement, wondering whether she should just leave rather than watch the tragic scene unfold any further.

Antony was now calmly answering all the journalists' questions with a look of quiet relief on his face. Suzie couldn't help admitting he'd handled it well, although she assumed that he'd been coached at length by Westminster's finest spin doctors. He repeated over and over again the key words he had obviously been told to focus on: mistake, honesty, public servant.

Suzie couldn't bear it. Charlie was still staring at the ground, ignoring all the questions flying in her direction, as Antony took centre stage and seized his moment in the spotlight.

She couldn't get Tammy Wynette out of her head. 'Stand By Your Man' was whirring round and round in a maddening fashion. She had to do something. Desperate measures were called for. She stuck her elbows out and managed to push her way through to the gate so she was just a few yards from Charlie. She called her name, but Charlie flatly refused to look up. In fact, she appeared to be edging backwards, as if she was trying to pull Antony away from his transfixed audience.

Suzie took a deep breath and decided there was only one option. She would have to turn to the only person whose words could possibly get through to Charlie at this time. The words of someone Charlie had been obsessed with back in the Nineties, when they'd still been friends. The words of the one and only . . . Gary Barlow.

So on that chilly winter's day, surrounded by the journalistic great and the good, Suzie took a deep breath and started to sing the words to 'Promises', written by the great man himself.

Charlie looked up at Suzie by the second line, so familiar were the words of her beloved Take That. Suzie struggled on, trying to remember the words. One by one the journalists surrounding her turned to stare. A couple of moments later Antony spotted her as the entire crowd went silent, wondering what on earth was going on. A look of absolute panic crossed his previously relieved face and he glanced towards Charlie nervously.

'Well, thank you very much for coming,' he interrupted as Suzie drew breath at the end of the chorus. 'That concludes the press conference. I would ask now that you allow both my wife and me some privacy in order to rebuild our marriage.' He turned to go but Charlie remained rooted to the spot, still staring at Suzie.

Keep going, thought Suzie. Last chance. She launched into the chorus again, putting in her own words to make her point hit home.

'*He's telling lies it's plain to see, he's trying to make a fool of Charlie,*' she sang, looking Charlie straight in the eye, willing her to respond.

'What is that song?' asked a man standing next to Suzie.

'Take That's second single, "Promises". It only got to thirty-eight in the charts, which might be why you don't recognise it,' she said out of the corner of her mouth, still staring hopefully at Charlie.

Charlie stared back at Suzie before turning to survey the bewildered crowd of seasoned hacks who had clearly never encountered such a bizarre scene in their reporting careers.

'I have something to say,' she said quietly.

'Speak up, love,' came a shout from the back.

'It's okay, Charlotte, you don't have to say anything. Let's just go inside, shall we?' interrupted a very bothered-looking Antony, pulling at her hand.

'Will you be quiet for once and let me speak,' said Charlie, wrenching her hand away from his and reaching into her coat pocket to pull out a piece of screwed-up paper. She slowly unfolded it in front of the now silent crowd.

'I didn't think I was going to be able to do this but someone has just reminded me why I should.' She looked up and smiled weakly at Suzie before removing her sunglasses and turning to face a hovering TV camera.

'This is what I have to say about my husband,' she said, staring steadily ahead.

'He's a shit.'

After a moment's shocked silence the journalists went crazy, bombarding Charlie with requests to elaborate on her brief statement. After waiting patiently for the noise to die away she continued.

'I have nothing more to say about him and that's all you need to write. I ask that you do not give him the satisfaction of writing pages and pages, scrutinising his entire career and his every move. He's not worth it. He is a second-rate MP who couldn't organise a pensioners' tea party. So ignore him and hope he goes away, for everyone's sake.'

The crowd listened intently to Charlie's every word whilst Antony stood in shock, not knowing what to do.

'I would, however, like to say something about myself. I have supported Antony in his career for nearly ten years. I sacrificed all my ambitions in order to stand by his side and act the perfect political wife. I did this because I loved him. But I am sad to admit that I also did it because he was a man with ambition – a man with a goal in life and a desire for power – and I found that hugely attractive. But it is a sad fact of life that men with power can be dangerous, because for some reason that sense of power goes straight to their penis.' Charlie paused and looked Antony in the eye as he took a sharp, shocked intake of breath. A titter went around the crowd as the journalists scribbled furiously and photographers flashed mercilessly at the beetroot face of Antony Barwood.

'Sadly this leads to a desire to prove their power status by manipulating as many women into bed as they possibly can. And even more sadly, women succumb, often feeling honoured that such a man has bestowed his attention.' Charlie paused for a moment, looked down at the crumpled piece of paper in her hand and appeared to falter before she screwed it up and put it back in her pocket.

'To those women I would like to say this,' she said, looking almost calm. 'Particularly to the girl who has been sleeping with my husband.' All heads rose and the journalists held their breath to listen to what the wronged MP's wife had to say to her husband's mistress. 'Don't bother. The power may go to their penis but sadly this does not lead to a performance improvement.'

There was a moment of silence before the place erupted in laughter and excited chatter. Suzie looked on amazed as jaded hacks turned to nod at each other in an approving manner. Charlie had unwittingly delivered a piece of great news which the entire universe wanted to hear. Powerful, seemingly successful men were crap in bed. Even if it was a gross generalisation, the assembled, largely middle-aged men, who no doubt had all suffered at the hands of power-crazed male bosses, approved wholeheartedly. As Charlie paused, a clatter of questions filled the air once again but she raised her hands for silence.

'That is all I have to say for now. Other than to pay

special thanks to someone without whom I would not be standing here today. I would like to thank Suzie Miller, who writes the absolutely fantastic Dear Suzie column in the *Manchester Herald*. Come over here, Suzie.'

Suzie wanted to run away and hide. She didn't want to stand in front of a legion of professional journalists and be congratulated on her advice column. She shook her head at Charlie, hoping she would leave her be.

'Come on, Suzie, come over here,' Charlie urged. Suzie caught sight of Antony looking daggers at her and her confidence returned. She opened the side gate and strode up to Charlie, throwing her arms around her as if she had just won an Olympic medal.

'Dear Suzie is the first advice column I have ever read that gives the brutal truth on how to handle relationships and how to fight back when they go wrong. Everyone who is having relationship issues should read her column because, as she said to me, you should not roll over and die; you should roll over and crush him to death.' Charlie turned and engulfed Suzie in a bear hug and whispered in her ear.

'Thank you so much. You were right. I feel amazing.'

Suzie hugged her back, speechless. This was not what she'd expected at all.

Holding Suzie's hand tightly, Charlie concluded the press conference.

'I will not answer any further questions now. I will, however, be giving an exclusive interview to the *Manchester Herald*, so make sure you buy a copy tomorrow.' She turned and gave Suzie one last kiss, then strode back up the gravel drive without looking back, leaving Antony still gaping in her wake.

He directed a vicious stare at Suzie, then pulled his mobile phone out of his pocket, no doubt to place a call to his advisors, and stormed angrily up the drive after Charlie. Suzie wondered for a moment if she should follow before deciding that Charlie was now more than capable of dealing with anything Antony, the disgraced and sexually challenged MP, had to throw at her.

Chapter 18

'Secrets and lies are the poison that kills a marriage,'
said Charlotte, the wife of disgraced MP Antony
Barwood, yesterday as she reflected on the demise of
their ten-year marriage after he admitted having an
affair. 'Once you lie to your spouse you show them the
deepest form of disrespect, and without respect, how
can a marriage survive?' It is clear that her refusal to
stand by her man yesterday has given her renewed
self-respect and the confidence to pick up the pieces of
her life and start again.

Suzie stopped reading from the front page of the

newspaper and turned to look at Drew, who was leaning back in his office chair sipping on a triple espresso, having stayed up all night to complete the article.

'Very nice,' she said. 'You're really good at the girly stuff. You should do these in-depth pieces more often.'

'I still think you should have done the interview,' he said.

'No way,' she replied. 'I owed you one and I knew you would do it so much better than me. Just look what you've written here,' she said, stabbing at the paper with her finger. '*Charlotte Harwood is clearly already showing signs of bursting out of her chrysalis. Shrouded for too long by the heavy cloak of a self-obsessed man, a megawatt grin breaks through, if somewhat shyly, whenever she recounts her brave statement at the morning's press conference.*'

She looked up and sighed. 'That is so right. So beautifully put. You didn't fancy her, did you?'

'What? No, you idiot. I felt sorry for her, that's all,' said Drew, going bright red. He was dog-tired and the last thing he needed was for Suzie to make stupid statements like that. Listening for three hours to Charlie and her account of their flawed marriage had mixed his head up enough as it was. One particular statement was playing on a loop in his mind. She'd broken down in

239

tears and told him that she knew he didn't love her the day they got married. She knew in her heart of hearts that they were great friends but he wasn't in love with her. He had merely recognised a good political wife with the right connections. How can anyone marry someone they're not in love with? she'd sobbed. Indeed, he'd wondered, and then tried to shelve the question in the back of his mind.

But now he'd finished the article, and having been awake for nearly twenty hours, his mind was mush and he had no barrier against random thoughts. He had to get out of here, get some sleep and get his head straight.

Suzie was still devouring the article as he started to tidy his desk. Her phone rang and she idly picked it up without looking away from the paper.

'Hello . . . Yes, it is . . . From where, sorry? . . . I see.' She dropped the paper and sat up. 'Well, I've been doing the column this way for a while now and my letters have actually quadrupled since I changed it.' A pause. 'Yeah, that's right.' Another pause. 'Well, er, yeah. I think I'm free, just let me check my diary.' She cupped the mouthpiece of her phone and held it away from her before emitting a small scream. She took her hand away and returned to speak to the caller. 'Yes, actually I am free.' Final pause. 'Right, I'll see you there then. Thanks very much. Bye.'

She carefully replaced the receiver then looked up at Drew with wide, manic eyes. She stood up slowly then ran around the office waving her arms and shouting 'Oh my God!' at the top of her voice. After three laps she finally came to a screeching halt next to Drew's chair, grasped the top of his head and firmly kissed him on his forehead. She then took a step back and bounced on the spot chanting, 'Guess what, guess what, guess what?'

'What?' he finally shouted. She was giving him a headache and his nostrils were still chasing the faint perfume she had left lingering over his head.

'I'm going to be on the telly!' she shrieked, giving a huge jump in the air. 'Like, real telly, not pretend YouTube stuff, real telly!'

'Why?' he asked, bewildered, wishing she would stop jumping up and down.

'*Granada Reports* want to interview me tomorrow morning about my column. Me, me, me!' she said, right in his face.

'Wow,' he said, pulling back, her sudden proximity really unsettling.

'Isn't it great?' she said. 'Who would have thought

241

that the minute I decide to give up the relentless pursuit of men my entire life would get better? I don't know why I didn't do it sooner. Maybe I could have been a celebrity years ago if I had.'

'You're not quite a celebrity yet,' Drew pointed out.

'But who knows where this could lead?' she said. 'Everyone has to start somewhere. Who knows who might pick up the story once it's been on the local news?' She paused and suddenly looked sad. 'Oh bugger,' she said, her enthusiasm suddenly evaporating.

'What's wrong?' Drew asked.

'Bloody Richard and Judy.'

'What have they done?'

'They're not on the telly anymore, are they? I dreamed of being a guest on *This Morning*, and now the minute I get the chance they screw it up for me. It's like *Wogan* all over again.'

'*Wogan*?'

'Yeah, *Wogan*. In my graduation yearbook I stated that my ultimate ambition was to be on *Wogan*, then the fool gets taken off the TV. Why can't these celebs stay on air long enough to interview me?'

Drew realised he definitely had to leave and inhabit a saner world.

'Well,' he said. 'Gotta go and get some sleep. Text me to tell me when you're on, okay?'

'Of course.'

Just as Drew was picking up his bag the Editor came rushing over.

'So here's my dynamic duo,' he said, grinning from ear to ear and placing a hand on each of their shoulders.

'I've just come to tell you that between your exclusive and the interest in Dear Suzie we have doubled sales today already. Hits on the website have trebled and Alex tells me he now needs an assistant, so many advertisers are calling him.'

'Seriously?' said Drew, sitting down again.

'Seriously,' said Gareth. 'Plus I have some fantastic news for you, son.' Drew couldn't help wincing. As good as the news might be, being called *son* by a man younger than him really wasn't right.

'You are going to get syndicated. The desk is getting calls from websites and newspapers from all over the world wanting to use your article. That little lady made quite a splash yesterday. I guess she struck a nerve. She did what everyone has always dreamed would happen to a stray politician. This is really big.'

'Wow, syndicated,' was all Drew could say. Now *his* dreams were coming true, never mind Suzie's.

'Drew, that's brilliant! You're going to be famous too!' said Suzie, jumping up and down again.

'I don't want you getting ideas above your station,' said Gareth, suddenly stern. 'You're not to start getting starry-eyed and leave the *Herald*. Now, well done and . . . back to work.' He strode off, leaving the two of them in stunned silence at his sudden change in mood.

'Wow,' whispered Suzie. 'He thinks you're going to get poached. About time, matey. Just think, you and Emily can head off to London and become one of those mega-couples – you the hotshot journalist and she the successful lawyer. You'll have nannies and maids and . . . and clean cars and everything. Ring Emily. Ring her now and tell her you might be moving to London.'

Drew thought his eyes were about to sink back into his head. The tiredness and the information overload were too much for his body to take.

'I'm so happy for you, you so deserve it,' he heard Suzie saying to him.

He looked at her for a moment, then his mouth started to move without his being able to stop it.

'Wouldn't you miss me?' he asked.

'Of course not,' she exclaimed. 'You and your perfect life can push off down south for all I care. About time I got to sit next to someone who screwed up as much as me.'

Truth discovered. She wouldn't miss him if he wasn't there. The thought was still bouncing around his head when they were interrupted by Diane the receptionist sticking a waste-paper bin under his nose.

'Pick one,' she urged.

'What?' he spluttered. Sleep deprivation sure made the weirdest things happen.

'A name,' she said, rattling the bin.

'Er, Gordon,' he said.

'No-one who works here is called Gordon, and anyway you pick a name out in secret. Don't say it out loud, that ruins it.'

Drew thought he actually might burst into tears. What was happening? He looked at Suzie for some assistance.

'Secret Santa,' she mouthed, pointing into the bin at the mound of neatly folded squares which held the names of every employee in the building.

'Oh, I see,' he said, relieved there was a logical explanation.

'I hate Secret Santa,' Suzie declared. 'Creates so much waste. You give crap, you receive crap and then it lingers somewhere in a drawer for hundreds of millions of years refusing to go away and decompose.'

'So what did you get last year?' asked Drew.

'Men's aftershave gift pack,' said Suzie.

'For under a fiver?' exclaimed Drew.

'Precisely,' replied Suzie. 'Wrong on so many levels. It would be more useful to take a fiver and flush it down the toilet. Secret Santa should be banned.'

'Look, just pick a name,' said Diane, losing patience and rattling the bin again.

Drew and Suzie both dived in and pulled out a piece of paper. Suzie opened hers first and gave a deep groan. Drew opened his and stared at it.

'Well, at least it's probably the last time you'll have to do this,' said Suzie after Diane had moved on to the next desk. 'I can't imagine those swanky nationals do Secret Santa. It'll be more throw your keys in the pot kind of dos, I reckon. So who you got?'

He carefully folded the piece of paper back up and put it in his pocket.

'It's a secret,' he said, before picking up his briefcase and setting off for the door.

Chapter 19

Drew stared at the orange woman sitting opposite him. He'd thought that after all the weirdness at the office and only a few hours' sleep there was no way his day could get any more bizarre. But as he listened to the woman in the green polyester suit and fake-tan-smeared cream cravat, he wished with all his heart he was back in the relative sanity of the office.

'Now I highly recommend that you do not overlook our Decorative Accessories Department. We have some wonderful items in there that can really add your own sense of personal style to your newly-wed home. And of course, because of the time of year we have some gorgeous festive items. Many of my couples have already chosen our adorable reindeer draught excluders. How much fun would it be to celebrate your first Christmas as newly-weds with Christmas-themed draught excluders?' The woman giggled to herself as Drew glanced at Emily, who thankfully was also looking somewhat nonplussed.

'Actually,' Emily finally said to the wedding-list coordinator, who seemed to be turning a deeper orange the longer they sat there. 'I've already been through your website and I have a list of exactly what we want bar choosing colours on a few things. I also wanted to check that your Egyptian cotton sheets are actually five hundred thread count.'

'Madam,' said the orange lady, running a finger around the inside of her cravat, smearing it with even more fake tan, 'I can assure you that I would not be able to sleep at night if I thought that my newlyweds were sleeping in anything less.'

'Good,' said Emily brusquely. 'So shall we get started then?' She tapped the folder she had laid out on her knee, containing her neatly typed wedding gift list.

'If you could just bear with me a few more minutes I can explain where all the departments are. I can't tell you the amount of times that, in the excitement of choosing their wedding gifts, some of my couples actually forget table linen entirely,' chuckled orange lady. 'And you can't start married life without table linen, can you?' she said, directing her question at Drew.

'Absolutely,' he replied, shrinking back in his chair. He looked round the third-floor room to see if anyone else was scared of these weird wedding creatures. There were four other couples sitting in cubicles being harassed by women in polyester. Actually, he noticed, they didn't look at all uncomfortable. The women were leaning forward eagerly, lapping up every word they were being preached by these gift mercenaries, whilst their partners clutched their hands tightly and grinned inanely.

'There's no need to tell us where anything is,' Emily told the woman. 'I've mapped it all out.' She turned to Drew. 'I think the most efficient way is for you to take the ground floor. Here's the list done in order of when you come out of the lift so it should take you no more than half an hour. I'll do this floor.' She turned back to the woman sitting across the desk. 'Now, can we have two scanners, please, so we can make a start?'

The orange lady stared at Emily with a look of utter confusion. Drew had to admit he felt proud. Stick that up your reindeer draught excluder, he thought.

'Well, of course, if that's the way you want to do it that's fine,' she said curtly. 'I do find however that most of my couples like to go around together in case they need to make any decisions as they go along. These are your wedding gifts, after all. You will be living with them for the rest of your lives.'

'No need,' said Emily, standing up. 'The decisions have been made; we just want to get on with it. Now please give me the scanner.' She held her hand out.

The orange lady rather begrudgingly handed over the scanners, but just as Drew was about to walk away she grabbed his arm.

'Why don't I come round with you? I don't have another couple in for half an hour. You never know, I might help you find something that's not on your list.'

'No,' said Drew and Emily in unison, almost shouting. 'Thank you,' said Drew. 'I think I can manage.'

Outside the lift Emily handed Drew his list and a pen.

'If there's anything you can't find then just mark it with a cross and I'll come down and choose an alternative. Okay?'

'Super,' smiled Drew. 'Choosing wedding presents is the best thing ever.'

'Got to be done, Drew,' she said seriously. 'Or else

we're going to get a house full of rubbish we can't chuck away. I'll come down and find you when I'm finished.' With that she turned and a headed straight for a pillowcase stand.

He studied the scanner as he went down in the lift. He pressed the trigger a few times and discovered that if he aimed it at his hand it beamed a red light onto his palm. He then did what any man would do when armed with such an object. He pretended it was a lightsaber, swishing it dramatically from one side of the lift to the other until the doors opened just as he was in the middle of slaying the overbearing orange lady.

It didn't take long for Drew to start feeling really uncomfortable. He was lost in a sea of white porcelain in the dinnerware department. Everywhere he looked, glaring white dinner plates bore down on him, so pristine and perfect that he felt grubby and out of place. And now, with every highly irritating beep of the gruesome scanner, he winced as he peered into the tiny display window to look at the price. How could one saucer cost nearly twenty pounds? The most irrelevant item known to man, a plate to hold a cup that already has a handle, costing that much – how so? And what in heaven's name was a 'creamer'? He had never heard of such a thing, never mind used one, he was sure. So why did he need one of his friends or relatives to spend their hard-earned cash buying him one? What he was also starting to realise was that Emily, for all her immense organisational skills, had completely overlooked the fact that his family didn't have this kind of money. In fact he had never known anyone in his family have a wedding list, unless you counted his cousin Catrina who got married in a rush and had her list at Mothercare. He knew he would have to talk to Emily. Maybe they could have a list at Argos as well, or even no list at all. He looked over to see one of the couples that had been sitting upstairs in a cubicle, studying coffee machines. The man reached over and grabbed a small cup, then pretended to make his lady an espresso before handing it over with a flourish, saying, 'For you, Mrs Pemberton to-be.' The girl giggled and gave him a quick peck on the cheek before telling him to put the cup back and concentrate.

That was what was wrong, he realised. They shouldn't be doing this separately. Sod efficiency. If this was what you had to do then you might as well enjoy doing it together rather than looking like a moron on your own, pointing a stupid stick at a teapot. Pleased that he had spotted an escape route from the torture, he scuttled back to the lift and jabbed the button to go up.

It took him some time to find Emily, as she was hiding behind a mountain of Teflon and a full-size cardboard cut-out of Jamie Oliver grinning inanely holding what looked like a designer vibrator.

'You getting one of those?' Drew shouted over to Emily, pointing at the sleek, moulded item clutched in Jamie's hand.

Emily glanced over. 'Yes. In red hot.'

'Wow,' said Drew with a grin. 'I'm beginning to get excited about the wedding list thing now.'

'So have you finished already?' she asked, getting up off her hands and knees and walking over to him.

'Not quite,' he replied. 'To be honest, I wasn't enjoying it on my own. I think maybe orange lady was right. We should do it together seeing as it is our wedding list.'

Emily looked at him for a moment without saying anything. Then she consulted her watch before explaining that was all very well but they had to be quick because she had to leave for a meeting in twenty-five minutes.

'No problem,' he responded. 'Tell you what, you read the list out and I'll scan. My laser control is second to none.'

She looked at him again for a few moments before giving a small sigh and handing over the scanner. She traced her pen down the piece of paper until she found her place.

'Okay then. Next is a Pyrex Pyroflam Round Casserole in white, one litre,' she read out.

'Excuse me?' asked Drew without moving.

'I said a Pyrex Pyroflam Round Casserole in white, one litre,' she repeated without having to refer back to her list.

Drew didn't move.

'What's the matter?' she asked.

'We never eat casserole.'

'So?'

'So why are we asking for a casserole dish?'

'Because we might want to eat casserole one day,' she replied a little shortly.

Drew still didn't move.

'You're telling me that we're asking someone to spend money to buy us a casserole dish just in case one day we wake up and say, "Crikey, I just fancy a casserole. Isn't it a good job that Auntie Mavis bought us one for our wedding or wouldn't we be in mess,"' said Drew, his voice getting higher and higher.

Emily looked around, exasperated.

'Just scan the bloody dish,' she said finally through gritted teeth. 'I haven't got time for this.'

'No,' said Drew.

Emily looked taken aback for a moment, but then she lunged forward, took the scanner out of Drew's hand and strode off towards a large stand of cooking dishes.

Drew stood with his mouth open before he shouted after her, 'If you scan that casserole . . .'

Emily turned and paused right next to the stand, holding the scanner over a large white dish.

'What?' she said. 'Please don't you tell me what I can and can't scan.'

'If you scan that casserole I'll . . .' he repeated.

'You'll what?' she asked.

Drew stared at her as she looked coolly back at him, her face set, determined at all costs to complete the task she had planned so meticulously. How had it come to this? he thought, his tiredness sweeping over him once again. What on earth had happened to him that he was standing in a shop with his fiancée arguing over a casserole dish?

'You'll what?' she asked again.

'I'll call the wedding off,' he replied quickly, the words jumping out of his mouth before he had time to think properly. He heard them out loud for the first time, words that had hovered around his brain for so long but had thus far remained private and unsaid.

'What did you say?' said Emily, cutting through his thoughts.

Could he say it out loud again? he wondered. The leap between thinking it and saying it had seemed impossibly wide, and yet he had done it. Just like that. Emily was advancing towards him now, brandishing the scanner like some kind of gladiator's sword.

'What did you say?' she asked again.

'I'll call the wedding off,' he whispered, not even looking at her, barely aware that she was there, he was so in awe of the sound of those words out in the open.

Emily stopped in her tracks, then burst out laughing, shaking her head and focusing her attention back down on her list. 'You are hysterical, you know that?' she said. 'Tell you what. I'll ditch the casserole and add in an extra milk saucepan instead, how's that?'

'Milk saucepan?' he asked slowly.

'Yeah, you know, a small pan you boil milk in.'

'Milk for what?'

'Well, like for coffee,' replied Emily. 'Look, time is running out, Drew, we have to get on with this.'

'We both take it black,' he said, shaking his head.

'Drew, you're being stupid. Can we just get on, please. You're totally overthinking this. It's just a wedding list, that's all.'

'Just a wedding list,' he repeated.

'Yes,' she said, taking his hand and putting the scanner firmly back in it. 'Just a wedding list.'

'And we're just getting married,' said Drew.

'Yes,' hissed Emily, completely exasperated now. 'We're just getting married. No big deal. Now come on, I'm going to be late at this rate.'

Drew felt on the verge of tears.

'We can't,' he said.

'Can't what?' she asked.

'We can't *just* get married,' he replied, stepping forward and taking her hand.

'Drew, you're making no sense today. What *has* got into you?'

'No-one should ever *just* get married. We're doing it because it's the next logical step, because we've been together so long, why wouldn't we get married? But we've never stopped to really think about why *should* we get married?'

'Why should we?' said Emily. 'Why should we?' she

repeated more loudly. 'You want to know now, why should we get married?'

'Yes. I do,' he said, barely whispering.

'Because it works, Drew. It's worked for sixteen years,' she shouted, finally losing her temper. 'I really don't understand what the hell you're asking here. We get on. We allow each other to live our lives the way we want to live them. We support each other. That's why we should get married. My God, Drew, what the hell has been going on with you lately? This is what we have spent our lives together building up to. Look at us, we're the perfect couple. We were meant to be together. There is absolutely no reason why we should not get married.'

Drew bit his lip. The other sentence that had been swirling around in his head for the last few weeks was threatening to make a break for it and he wasn't sure whether he should let it escape.

'Give me one good reason why we shouldn't get married,' pressed Emily.

Bollocks. That was it, game over. She had asked him the direct question so there was nothing he could do but let the thought go free.

'I don't think I love you,' he said, squeezing her hands tightly as if that might help quell the reaction.

The colour drained from Emily's face. She said nothing.

'I'm so sorry,' he said.

Still Emily said nothing, just blinked rapidly.

'Aaah, are you having a moment?' came a voice from behind Drew's shoulder. 'Most of my couples get quite emotional once they start selecting the gifts their loved ones will buy them for their special day.' The orange lady appeared out of nowhere. 'Is there anything you can't find? The scale of the task can be quite intimidating.'

Drew searched Emily's blank face for the first signs of reaction to his confession. Suddenly she took a sharp intake of breath and appeared to collect herself.

'I'll be late,' she murmured, bending down to pick up her bag without taking her eyes off him. She turned and walked slowly but steadily to the stairs without looking back. When she finally disappeared Drew sank to the floor and buried his head in his hands, allowing the scanner to clatter noisily onto the tiles.

The orange lady bent to pick it up. 'I know, it's exhausting, isn't it?' she said, patting him on the back. 'I'll just go and download this and when you're ready you come up and I'll have a nice cup of tea waiting for you.'

Drew waited for the clatter of her stilettos to die away before he allowed himself his first sob.

Chapter 20

'And our next caller on the line to Granada Reports this morning is Marion from Alderley Edge. Hello, Marion. What would you like to ask Dear Suzie?'

'Hello, Andrew, hello, Suzie. I just wanted to call and thank Suzie for the marvellous advice she gave me some weeks ago. I'm so grateful. She saved my marriage.'

'That's brilliant news, Marion. Would you mind sharing with us what your problem was?'

'Not at all, Andrew. Anything to help other women who might have suffered the same as me. I'd become a golf widow, you see. Since my husband had taken early retirement he spent all his time on the golf course and barely had two words to say to me, let alone provide for my other needs, if you know what I mean?'

'No need to elaborate there, I think, Marion; this is a family show.'

'Well, just because you hit over fifty doesn't mean that . . .'

'We know exactly what you mean, Marion. Why don't you tell us what advice Suzie gave you?'

'Well, it was quite brilliant really. She told me to tell my husband that he had forced me to turn lesbian because he was so boring in bed. It was like a magic spell, truly. I am now having the best you-know-what of my life.'

'Hi, Marion, Suzie here. I remember your letter. So it worked then, did it?'

'Like a treat, dear. As you predicted, his competitive streak came to the fore when he thought his golf buddies might find out that he'd turned his wife gay. He totally upped his game. Now all I have to do is mention the words "Billie Jean King" and he's laying the passion on with a trowel.'

'That's wonderful, Marion. I'm so happy for you.'

'I just wanted to tell everyone what a genius Suzie is, and men – beware. We're coming after you.'

'Well, thank you, Marion. We've been inundated with calls but sadly that's all we have time for today. So thank you for coming in, Suzie. Judging by the calls, I'm sure we'll be seeing a lot more of you in the future.'

'Look, Drew, look! I'm wearing TV make-up and everything,' said Suzie, bounding up to Drew's chair and thrusting her face in front of him on her return from the studio.

Drew stared at her, feeling even worse than he had the day before.

'You look awful,' she exclaimed before she was overcome by excitement again. 'So did you see me? Was I okay?' she asked, spinning round on her office chair in glee.

'See you where?' asked Drew, looking almost haunted.

'On TV, you idiot,' she said, stopping dead in her tracks. 'I was on *Granada Reports* this morning. Don't tell me you forgot to watch it?'

'Oh, I'm so sorry, Suzie, really I am. I forgot, I . . .'

'It's okay, I got my mum, my Auntie Dorothy and

Malcolm next door to record it so you can come over tonight and we'll watch it together.'

'Great,' said Drew, nodding distractedly. 'Not tonight, though, I, er . . .'

'Need some sleep by the looks of you,' Suzie interrupted. 'Did you pull another all-nighter or something?'

'Yeah, something like that.'

Suzie stared at him for a moment. Something was up. Normally Drew would be full of questions about such a major event in her life. She'd been so excited to get back and tell him all about it because she knew he'd want every detail, and here he was looking completely uninterested.

'You okay?' she asked, as he rested his chin in his hand, staring blankly at his email. He sniffed a couple of times then slowly turned to face her. He looked so weird. His face was haggard and as he lifted his hand up to rake through his hair she noticed a slight tremble. She had never seen Drew like this. He was the cool, calm, collected one and she was the gibbering wreck. That was why they got on so well. They were like yin and yang. She did all the screwing up and he sorted her out. She never had to sort him out. She didn't know *how* to sort him out. At a loss as to what to do, she reached forward and took his hand. She leapt in surprise as he clutched it, then marvelled at how big and safe it felt. She stared down at the unfamiliar sight of their fingers intertwined until the loud trill of her phone interrupted the prolonged silence.

'I'll just get rid of that,' she said, using her free hand to pick up the phone.

'Hi, Suzie Miller,' she said tersely.

'Hello, this is Bruce Whitaker from the *Mirror*. Are you okay to talk? I have a proposition you may be interested in.'

Suzie's mind raced. A national newspaper calling a journalist with a proposition normally meant only one thing. A job. His clandestine tone added further encouragement. She looked at Drew, who was staring blankly at their clasped hands, and gave him a squeeze in a way she hoped approximated a wordless apology for keeping him waiting.

'Er, yeah, I can talk,' she said.

'Good. Now I won't beat about the bush. We've been following your column for some weeks now and are extremely impressed with the attention you've been getting, not to mention the reaction from Joe Public. I caught you on *Granada Reports* this morning and I can see that women just love you.'

'Thank you,' croaked Suzie.

'Anyway, our female readership has been sliding dramatically and we've been looking for a solution for some time. We think you're it. How do you fancy coming and doing your column for us? Full page, first half of the paper, it's yours. What do you say?'

Suzie almost dropped the phone in shock. A national offering her a full page. Never in her wildest dreams had she thought that would happen. Even Kate Adie never got a full page. She would be so proud.

'I don't know what to say,' she choked, trying to fight back the tears.

'I know. A lot to take in, probably. At least you won't have to ask your boyfriend if it's okay to move down to London. You must be single, I assume,' guffawed the executive.

She giggled slightly hysterically before managing to gather her wits.

'Well, there are things to consider other than my relationship status,' she managed to say. 'But I do have to confess that I always dreamed of having a column in the *Sun*.'

There was a short silence before the man spoke again. 'The *Mirror*,' he said grimly. 'I'm calling from the *Mirror*.'

Suzie froze in horror. Shit, she thought, I may just have thrown away the job of a lifetime.

She laughed hysterically. 'Just my little joke,' she giggled. 'I can see you're going to have to get used to my quirky sense of humour.' She held her breath as she waited for his response. There was an awkward silence.

'Very funny,' he said finally, completely deadpan. 'I have another call. We should meet for lunch and discuss this further. My PA will call you later with details.'

'Yes, yes, of course,' said Suzie. 'Thank you so much.'

There was no reply. He had already cut her off.

She put down her receiver slowly and tried to bring her heart rate under control.

She turned to Drew, who was looking at her intently.

'That was the *Mirror*,' she whispered. 'They've offered me a job. Full-page column.'

He looked blank as if he couldn't take in what she was saying.

'They want me to do Dear Suzie in the *Mirror*,' she spelt out.

'Wow,' said Drew, reeling back in his chair as if she had just hit him.

'Oh God, Drew, I'm sorry,' she said, realising this

wasn't the time. 'What were you going to tell me? What's happened?'

He just stared at her manically, his hands clutching his head.

'You can tell me, really you can,' she said, putting her hand on his shoulder. He flinched and pulled away. She stared at his pain-filled face, but for the second time that morning he was prevented from saying anything as the doors to the floor burst open and the air was filled with the sound of pulsating music.

'What the . . .' began Suzie as they both turned to see what the commotion was all about.

A lifetime of watching Jerry Springer could not have equipped either of them for the sight that greeted their eyes. Suzie heard Drew gasp as he knocked his coffee into his lap.

A woman stood dramatically in the doorway looking wildly around the open-plan office until her eyes rested on Drew. Then she reached behind her to gather up a voluptuous ivory satin train and advanced towards him. She was wearing her complete wedding outfit, including tiara and veil, and on her left shoulder she carried an Eighties-style ghetto blaster that was banging out the Billy Idol classic, 'White Wedding'.

Suzie managed to drag her eyes away from the vision approaching them just long enough to take in the fact that Drew was white as a sheet.

'Doesn't she know that it's bad luck to see the bride in her dress before the big day?' she hissed just as Emily reached his desk. Drew said nothing, just sat shaking in his seat. By now quite a crowd was gathering at the outskirts of the room, the word having travelled round the office in a flash that there was a mad woman on the loose wearing a wedding dress.

Emily slammed the ghetto blaster down on Drew's desk and killed the sound. There was complete silence in the office. The assembled crowd stood poised for action, waiting for the spectacle to evolve.

'I know it's bad luck for the groom to see the bride in her dress before their wedding day,' Emily announced.

'That's exactly what I just said,' muttered Suzie. Emily glared at her before continuing.

'But I figured that seeing as there isn't going to be a wedding then it didn't matter.' She locked Drew in a deadly gaze.

There was a gasp from the entire room followed by low-level muttering. As that died down, all that could be heard was Drew's laboured breathing.

'How do I look?' she demanded.

'Beautiful,' he said quickly before swallowing hard.

'I wanted you to be able to see me as you would have done on our special day. So the image of me in my wedding dress could haunt you for the rest of your life,' she spat out.

'I'm so sorry I've put you in this situation.' Drew looked as though he was about to throw up. 'But I was trying to do the right thing. I was trying to be honest with you. You have to believe that, Emily.' He looked over to Suzie. She stared back at him, horrified.

'Well,' said Emily, tossing her hair confidently over her shoulder. 'You didn't expect me to just walk away quietly, did you? You don't throw away all those years we spent together and not expect me to have something to say about it. This, Drew, is me showing you that you have just made the biggest mistake of your life.'

'I'm sorry,' he said hopelessly. 'I never meant to drive you to this.'

'Well, you can blame her for that.' Emily turned and extended a perfectly manicured fingernail in Suzie's direction.

'What?' exclaimed Suzie, recovering from her awe-struck gaze. 'I haven't done anything.' She looked at

Drew, distraught. He was rocking backwards and forwards in his seat, glancing like a frightened rabbit between Suzie and Emily.

'She . . . she . . .' His voice sounded strangled.

'She is so right,' said Emily, slamming her fist on the desk. 'What you said this morning on the TV,' she continued, pointing wildly again at Suzie. 'That bit about the fact that we complain about men when they hurt us but we never punish them, so how do we expect them to learn. This is me punishing you, Drew, for dumping me well and truly at the altar, and I hope you never, ever forget how you feel at this moment.' She ripped off her veil and tiara and threw them at Drew.

Suzie was beside herself. What had Drew done? This was so out of character. It didn't make any sense.

Emily bent to pick up her ghetto blaster and flicked the switch back on to blare out the last few bars of the song. Then she turned and stalked out of the room, past the awestruck crowd, without giving Drew a backward glance.

Suzie turned to face him and came to the only conclusion that made any sense.

'You slept with someone, didn't you?' she said, not

waiting for an answer. 'How could you, Drew? And I thought you were one of the few good ones.'

He looked back her, a totally broken man, then slowly raised himself from his seat and walked out of the office.

Typical, she thought to herself.

Chapter 21

Drew stared into the grubby mirror of the Gents' toilets at the Majestic Hotel. He felt sick and he hadn't even touched the free bar yet. The office Christmas party would be the first time he'd seen his colleagues since Emily's performance. He'd taken a hasty week off to attempt to gather up the shreds of his life. He'd gone straight to his mum's and literally stared at the wall for four solid hours and tried to stop shaking whilst she fed him sweet tea and French Fancies. When he'd eventually managed to explain to her what he had done and why, she had put her arms around him and cried with him. Tears for his sadness, no doubt mingled with tears for her own sorry love story. His dad had arrived home at some point and his mum had swept him into the kitchen and filled him in via urgent whispers. When he'd finally come in his condolences were non-existent.

'About time, lad,' he'd said, slapping him on the back. 'Knew you'd have to get out and sow your wild oats sooner or later.'

Drew had fled following a desperate look between him and his mother. His dad and his cockeyed view on relationships was the last thing he needed.

Forced to decamp to a mate's sofa for a few days, he realised he had to sort his life out when he caught himself recording World Poker TV whilst he went to the toilet. And so he walked. He walked and walked, hoping to reduce the relentless grip the guilt had over him. It wasn't until he started to see his future stretching ahead of him as a wide open space, rather than a brick wall erected on the day he was due to get married, that relief started gradually to kick in and soothe his pain. What he hadn't expected was for it to be followed by anger. He had wasted so much of his and Emily's time. He'd spent years merely existing, in a bubble that was stable and didn't make him sad, but certainly didn't make him happy either. He realised now that he wanted to live. He wanted to feel alive. He wanted to experience his emotions beating through his entire body, not to bury them as he had been doing, to the point where he'd become a wooden, boring man.

Tonight he would start living again, he told himself. Tonight was the start of the rest of his life. He stood up straight and cleared his throat before striding out of the toilets in search of Toby, who had agreed to DJ for a knock-down price and who was instrumental in kick-starting the dawn of the new Drew.

'You look like a tit,' said Toby, dragging a speaker across the makeshift stage.

'Thanks. I feel like a tit. Everyone else had already rifled through the costumes and taken all the best dwarf bits, leaving me with the crap.'

'So which one are you meant to be?'

'Tramp dwarf by the looks of it.' Drew pushed the grubby grey-white bobble on the tip of his hat out of his eyes for the hundredth time. 'Perfect for tonight's proceedings, don't you think?' he said grimly.

Toby didn't answer as he struggled to set the speaker up on its stand. Mission accomplished he climbed over the tangle of wires to sit with Drew on the edge of the stage.

'Look, mate,' he said, putting his arm around his friend's shoulders, 'are you really sure about this?'

'Yes,' said Drew, nodding his head vigorously.

'But . . .' Toby began. It was the first time Drew had known him struggle for words.

'But what?' asked Drew. 'Spit it out.'

'But it's just so out of character, mate. You don't do things like this. I hardly recognise you at the moment.'

'That'll be because I'm dressed as a fashion-challenged dwarf.'

'You know what I mean. One minute you're dumping the woman you've spent your entire adult life with just as you're about to get married, and the next you're calling me up in the middle of the night with a hare-brained scheme like this. You're behaving like me, not you. And quite frankly I'm not very happy that you're forcing me to behave like you.'

'What's that supposed to mean?'

'Sensible,' grimaced Toby, 'normal, trying to talk sense. It's making me nauseous.'

'Sorry. I didn't mean for all this to upset your stomach.'

'Look,' said Toby. 'I know you just dumped your fiancée and it's Christmas so you're feeling lonely, but are you really sure you want to go through with this? Why don't you just get into the true office party spirit? Drink a bottle of less crap wine and shag some secretary instead of all this grand gesture stuff?'

'Secretaries don't exist any more. They're called personal assistants these days.'

'Even better,' cried Toby. 'Get one of them to personally assist you in getting over this bizarre rocky patch by shagging you senseless.'

Drew bent over and polished the gold-coloured buckle on his dwarf boot then straightened up to look at Toby.

'I don't want mindless sex,' he said. 'I just want her.'

Toby gave a deep sign. 'So just tell her. Why go to all this trouble?'

'You've read her column. She thinks we're all bastards, including me after what I did to Emily. I can't just tell her. I have to convince her that she's not going to end up having her hopes dashed as she has before.'

'Wow, man, you've sure got it bad,' sighed Toby.

'Well, I happen to think she's worth it.'

'Just you be careful, that's all.'

'What do you mean?'

'I don't know,' said Toby, shuffling his feet. 'I don't want you to get hurt, mate. You never know with these chicks. She might not be who you think she is. Chicks do crazy things. They can be unpredictable. I don't want this ending badly for you.'

'I think it's worth the risk,' said Drew solemnly.

'And are you sure it's her, absolutely sure?'

'One hundred per cent.'

Toby opened his mouth as if he was about to say something serious before obviously thinking better of it. He gripped Drew's shoulder.

'Well then, off you go, Dopey. Go and get your Snow White if you must. I'm all primed at my end.'

'Thanks, mate. If this works I owe you big time.'

Drew left the misnamed Grand Ballroom to go in search of the bar and face the rest of his colleagues. He hoped they would already be hyped up over the free drinks and the hilarity of seeing each other in full-on fairy-tale fancy dress and so be distracted from asking him about his spectacular last meeting with his ex-fiancée.

'*We're not getting married in the morning, ding dong the bells ain't gonna chime,*' chorused the other six dwarves as he approached the bar.

'Thanks, guys,' he muttered, grabbing a free drink and looking for an escape. He headed out towards the reception area, intending to get some fresh air, but got

TRACY BLOOM

nobbled by the photographer hired to record the staff of the *Manchester Herald* as they arrived, in advance of them getting completely legless.

'Come on, son, I've not done you yet, have I? Stand over there.'

Drew shuffled over to the backdrop set up by the photographer. As he stood there alone, feeling utterly miserable, he realised that a night on which you were dressed as a dwarf and forced to have your picture taken standing in fake polystyrene snow next to a stuffed reindeer did not have success written all over it.

'Tell you what,' said the photographer, 'I've been wanting to try this all night. You take your shoes off and get down on your knees and put them in your shoes, so you look like a real dwarf. Come on, it'll look hilarious.'

Drew was stopped short of punching him by the sound of Snow White arriving.

'Christ, you can't get the dwarves these days, can you?' said Suzie, appearing from behind the photographer dressed in a picture perfect costume complete with jet-black wig.

'Just in time,' said the photographer. 'Come on, we need you in this photo, and tell him to get on his knees,' he said, pointing at Drew.

278

Suzie clutched her full skirt and swooped into the frame. Drew's heart was pounding at full throttle. She looked as if she'd stepped straight out of a fairy tale. How on earth was he going to pull off his plan tonight, especially looking more like a troll than a dwarf? Suzie *really* hated trolls. He must be mad. This wasn't a fairy tale; it was real life, where the dwarfs don't get to be with the princesses.

'Come on, on your knees,' she said, interrupting his panic. 'If you stand up you'll just look like some homeless drunk who staggered in from the street. At least if you're on your knees people will realise you're supposed to be a dwarf.' She grabbed his hand and gestured for him to sink to his knees.

He realised he couldn't speak so he did the only thing he could do. He sank to his knees and tried not to gaze up at Snow White.

'Great,' said the photographer, snapping away. 'One for the mantelpiece,' he said when he had finished.

Suzie hauled Drew up and waited in silence as he struggled with his buckled shoes.

'So, how've you been?' she asked as they made their way towards the bar. 'I was going to call but I figured you probably needed some space.'

'It's been a rough week, put it that way,' he said, trying to make saliva return to his dry mouth.

'But probably rougher for Emily,' she replied.

'Yes, of course,' he said quickly.

Just outside the bar she stopped and turned to him.

'Look, Drew,' she said. 'I want to say thank you for helping with everything over the last few weeks. I couldn't have done half the things that I've done without you.' She was looking at him so intently that Drew wondered whether now was his chance. Perhaps he should get it over with and confess everything. Ditch all the fancy stuff.

'I should tell you, though, that I've planned to do my last revenge tonight,' she continued. 'I know I haven't mentioned it before but I figured that you had enough on your plate.'

Drew's mind started to race. She's doing her last revenge tonight? So that has to mean Spanish guitar troll is here. Who could it be? The men who worked at the *Herald* were all generally such a shambles that he couldn't imagine Suzie getting involved with any of them. Unless. No, she wouldn't, would she? His mind went racing back to that morning in the café when he'd been checking out Gareth's blog in a jealous rage. He recalled that Gareth listed guitar as one of his hobbies. He remembered because he'd instantly pictured the stomach-churningly romantic sight of Gareth serenading a love-struck Suzie. So Suzie had had some secret liaison with Gareth. That's why she'd said it was complicated and she wouldn't talk about it. What didn't make sense was why Gareth was so supportive of Suzie's revenge column. Surely he saw himself as a target. Then again, he was so blindly ambitious that he would deal with anything that helped in his climb to the top.

'Drew, are you listening?' asked Suzie, cutting through his thoughts. 'I just wanted you to know so you're not surprised when it happens.'

'Yeah, sure,' he said, still reeling. He realised he had to stop his plan right now. He couldn't do it tonight. Not if she was planning all this.

'Right, I just need to go to the Ladies and then let's go and get a drink before we torture ourselves with what lovely surprises Secret Santa has in store.'

Drew stood rooted to the spot in a daze, then he let out a cry.

'Fuck!' He raced off in hot pursuit of Suzie. He had to get to Secret Santa before she did.

Chapter 22

'Dear Suzie, thank God you're here,' wailed Clare, the new trainee reporter, as soon as Suzie stepped into the toilets. 'What am I going to do?' She flung her arms around Suzie's shoulders and started sobbing into her neck.

Suzie was at a loss. She'd barely said two words to the girl since she'd started, let alone had any bodily contact. Awkwardly, she patted Clare's back in what she hoped was a consoling manner.

'Clare's boyfriend, Theo, has been chatting up Becca since he arrived,' explained Maddie from Sales. 'He can't keep his eyes off her. He even bought her a Cosmopolitan and just got Clare a Bacardi Breezer.'

Clare raised her head. 'P . . . p . . . p . . . pineapple,' she choked out. 'He bought me pineapple and he knows I hate pineapple. What am I going to do, Suzie?'

Suzie looked over her shoulder for some assistance only to find that a small crowd had gathered to observe the commotion. They all stared back at her expectantly and she realised they were waiting for her to solve Clare's dilemma on the spot.

'It's all right,' said Maddie, stroking Clare's back. 'Suzie's here now. She'll tell you what to do.'

Suzie was knocked sideways. It wasn't that long ago that she'd had been mostly ignored by the younger females of the office, written off as a failed journalist who was blocking their upward career path. And here they were gazing at her like some kind of Yoda of Romance, patiently awaiting her pearls of wisdom.

Well, if that was what they wanted, that's what she'd give them. She was Dear Suzie, after all, soon to be tabloid columnist and TV mega-star.

She grasped Clare by the shoulders and pushed her gently away so that she could look her in the eye.

'Firstly I want you to give up alcopops,' she said firmly. 'Nothing good can ever come of a girl who drinks alcopops, okay?'

'Yes, of course,' sniffed Clare, nodding her head vigorously.

'And secondly . . .' She paused for dramatic effect, sensing her audience lean forward. 'I want you to go out there and tell him to leave immediately.'

'What?' said Clare, looking taken aback.

'Tell him to leave,' repeated Suzie. 'He's your guest here. He's behaving inappropriately, so ask him to leave. It's your only hope of enjoying yourself tonight, believe me.'

Clare stared at Suzie wide-eyed. There wasn't a sound from behind them as they all waited for Clare's response.

'Of course!' she shrieked. 'I just tell him to go. Simple as that. He has no right to make me feel miserable at my office party, has he? Oh Suzie, thank you.'

'Don't mention it. Just remember, no Bacardi Breezers,' said Suzie, feeling a warm glow of smug self-satisfaction start to spread over her.

She turned to the mirrors to check out her make-up when the door burst open and Sandra rushed in. 'Am I too late?' she gasped. 'Di just said that Suzie was giving out free advice in the toilets.'

Wow, thought Suzie, she'd need her own TV show soon. *Suzie's Party Nightmares.*

'Oh Suzie, thank goodness you're still here. Listen, my husband's ruined my night. He just told me my Miss Piggy outfit suited me. What shall I do?'

Suzie sighed. Really, this was too easy.

'Go back out there and tell him that when you have sex you fantasise about Kermit the Frog, because anything would be better than looking at his pathetic, overweight, saggy body.'

The room exploded into laughter.

'Perfect,' said Sandra and promptly turned round and ran back out again.

'At least her husband came,' muttered Brenda. 'Mine refused. Said he would rather stay in and watch paint dry than come out with me.'

Suzie turned around to face their sixty-year-old cleaner.

'Go home,' she bellowed at her.

'What?'

'Go home right now. Collect a pair of your skimpiest knickers and your toothbrush then tell him you'll see him in the morning. You're staying here tonight. And when you go home tomorrow you refuse to tell him where you've been. Let him stew for twelve hours. No, let him stew for a week. That'll teach him to take an interest in what you're doing.'

Brenda blinked back at Suzie for a moment and then did an about-turn.

'I won't be long,' she shouted over her shoulder.

Suzie looked around her at the sea of raised hands. More women had materialised and they all seemed to be shouting her name. How many male-related disasters can you get at your average Christmas do? she thought. It was a minefield. She raised her hands to quell the cacophony of problems. When she had silence she told them all the answer to everything in one fell swoop.

'If in doubt, dance,' she shouted. 'They can't upset you on the dance floor. Come on, what are we all doing in here when there's dancing to be done?'

They followed her as though she was the Pied Piper out into the Grand Ballroom and within moments she was surrounded by a jumping mass of joyous hormones. Suzie felt she was on top of the world. These women adored her. She made them happy. Who would ever have thought that her horrendous relationship history would end up being the making of her? Who needs men? she decided. And the high point of the evening was still to come: her final revenge in front of her adoring fans. She couldn't wait.

Three songs later and a riot nearly broke out when the

DJ, misjudging the mood, started to play a soppy version of 'All I Want For Christmas Is You'. Suzie felt so proud as she watched an angry army of women demand it be taken off immediately and replaced with 'I Will Survive'. Confident they had the DJ under control, she decided she'd go and get Secret Santa over with before dinner was called and wandered back into the bar to find the makeshift grotto.

If the concept of Secret Santa wasn't bad enough, it had been made infinitely worse by being forced to sit on the knee of Chris from IT, his enormous belly bursting through fake fur as he got cheap thrills asking female colleagues if they had been good little girls all year. The only bonus was that Chris had utilised his team to produce an über grotto. Digital images of the North Pole were projected onto a screen behind him and neon snowflakes appeared to fall from the sky and disappear into nowhere, creating an impressively magical effect. One of Chris's minions sat behind a laptop orchestrating the whole tableau whilst two others looked grim, dressed as Santa's little helpers clutching sacks full of presents that nobody gave a toss about.

'Suzie!' cried Santa Chris as she came into view. 'You look hot as Snow White.' His eyes were wide with pleasure. Out of nowhere a loud wolf whistle rang out. The minion behind the laptop looked sheepish.

'Inappropriate, Santa,' said Suzie, shaking her head at him. 'Can we get this over with as quickly as possible?' She held her hand out. 'Hand it over and let me go, okay?'

'Sorry, Suzie. Santa needs you to sit on his knee and tell him that you've behaved yourself this year first,' said Santa Chris, his eyes gleaming.

'Fuck off, Chris,' she said. 'I'm not letting you have some weird Snow White fantasy for the rest of the decade just because I sat on your knee. Now hand it over.'

'Or what?' he asked defiantly.

'I'll report you to the Secret Santa Union for withholding crap gifts.'

'You do that,' he said. 'See if I care. I don't need you. I've just had Cinderella on my knee for two and a half minutes.'

'Two minutes thirty-six, actually,' chirped the minion laptop operator.

'You mean you're timing how long we sit on your knee?' asked Suzie.

The minions sniggered.

'We're running a tab on it,' said Chris. 'We've got you

down to be in the top three seeing as you're single and desperate. So come on, there's money riding on this.'

'You're all disgusting. You can keep your Secret Santa,' she said, turning away.

'So you don't want this gold envelope then?' he said, holding one up.

Suzie stopped in her tracks. An envelope? Now that was different. An envelope had potential. It could be cash, which would be such a sensible thing to put in a Secret Santa gift, or it could be a voucher for something like a manicure. Envelopes didn't involve packaging that would no doubt contain some hidden horror. She turned around and moved forwards to take it, but Santa Chris pulled it quickly out of her grasp.

'Oh no you don't. For being a naughty girl you have to sit on my knee and open it.'

'Stop messing about.' She tried to grab it again but he quickly whisked it out of the way. At that moment she noticed Dwarf Drew appear, looking flustered. 'Drew, tell him to give me my Secret Santa,' she demanded. 'He says I've got to sit on his knee to get it.'

'Tell him to keep it. It'll be crap anyway,' urged Dwarf Drew.

'But it's an envelope,' pleaded Snow White. 'Envelopes

can be good. They're not like wrapped presents, they have potential. I need to see what's in it.'

'You're being sucked in,' he said. 'This is Secret Santa; it will not be any good. Remember what you said the other day.' He held his hands out towards her. 'Just walk away from the Secret Santa, you can do it.'

Snow White looked from Santa Chris to Dwarf Drew. She should walk away, she knew she should. But what if it was good? What if someone had finally nailed the perfect Secret Santa gift and she walked away? She knew she couldn't do it. She had to know what was in the golden envelope. She turned towards Drew, letting her shoulders sag as if in defeat, before twirling around at lightning speed, her bright yellow skirt knocking over a decorative silver Christmas tree. She leapt up and grabbed the envelope clean out of Santa Chris's hand.

'I got it!' she shrieked, jumping up and down.

'Why don't you open it tomorrow?' Dwarf Drew suggested. 'Or save it for Christmas Day.'

'No way,' cried Suzie. 'The only good thing about Secret Santa is that you get to open them straight away.' She tore at the envelope, dropping pieces of gold paper on the floor, then pulled out a stiff white card and read the typed words that had been painstakingly glued onto it.

'What does it say?' asked the three minions in unison as they gathered round her.

'*Be on the dance floor below the glitter ball at midnight for your extra special delivery from Secret Santa,*' she said slowly. There was silence as they all tried to understand the cryptic message.

She turned on Santa Chris. 'This better not be you after a grope in the dark,' she barked.

'Not me,' he said, his hands held up in submission. 'Great idea, though. Perhaps I'll try that on Debs in payroll next year,' he said thoughtfully.

'I don't understand,' said Snow White, staring at the message. 'What on earth could it mean?'

'Secret admirer,' muttered one of the helper minions. 'Got to be. He's going to reveal himself at midnight, don't you see? So romantic,' he sighed.

'Do you really think so?' asked Snow White.

'No, it's not,' said Dwarf Drew, grabbing the card away from Suzie. 'It's someone winding you up, bound to be. It is you, isn't it, Chris? Don't let them con you, Suzie. Just forget all about it.' He tried to put the card in the top pocket of his jacket until he realised he had no top pocket, just a wine-stained tabard.

Snow White grabbed the card back off Dwarf Drew so she could read it again.

'Remember what you said,' he urged. 'Secret Santa disappoints without fail. Santa is a man, after all, so let's bin it, shall we?'

'Yes,' she said finally, looking up. 'You're right. Chris, you're a dead man.' She swooped out of the room holding her Snow White chin up high and trying to ignore the fact that, for just a moment, her heart had soared when the words secret admirer, midnight, glitter ball and dance floor had come together in one conversation. No soaring hearts, she said to herself quietly. This was the office Christmas party, after all. Fertile ground for soaring hearts to be crushed in an instant. The session in the toilets was testament to that. No, she must focus. Tonight the last troll would be well and truly buried. That was what mattered this evening, not someone's idea of a sick Secret Santa joke.

Chapter 23

By the end of the meal Drew was almost feeling relaxed, relieved that he wasn't going to confess all to Suzie that night. Although it had been a close shave with Secret Santa. He'd realised that asking Chris for Suzie's present back would reveal his identity and rouse too much suspicion. Better to convince her that she was being wound up by someone else, get her to dismiss it and leave it at that. Present his pumping heart to her another day.

Just as he was considering making his excuses and leaving, Suzie plopped herself into the chair next to him.

'I take it we spent the party budget on the free booze

and not the food.' She prodded a rock-hard piece of Christmas pudding that had been left on a plate.

'Mmm,' he muttered, trying not to stare at her lips in his cheapo-wine-fuddled state.

They fell silent watching the hideous display of jiggling around that had now filled the dance floor.

'You know, it's really weird but I've never noticed a glitter ball in here before,' she said, nodding towards the ceiling. 'Even though we've been coming here for our Christmas do for years.'

Drew didn't dare speak, so he watched Suzie stare at the glitter ball, completely mesmerised, a small smile hovering on her lips.

'Are you thinking about that Secret Santa card?' he had to ask.

She turned to look at him. She was heartbreakingly beautiful. He wanted to take her in his arms and kiss her right now.

'Nah,' she said. 'You were right. Some dipshit just trying to wind me up. What a wanker, eh?'

Kiss her, kiss her, something inside Drew pleaded.

'Yeah, wanker,' he muttered, looking away.

Kiss her, his whole body was shouting at him.

Her arm brushed his as she stood up abruptly.

'You're not leaving, are you?' he cried.

'Stuff to do,' she replied. 'I'll see you later.'

'Yep, sure, fine, I'll see you later then.'

Drew watched her as she turned and walked away. Idiot, he thought. He should have just gone for it. He'd promised himself he was going to start living, start showing his emotions, and here he was burying them as usual. And he'd seen her gaze at that glitter ball. That was hope in her eyes, he was sure. He had to act tonight. He couldn't waste this chance. Her last revenge was no excuse. Besides, Suzie would forget all about revenge when he told her how he felt. It wouldn't be important any more.

The clock was fast approaching midnight and the mood in the room changed as the DJ took it down a gear and effortlessly slid into a slow number. The ladies who earlier had been euphoric in the sisterhood of female-only dancing were now merging into the bodies of their male escorts as the alcohol and romance of the moment overcame them and they succumbed to the sexy tones of Barry White.

Suzie checked her watch: 11.58 p.m. Time to get into position and deliver her last revenge before the night came to an end.

She went to fetch the suitcase that she'd stored under a trestle table at the back of the room earlier. The plan was simple, swift and, with luck, effective. She was about to stride across the dance floor when the song ended and the DJ's voice could be heard cutting through the moment.

'We're coming to the end of the night now, ladies and gentlemen, and I have been asked to remind you to make sure you've collected your Secret Santa gifts. Santa says his sack is still full and he'd like to make sure you ladies empty it before you leave.' Toby completed his request with a drum roll. No-one laughed.

'Now, I've been asked to present one of the Secret Santa gifts personally. So, at very great expense, we would like to present Suzie Miller with her very own special Secret Santa.'

Suzie stopped in her tracks at the edge of the dance floor and dropped the suitcase to the floor. What was going on? She had a job to do; she couldn't be faffing around with Secret Santa now. Especially if it was someone's idea of a sick joke. Music struck up and she immediately recognised the first few bars of Rick Astley's 'Never Gonna Give You Up'. A million thoughts flowed like a waterfall through her mind. What the hell was going on? Why were they playing this song? God, she missed Rick Astley. Was he still sexy, and did he still wear purple suits?

As the song continued she suddenly felt like crying. The words of the chorus took her straight back to her teenage years when she'd had her first ever kiss. Hang on a minute. Who on earth would know that? She gazed at the dance floor, now empty since the smoochers had tried but failed to continue their love fest to the upbeat track. There was just one person remaining, right in the middle, standing under the glitter ball dressed as a dwarf. Drew raised a plastic cup in her direction. What was he doing? Was he behind the Secret Santa message? Surely not. She gathered up her skirt in vague annoyance and hurried across the dance floor.

He smiled and pushed the plastic cup towards her.

'It's a weak Cinzano and lemonade,' he said nervously.

She stared down at the cup and noticed it was shaking violently.

She looked back up at the now white-as-a-ghost Drew.

'What are you doing, Drew?' she asked, annoyed that he was making such a show of her and getting in the way of her revenge.

'I wanted to take you back,' he whispered.

'You'll have to speak up, I can't hear you,' she shouted above the din of the disco.

He looked down at the cup and knocked back the contents before throwing it over his shoulder. Then he stepped forward and took both of her hands.

'I wanted to take you back,' he repeated. 'To when you were a teenager, in that community hall you talked about. You know, the one with the glitter ball and the dodgy disco and the watered-down drinks.'

'But . . . but why?' she asked, completely bewildered.

'Because you said that was the best time of your life. When a song came on, your song, and you got up and danced and you felt like you were in the best place in the entire universe. When you danced because you were happy, not because you were pissed. When a smile from the right person could send your heart into the stratosphere for an entire week.' He paused as if waiting for a reaction. When she didn't speak he ploughed on. 'When you still had hope, Suzie. When you still believed in love. That's what I wanted your Secret Santa gift to be. For you to hope again, and believe in love again, because . . . because . . .' He was breathing really quickly now as if he could quite easily hyperventilate.

Suzie was staring at him, trying to take in what he was saying. The words were entering her ears but getting jumbled up once they were lodged in her head. She tried to concentrate on making sense of it all, but then she caught sight of someone over Drew's shoulder, and suddenly his words were sucked out of her brain to be replaced with something she could make some sense of. Completing her task for the evening.

'Drew,' she interrupted, placing her hands on his shoulders. 'This is all very nice and I will be sure to download Rick to my iPod. Thank you for reminding me how great he was. This is a great Secret Santa gift.' She threw her arms around him in an effort to complete the conversation.

'Oh Suzie,' she heard him whisper desperately in her ear. He pulled away from her. 'What I'm trying to say is . . .'

She held up her hand and signalled him to stop. 'Drew,' she said. 'There's something I need to do first, and then I promise you we can reminisce all you like about the merits of Mr Astley.'

'But Suzie,' he said, beginning to look frustrated.

'I just wanted to say I'm really happy for you,' said Toby, suddenly appearing and looking nervously from

Suzie to Drew. 'And I'm looking forward to us all being friends,' he said, giving Suzie a pointed look.

Suzie stared at Toby. Now he was talking in riddles. Was she dreaming?

She turned to Drew, who for some reason was shaking his head violently at Toby. 'Drew,' she said steadily, 'I'm trying to do my last revenge.'

'Suzie, no,' said Drew and Toby in unison. 'You can stop now,' continued Drew. 'You don't have to get revenge any more. You have to listen to me.'

'Yeah, just drop it,' said Toby.

'Oh, that would really suit you, wouldn't it?' said Suzie, turning to Toby.

'Don't do it, Suzie,' he said.

'What's going on?' said Drew, suddenly looking confused.

'Toby is my last troll,' said Suzie though gritted teeth. 'And now you've ruined my last revenge.'

'Mate. It was nothing,' said Toby, looking at Drew, terrified.

'What?' said Drew, staggering back. 'I don't understand.'

'He called me after we met at your engagement party,' said Suzie. 'He said he wanted to get together to do some early planning for his best man's speech, and he needed some good work stories so I wasn't to tell you. We met in a bar at happy hour and, well . . .'

'You slept together?' said Drew, incredulous.

'Mate, it was nothing, really,' protested Toby.

'But you were engaged then,' Drew said, aghast.

'It was like I said – you know, when we had our suit fitting. I just needed to get it out of my system. It didn't mean anything; I wasn't to know that this was going to happen.'

'It didn't mean anything?' screeched Suzie. 'You said you were going to break up with her but it was a lie. You never meant it, you just wanted to string me along for a bit longer.' She turned round and went to the edge of the dance floor to collect the suitcase she had left there. She dropped it with a bang at Toby's feet.

'See this suitcase,' she said, pointing at it. 'This is the suitcase I packed on the night you said you were going to leave Chloe. I was going to tell you that after all this time I'd never unpacked it. That I was still waiting for you. I wanted to freak you out to the point where you vowed never to stray again.'

There was silence now. The music had stopped in the absence of the DJ. Everyone was watching them.

'Did you know he was engaged?' asked Drew, staring at her in horror.

'No, of course I didn't. Not to start with. Not until he'd hooked me in. And then . . .' She trailed off, not knowing what to say.

Drew shook his head in despair.

'It was him that was engaged, not me,' she protested.

'No, no,' he said, staggering back and staring at her accusingly.

'What are you looking at me like that for? He's in the wrong, Drew, not me. Why aren't you having a go at him? Or is it that you've done the same thing so you have total sympathy? Is that it?'

Drew looked as though he was about to cry and he was breathing so hard it was as if someone had punched him in the stomach.

'No,' he said finally. 'I realised I didn't love Emily and I had to do something before I ruined her life. I was trying to do the right thing.'

'Oh really,' said Suzie sarcastically.

'Yes, really,' said Drew. He paused and looked at the floor. 'And I also realised that I had feelings for someone else.'

'You see,' she cried in triumph. 'You are such a cliché,

Drew. You slept with someone else and thought the grass might be greener. What more can I say?'

'I did not sleep with anyone.'

'Yeah, yeah, whatever you say. You can't tell me you didn't sample the pie before deciding to jump ship. You're a man, for God's sake, Drew. That's what men do.'

'It's not what I do!' shouted Drew.

'Well, we'll see, shall we? The truth will out when you turn up with some gormless twenty-year-old in a few weeks when you think it's a decent enough time after getting rid of Emily.'

'There is no gormless twenty-year-old,' said Drew angrily.

Suzie merely raised her eyebrows.

He stared at Suzie and the seconds ticked past as she stared defiantly back.

'Look at you,' he spat at her. 'You've got so caught up in all this Dear Suzie stuff you can't look at any man without contempt and without assuming the absolute worst, and yet . . .' He faltered, the tears now streaming down his face as he glanced from Toby to Suzie. 'And yet you, Suzie Miller, are certainly no Snow White,' he finished, sweeping past her and out into the night.

Toby ran after him and Suzie was left all alone,

clutching her shiny blue silk pouch in the middle of the dance floor whilst tiny specks of light glided silently around her.

Chapter 24

She trudged along the damp streets of Manchester, her silky yellow skirt soaking up the pavement grime, her suitcase squeaking behind her. She'd stood in the middle of the dance floor after Drew's departure and looked round as the entire office looked on in heavy silence. The revenge had been a disaster; there was no applause, just silent stares. No-one came over to help her as she struggled with her case, not even the women who'd she'd helped in the Ladies earlier that evening. The silence continued as she walked through the door and found herself alone on the streets after a works Christmas party. Somewhere no-one wanted to be.

How dare he, she kept asking herself. How dare he take it out on her and make her feel like she was a bad person, just because he'd screwed up his oh-so-perfect life? Who the hell did he think he was? She'd thought he was her friend but clearly he wasn't. He'd turned out to be a twat, just like the rest of them.

She turned up a garden path and stopped at the bright red door, then rang the doorbell, still muttering under her breath.

'All men are bastards,' she declared, shivering violently, as Jackie flung open her front door.

Jackie stared at her and shouted over her shoulder.

'Dave? What the hell did you put in those cocktails?'

'Why?'

'Because Snow White has just turned up on the doorstep.'

'Must be Christmas,' came the shout back. 'Bring her in. I've always fancied a threesome with Snow White.'

Jackie raised her eyebrows and motioned for Suzie to come in.

Dave was in the lounge head-banging to Deep Purple, clearly off his head.

'Snowy,' he cried, throwing his arms out. 'Santa obviously got my letter. The one I sent when I was twelve.'

'Shut it, Dave,' said Jackie. 'I think something has happened.'

'All men are bastards,' repeated Suzie, throwing herself down on the sofa and burying her head in her hands.

Jackie sat down next to her and put an arm around her. 'Have them dwarves been playing you up again, love?' she asked.

'Yes,' cried Suzie. 'I've had it up to here with bloody dwarves.'

'Oh no,' said Dave, 'I'm not having that in this house. You can come here quoting all the Dear Suzie claptrap you like but you leave them dwarves alone. Sound as a pound, they are.'

Suzie looked as if she might burst into tears.

'Ignore him,' said Jackie, rubbing Suzie's arm. 'I can't bear those bloody dwarves either. Especially Sleepy. Typical bloke with the old sleeping trick when there's work to be done. Lazy git.'

Suzie looked up at Jackie gratefully. A hint of a smile hovered on her lips.

'And as for that Doc,' continued Jackie. 'Pretends to know everything and actually it's all bullshit. He's making it all up.'

'You're right,' agreed Suzie. 'Doc is a complete bullshitter.'

'And Bashful, well, complete and utter fuck-up in all social situations. You can't take him anywhere.'

'Stop,' shouted Dave. 'This is wrong.' He disappeared off into the kitchen and returned with a dog-eared children's book.

'Here we go,' he said, flicking through a few pages. 'What about Sneezy?' he asked accusingly. 'I suppose you have something against Sneezy, do you?'

'Oh, he's the worst,' said Jackie. 'Permanent case of man flu, him. Not a thing wrong with him, just wants constant sympathy. Pathetic. Next?'

Dave stared at them, speechless.

'Dopey's just stupid,' said Suzie. 'He tries to be all cute but actually he's just thick, which is really irritating.'

'Happy,' exclaimed Dave, who had been quietly flicking through the book looking for the dwarf that was going to prove them wrong. 'Happy is not a bastard. How can you not love him?' He thrust a picture of the smiley cartoon character under their faces.

'He's only bloody Happy because he doesn't give a shit about anybody or anything but himself, and hasn't got a care in the bloody world. Selfish bastard,' declared Suzie.

Dave threw the book on the floor in frustration.

'So,' said Jackie. 'All men are bastards, including the seven dwarves. Has that made you feel better, Snow White?'

'Much better,' replied Suzie. She knew she'd been right to come here. Jackie always knew how to cheer her up.

'No, no, no, no, no, I can't have this,' Dave interrupted. He walked across the room to where a child's blackboard on an easel stood. He dragged it over to where Suzie and Jackie sat and picked up a piece of pink chalk.

'Right, ladies,' he said. 'We are going to make a list of all the men who are not bastards.'

'Why?' said Suzie and Jackie in unison.

'To prove the point to Dear Suzie here that all men are not bastards, okay?' Jackie and Suzie watched dubiously as Dave wrote MEN WHO ARE NOT BASTARDS across the top of the blackboard.

'Right, I'm sure there is at least one who instantly springs to mind,' said Dave, turning to look at them.

They stared back at him blankly.

'Me!' he shrieked. 'Come on, love, I did buy you that Deep Purple original.'

Jackie glanced at Suzie, who just shrugged.

'Go on then, you can go on the list,' she said.

'You're too kind, really,' said Dave, turning to write his name down. 'Now come on, let's have another one.'

Jackie flung her head back and screwed up her eyes in concentration. All was quiet until she flung herself forward. 'Barry,' she cried. 'He's okay.'

'Barry,' exclaimed Dave. 'Who the fuck's Barry?'

'Barry Obama, of course,' said Jackie.

'He's that chap who's taken over the offy, isn't he?' demanded Dave. 'The one who always looks at your tits whenever we go in. I'm gonna kill him.'

'No, that's not him. I mean the President of America. He seems like a nice guy.'

'It's Barack, you idiot,' said Dave. 'Barack Obama.'

'I know. I just think Barry suits him better.'

Dave stared at Jackie before sighing heavily and turning to write Mr Obama on the blackboard.

'Right,' he said, kneeling down and taking Suzie's hands gently. 'I want you to think of a man who isn't a bastard to put on this list. Come on, it will do you good.'

The silence stretched out until Dave made a suggestion.

'What about that bloke from work who's been helping you with your revenges? He must be alright. What's his name?'

To Suzie's surprise, tears sprang to her eyes. She screwed them up in an effort to avoid embarrassment.

'He just dumped his fiancée a few weeks before the wedding,' Jackie told Dave, shaking her head sadly. 'An utter wanker, hey, Suzie?'

'Totally and utterly,' muttered Suzie. 'Do you know what he had the nerve to say to me tonight? He told me that I was no Snow White. And after what he did to Emily. I just can't believe it.'

'Guilt,' said Jackie. 'He's obviously lashing out to make him feel better about what he's done.'

'Of course he is,' said Suzie angrily. 'All I was trying to do was complete my last revenge, just like I said I would. He's been so supportive. I can't believe he was so mean to me.'

'You were trying to do your last revenge at the office party?' asked Jackie. 'You never said.'

'Yeah.'

'So who was it?'

'Do you remember me telling you about that mate of Drew's, the DJ who turned out to be engaged?'

'Oh yeah. He said he loved you and was going to leave her.'

'Whoa there,' said Dave after a moment. 'My brain isn't keeping up with this one. Are you saying you slept with a mate of Drew's and he was engaged?'

'Yeah, but I didn't know to start with,' said Suzie.

'You wouldn't have done if you'd known, would you?' added Jackie.

'Oh no,' said Dave, wagging his finger. 'Extreme double standards, ladies.' He paused, swaying backwards slightly. 'You are telling me that Dear Suzie, *the* Dear Suzie who has been giving the male population extreme hell over the last few weeks, has actually done the dirty on her own sex and slept with another woman's man?'

Both Jackie and Suzie stared at Dave in silence.

'Dave, please do not interrupt. Suzie is telling us about her last revenge,' said Jackie, turning away from Dave to face Suzie. 'I don't understand. Why was this guy at your office party?'

'He was the DJ. Drew booked him cheap.'

'So come on then. Tell me all the gory details of the revenge,' said Jackie, rubbing her hands together in excitement.

'Well, you see me and Drew were on the dance floor at the end of the night because that was his Secret Santa present.'

'His what?' asked Dave.

'His Secret Santa,' repeated Suzie.

Dave looked between Suzie and Jackie, waiting for an explanation that didn't arrive.

'What, to have the last dance?' asked Jackie. 'Cheap or what.'

'No, actually.' Suzie shook her head, still confused as to what Drew's gift was all about. 'I didn't really understand it, to be honest, but he said something about trying to give me my hope back.'

'Right,' said Jackie, now also confused.

'Hope?' said Dave. 'What the fuck does that mean? Will someone tell me what the hell she's talking about?'

'I have no idea,' said Jackie. 'What the hell are you talking about, Suzie?'

Suzie reached into her bag and extracted the golden envelope, then handed the card to Jackie.

'Oh, I get it,' said Jackie after she'd read it. 'He's lost his fiancée and he's lonely, and it's Christmas, so he's preying on poor gullible women like you. I can't believe you actually danced with him.'

'I didn't actually dance with him, but Rick Astley was playing.'

'You mean "Never Gonna Give You Up"?' asked Jackie.

'Yep.'

'The song that you first snogged Patrick to?'

'Yep. Drew must have asked for it. Then he offered me a weak Cinzano.'

Both Jackie and Dave were now staring at her in amazement.

'Tell me you never used to drink Cinzano,' exclaimed Dave to Jackie. 'That is grounds for divorce. If I ever catch you . . .'

'Shut it, Dave,' shouted Jackie. 'I'm trying to think here. So what else did he do?'

'He just kept wittering on about this hope thing. Something about believing in love. I don't know, I can't really remember.' Suzie slumped back in the sofa.

Jackie and Dave stared at her.

'He inflicted Rick Astley on people who thought there were a good few decades between them and that mindless crap?' said Jackie, aghast.

'He went up to a bar and asked for Cinzano?' said Dave, totally horrified.

Suzie nodded.

'Wow,' was all Jackie could say.

Dave looked again from one to the other in total confusion.

'So why the hell did he do that?' he said eventually when neither of them offered him an explanation.

'Why do you think?' said Jackie.

'How the hell do I know? He wants to form a Rick Astley tribute band with her? Cinzano is the new bitter? He's a complete nutter?'

'No, you absolute idiot. Because he loves her, for God's sake,' said Jackie.

Suzie snapped her head round to stare at Jackie.

'Bloody hell,' breathed Dave.

'No,' said Suzie, leaping up. 'That's not it. He was just trying to prove to me you can give a decent Secret Santa gift or something. That's all.' She began pacing up and down.

'Oh Suzie,' said Jackie. 'No man on earth goes to all that trouble just to get a present right. He loves you. It's obvious.'

Suzie stopped dead in her tracks, the truth starting to dawn on her.

'He did say there was someone else,' she said slowly. 'That's why he broke it off with Emily. Oh my God!' she shrieked, dropping slowly to her knees, her head in her hands.

The only sound in the room now was Suzie breathing very heavily.

'So?' Dave finally dared to utter.

'What?' said Jackie before Suzie could speak.

'So what happened next?' Dave asked.

'I didn't get it,' moaned Suzie from behind her hands. 'I didn't see what he was getting at.'

'Well, that's understandable,' said Dave. 'Way too subtle if you ask me.'

Suzie threw her head up in the air, looking manic.

'I got distracted by Toby,' she continued. 'He was saying all this stuff and I was trying to shut him up so I could get on with my last revenge. Then Toby came over and it all came out about us sleeping together, and that's when Drew told me I was no Snow White . . .'

'I'm not bloody surprised,' exclaimed Dave. 'Dear, sanctimonious Suzie slept with his best mate who was engaged.'

'Dave,' Jackie said sharply. 'I think you're missing the point here. The point is that Drew is in love with Suzie. That is what we are dealing with.'

'No, incorrect,' said Dave. 'The point is that Drew

was in love with Suzie until he found out that she was a hypocrite. Drew was *so* in love with Suzie that he embarrassed himself totally by asking for Rick Astley and Cinzano on the same night, only to find out that she had slept with his best mate.'

Jackie and Suzie stared back at Dave.

'Oh, but it's fine, Suzie,' said Dave, throwing his hands up in the air. 'All men are bastards, right? You don't give a damn, right? Look at the list,' he said, spinning round and stabbing the blackboard behind him so hard it nearly fell over. 'Only me and the winner of the bloody Nobel Peace Prize are not bastards. So every other man must be, right?'

'Right,' she whispered.

'Except,' said Jackie quietly, 'you, Mr Obama and maybe the one that manages to turn Secret Santa, the stupidest invention in history, into something worth having. I don't think he's a bastard. I think he might just be a genius.'

Chapter 25

'*To my husband. There's no surprise that my work got better when I met you, because I never knew what it felt like for someone to have my back. So thank you . . .*'

Applause, applause, applause.

Cue picture of doting husband . . . NOT.

Suzie watched Sandra Bullock complete her moving tribute to her husband during her 2010 Golden Globe acceptance speech for the tenth time that morning on YouTube. She then clicked yet again on the headlines that emerged just a few short weeks later revealing Jesse James to be the biggest love rat in history. If ever you were going to convince yourself that happily ever after does not exist, then all you had to do was watch the queen of romantic comedy, whose life's work had been about showing millions of women that love does indeed conquer all, fall from a very great height at the hands of her Prince Charming. If Sandra Bullock does not live happily ever after then clearly happily ever after does not exist.

Suzie leapt up from her chair in front of her home computer and knelt down in front of the TV, pulling out the drawer containing all her old romcom DVDs. Why on earth had she kept these? she wondered to herself. They were all full of bullshit, with not a grain of reality between them.

'*You've Got Mail*,' she muttered under her breath, scrutinising the picture on the cover. 'He destroyed your business,' she declared to Meg Ryan, who was gazing adoringly into Tom Hanks' eyes. 'He is not a nice man, you idiot. What the hell do you think you are doing?' She flung the offending case at the waste-paper basket in the corner of the room, knocking it clean over.

'And as for you, Julia Roberts,' she said to the semi-clad picture on the front of a well-worn *Pretty Woman* case. 'He pays for prostitutes, you fool. Nothing good can ever come of a man who pays for sex. You are doomed.'

She picked up the next box. '*You had me at hello,*' she cried. 'Are you kidding me, Renée? A man says *hello* and all is forgiven? Not good enough, even if he is Tom Cruise,' she said flinging the copy of *Jerry Maguire* over her shoulder.

She was brought up short by the sight of her all-time favourite. She stared at the image of Meg Ryan and Billy Crystal walking easily through an autumnal Central Park on the cover of *When Harry Met Sally.*

'*And I love that you're the last person that I want to talk to before I go to sleep at night,*' Suzie muttered quietly to herself. '*And it's not because I'm lonely. And it's not because it's New Year's Eve. I came here tonight because when you realise that you want to spend the rest of your life with somebody, you want the rest of your life to start as soon as possible.*'

Unwelcome thoughts flooded her mind. She screamed in frustration. This is what happens, she told herself angrily. Just a few short hours ago she'd been on the biggest high she had ever experienced. Her career finally taking off, adored by the women she was helping with their men problems, she couldn't have been happier. And now here she was on a cold, grey Sunday morning feeling miserable, and surprise, surprise, it was all because of a man.

She got up and sat back at her computer once again. After a few clicks and some careful reading she felt better. Why hadn't she thought of this earlier? One look at the Dear Suzie section of the *Manchester Herald* website had extinguished any indecision she was harbouring over what she should do following the revelations from the previous evening.

As she scrolled through the emails flooding in and perused the chat forum she had set up to allow women to discuss their men problems, she felt a warm glow of reassurance that only pain could come of falling for a man.

She kept reading, feeling the ache somewhere deep behind her breastbone subside as she went through the tales of woe that were streaming in. Story after story of longed-for man proving to be a big disappointment.

Every click of the mouse calmed her further until she was forced to stop abruptly and re-read a problem sent in from someone signing themselves The Real Jay Kay.

The Real Jay Kay – I need to know how to help my friend. She is so anti-men that I have been forced to remove all kitchen knives from her home in case she goes on a penis-chopping frenzy. It appears a very

TRACY BLOOM

brave colleague of hers has fallen in love with her,
having recently broken off his engagement to his
fiancée with just weeks to go before the wedding.
What should I do? Give her her knives back or get her
a duster for her vagina?

Suzie was outraged. She would kill that Jackie. What
the hell did she think she was doing, putting her
problems up on the chat forum? At least she could rely
on her followers to back her up. She read on to see what
comments had been posted.

Ditched of Didsbury – Any man who asks a woman
to marry them and then gets cold feet is a pathetic
coward. Do not trust this man. Go with the knives
and lock up the dusters.

'Thank you,' said Suzie to the screen. The world
was starting to feel a little more sane. She continued
to read.

Salford Swinger – He's lonely. He's worried he's made
a mistake cancelling his wedding and he wants your
friend to take his mind off it. Tell her to use him for

sex and come and join the party! We have dusters, feather dusters!

Uuurgh, thought Suzie, shuddering.

Law Unto Herself – My fiancé just cancelled our wedding. I turned up at his office in my wedding dress to show him what he had thrown away. He was totally humiliated. I felt on top of the world. Whatever Dear Suzie tells you to do, listen, you will not regret it.

Suzie leapt back from the screen. Emily? What was she doing on her chat forum? Surely she had more important things to do, like getting women divorced or something. Scanning down she noticed that Jackie had posted again. Bloody hell, what beans was she spilling now?

The Real Jay Kay – Some good comments made, ladies. However, I feel I must give you more details. This guy ditched his fiancée before he made any approach to my friend. So he didn't take the coward's route, which is fair play in my book. And then he did the most romantic thing I have ever heard of. (I have to say I'm not really one for romance. My ex-husband bought me a bunch of carnations once and I hate carnations. I used his golf bag as a vase.) So this guy recreated the moment when my friend had her first kiss as a teenager at a local disco. Even down to the crap music and crap drinks. And he did this because she once told him it was the happiest time of her life. When she had hope that she might live happily ever after. He said he wanted to give her her hope back.

Suzie stared at the screen. There were no replies under Jackie's last posting. She must be following the chat in real time now.

'Come on, ladies,' she muttered. 'Cheesy, right? Truly desperate for sex? Sad loser? Come on, Emily, you give him hell.' What felt like an eternity ticked by as she waited for their verdict. Eventually responses started to appear on the screen.

Ditched of Didsbury – If she doesn't want him, can I have his number?

Salford Swinger – If I had him I would give up being a Swinger.

Law Unto Herself – My fiancé never did anything like that for me. If I ever find someone else I hope he loves me as much as that man must love your friend.

Suzie stared at the screen in amazement.

What were they all thinking? Had they learned nothing from her column over the last few weeks? Did they not realise that romance always starts like this, full of grand gestures and prolific promises? Did they not understand yet that all too soon it evaporates and all you're left with is crushing disappointment? Did they not know it was absolutely inevitable, even with a man like Drew? A man who she'd come to rely on so much recently. Who'd been the only person to care enough to tell her to stand up for herself with men in the first place. Who'd crucially told her he believed in her when her confidence had threatened to fail her with Alex and then with Patrick at the football stadium. The disappointment was still bound to come. Even with Drew, who'd gone so far as to lend her the shirt off his back to ensure that she triumphed. The powder-blue shirt that matched his eyes, which for some reason she had failed to return to him, preferring to hang it in her closet unwashed. Even with Drew, whose hand had clutched hers so hard after he'd split with Emily that it felt as though its imprint had remained on her fingers, making them glow and tingle. Even with Drew, who had left her feeling so bereft when his chair was empty all last week that she'd turned to talk to thin air every time she'd had something to say that she thought he might like to hear.

Even with Drew.

Or could it be apart from Drew?

She got up in a daze and went upstairs to retrieve his powder-blue shirt. She took it downstairs and went in search of her Secret Santa card, which had been chucked in the kitchen bin. Having removed a soggy teabag, she sat down at her computer clutching Drew's shirt and his gift in her hands.

'*Be on the dance floor below the glitter ball at midnight for your extra special delivery from Secret Santa,*' she read aloud, running her fingers over the words.

She put the card down and ran a Google search on the hotel they'd been at the night before. It didn't take her long to pull up their website and some overly flattering pictures of their Grand Ballroom. Her heart was suddenly beating fast as she scanned the room in cyberspace. There was no glitter ball in the Grand

Ballroom. She reached for her phone, fumbling as she tried to find a contact number.

'Majestic Hotel. Can I help you?' a voice replied after way too many rings.

'Do you have a glitter ball in your ballroom?' she blurted out.

'Excuse me?'

'Do you have a glitter ball in your ballroom?' she repeated urgently. Did this woman not realise how crucial this information could be?

'Er, no, madam, not usually, although a gentleman did have one installed last night for a special occasion, so it is possible if you'd like us to look into it for you?'

Suzie didn't hear the last part of her answer because she'd already put the phone down. Or rather, she'd dropped the phone on the floor, buried her head in Drew's shirt and wept until she could weep no more.

Chapter 26

It was the Monday, 22 December and she was wearing her favourite dress without tights, and six-inch heels. She had debated tights for a good hour that morning, trying the dress with and without them several times before finally deciding that she looked better without. The fact that she could no longer feel her toes as she pushed open the door of the *Manchester Herald* building barely registered. The only thing she was aware of that morning was her raw emotions, so utterly worn to shreds that she felt like she'd been on a coffee binge for the last twelve hours. The fact that she had indeed been on a coffee binge for the last twelve hours gave her a complete out of body experience as she watched herself slowly climb the stairs to the first floor where her desk was, next to Drew's. She paused again as she got to the top of the stairs, smoothed down her dress, rubbed her lips together to ensure maximum gloss coverage and painted a huge smile on her face.

The first sign that the morning could prove challenging came as she passed Clare on her way to the kitchen to get coffee. She paused to ask how her boyfriend was post the party but was greeted with a frosty glare followed by a pointed stare at the floor, avoiding all eye contact. After her initial shock Suzie carried on to her desk, determined to focus on the key task of the day.

She looked at the floor for the rest of her journey, unwilling to let any other distractions enter her mind as she approached Drew. Finally she saw the welcome sight of his waste-paper basket and allowed herself to raise her eyes, mentally repeating her carefully rehearsed first words.

'Drew, I am so sorry, I . . .' she blurted out until she clocked that his seat was empty.

Must be on a coffee run, she thought to herself. She sighed with relief. Time to gather herself.

After taking her coat off she sat down and nervously drummed her fingers on the desktop. What now? She was too wired even to attempt any work. She had to get this sorted before she could concentrate on anything ever again. She gazed at her desk, hoping for some kind of distraction, but the usual chaos urgently needing her attention only acted to further increase her impatience to see Drew. She looked at his desk and wondered at his organisational skills and capacity for neatness. It made her smile fondly, a reaction to thoughts of Drew she had slowly but surely woken up to over the last twenty-four hours. Twenty-four hours of watching the moment – the one in every romantic comedy when the couple fall in love.

As she'd watched, her heart had physically ached as she realised she wished with all her heart that she was Meg Ryan at the top of the Empire State Building when Tom Hanks arrives to start their life together. She realised for the first time that however happy she made herself getting her own back on the men who broke her heart, and however happy she made the women whose hearts she tried to mend, never in a million years could she make a woman as happy as that. But more than that, when she'd watched those films she'd realised that none of the heroes was a patch on Drew. None of them laughed at her jokes like he did, none of them believed in her like he did, none of them was her rock, none of them completed her – and every other cliché that exists in the world of love. Clichés that are irritating until you fall in love and then they become *your* clichés.

Of course, along with the realisation that Drew had given her her hope back came the knowledge that she had destroyed her own happy ending. Not just destroyed it, crushed it to death in the most horrific way possible. She'd spent a long time mourning, believing her life to be over. At the depths of her despair she'd found herself staring yet again at the image of Sandra Bullock on screen in *While You Were Sleeping* as she stood at the altar marrying the wrong brother. It was then that it struck her how stupid she was, and hope crept back. Happy endings don't just happen. There is always something that goes wrong, something that forces you to strive even harder to live your destiny. What would a happy ending be without the misery you have to experience as a prelude? She realised in her romcom-fuddled state that blowing off Drew's declaration of true love was merely the hurdle she had to overcome to prove that this was what she truly wanted. 'Thank you, Sandra,' she'd whispered. 'Thank you for reminding me.' Then she had stayed up all night preparing her speech,

331

preparing her outfit, preparing everything for the following morning when she would be able to reconcile with Drew and live happily ever after.

Still no Drew. It couldn't take this long to make coffee. Maybe he was out interviewing, which would be a disaster. She had so planned this moment that any blip was a cause for major upset. She leaned over to see if his computer screen was switched on so she could take a look at his calendar. Nothing happened when she moved the mouse. Nothing apart from her noticing that his Manchester City mug, containing his Manchester City pen and pencil set, was not perched on top of the hard drive as usual. Which was odd, because no-one was allowed to touch this small shrine.

Her hand flew to her mouth. She stood up so quickly that her chair tipped over behind her. She threw open his top drawer. Empty. His hanging file drawer. Empty. His drawer usually kept locked for fear of Suzie stealing his secret stash of gummy bears. Empty. The bears were gone. Which meant Drew was gone.

No, this could not be happening. Where the hell was he? What was going on?

She ran, as fast as she could in six-inch heels, up two flights of stairs and down a corridor until she got to the

Editor's door. It was closed but she didn't pause to knock, just flung it open, falling into the office completely breathless and having acquired a limp.

'Where is he?' she huffed, trying to control her breathing.

'Suzie,' exclaimed Gareth angrily. 'You cannot just come barging in here.'

'Where is he?' she repeated.

'I have no idea who you are talking about, but now you're here I want a word with you.'

'Where is he?' she said yet again, more desperately.

'Shut up and sit down,' said Gareth, looking very angry indeed.

She slumped in a chair and tried to get her breath back.

'So when were you going to tell me?' he asked.

'Tell you what?'

'That the *Mirror* have offered you a job.'

Mirror? Job? She couldn't even think about that now; she had much bigger things on her mind.

'I can't believe it, Suzie. I gave you such a great opportunity here with Dear Suzie, and you're going to throw it in my face and go and work for a competitor.'

Hang on a minute, she thought as Gareth's words sank in. Dear Suzie was all her idea and the *Manchester*

Herald was hardly competition to a national tabloid.

She opened her mouth to defend herself, but all that came out was her repeated plea for the whereabouts of her colleague.

'Drew?' he said, finally listening to her desperate request. 'You want to know where Drew is?' He laughed. 'He's gone, dear Suzie. And after the way you treated him on Saturday, I'm not surprised.'

'Gone where?' she asked, desperate now, feeling her future slipping through her fingers.

'I have no idea. He said he needed to get away. Get away from you, no doubt.' He stood and crossed his arms, relishing her anguish.

The tears started to fall then. Tears of exhaustion and extreme disappointment.

Eventually Gareth relented enough to hand her a tissue.

'Is he coming back?' she managed to sniff.

'Not sure,' said Gareth. 'He said he'd call in the new year. So thanks to you, dear Suzie, it looks like I've also lost my best reporter.'

She buried her head in her tissue, unable to meet his eyes. The room was quiet for a few moments as she sat reeling from the news, feeling as though she'd been stabbed in the heart with a blunt knife. Then Gareth spoke up and pushed the knife in even deeper.

'I'll print the story,' he said.

'What story?'

'The story of how Dear Suzie is not the female warrior she has pretended to be. How she stole another woman's fiancée and broke the kindest, most romantic man in the world. I'll print that story if you go to the *Mirror* and then Dear Suzie will be no more, because you'll never get another woman to trust you again.'

Suzie drew a sharp breath. How could he do such a thing to her? How could he do it to Drew?

'You are evil,' she breathed.

'I think you'll find that you're no Snow White yourself,' he replied with a smug grin.

She stared at him. She had started the day so full of hope and now Drew was gone and her boss was threatening to destroy her career.

Chapter 27

'What if I stay?' she asked, bursting back into Gareth's office an hour later. His threat and the news of Drew's disappearance had caused a cold hand of panic to clutch at her heart and she'd started to hyperventilate. Gareth calmly called for a first-aider and Diane came to the rescue, paper bag in hand, and led her down to the canteen, Suzie bawling her eyes out between desperate gasps for breath. Three bags later and a whisky miniature that Di kept for emergencies and she was starting to breathe normally. Sitting there in a daze whilst Di droned on about the over-fifties speed dating event she'd been to the previous week, a sense of determination started to override the panic. She'd cast herself as a romantic heroine now and she couldn't allow the disappearance of her leading man and the threats of the Evil Baron Editor to get in her way. She would get that happy ending if it killed her.

'Front half of the paper, full page, picture with byline,' Gareth replied without batting an eye when she burst into his office for the second time.

'Full editorial control,' she barked back.

'Yeah, yeah, whatever,' he said, waving his hand dismissively.

'In writing, in the hour, or else I walk,' she said, turning to leave.

'You got it,' said Gareth smugly. 'You won't regret it,' he shouted after her as she strode down the corridor.

'I won't, you might,' she muttered to herself as she dashed down the stairs to start work on her column immediately. She had no time to lose.

Chapter 28

'I am not printing this crap,' said Gareth the following day, slamming the copy for her latest column down on her desk.

'It's not crap,' said Suzie defiantly.

'No, you're right. It's actually pathetic drivel. Where's the hate? Where's the vitriol? Where's the blunt honesty?' He thumped his hand on the desk at the end of each sentence.

'This is what women really want,' said Suzie calmly.

'I don't give a shit what women really want,' said Gareth, turning red. 'I want Dear Suzie back, so you'd better start writing now.'

'Giving a shit about what women really want is what made the column so successful in the first place. *Now* I am telling you this is what women really, really want.'

'So you've changed your mind about what women want, is that what you're telling me?'

'Precisely.'

'Bloody women!' shouted Gareth, putting his head in his hands.

'And I'd like to point out that my new contract says I have full editorial control,' said Suzie, showing him where that particular clause had been highlighted in pink.

'Full editorial control to be as vicious as you have been in the past, not to submit this nonsense,' he said.

'Gareth,' she said calmly, 'this column will have the best response yet, believe me. This is going to work.'

'It had better, or your job is on the line, young lady,' he said, strutting away.

Suzie sat back and picked up the sheets of paper that Gareth had thrown on her desk. Chewing her lip, she read her copy for the millionth time. It certainly had better work, or *everything* was on the line.

Dear Readers,

I would like to end this year with my official Christmas message, knowing that it is crazy season out there when it comes to affairs of the heart.

Looking for love is a lot like Christmas. Endless build-up and huge expectations which inevitably lead to disappointment.

And yet every time we expect it to be different. Every time we hope and dream that this will be the one that lives up to the fairy tale.

For that reason I have decided that there will be no more Dear Suzie column as you know it.

Why? Because the last thing I want is for you to stop looking forward to Christmas. If that happens, you have lost all hope in the joy that life can bring. I don't know about you, but that is not someone who I want to spend time with.

And I have come to realise that I don't want you to stop looking forward to love. Dear Suzie has become so focused on the agony of failed love and how to fight that battle that it has forgotten the fundamental reason why you have all written those painful letters in the first place.

Because you all know that the biggest joy we can

*experience is to love and be loved, and the active
pursuit of that is our most important goal in life.*

*And so in future this column will focus on how to
find true love, not how to beat someone up who failed
to love you back. As satisfying as revenge can be, it
will never make you as happy as finding someone to
love and to love you. After all, there are a million love
songs but hardly any are written about revenge.*

*I realise that this may throw you into a blind panic
as to how you're going to cope, knowing that putting
yourself out there to find love doesn't happen without
agony, pain and disappointment. So here is my first
piece of advice to help you through the inevitable
torture.*

Just follow this basic rule.

*Look for your reflection. Just look into his eyes and
see what he sees. Honestly and truthfully. If you see
yourself in a way that you want to be seen, in a way
that makes you look your best, then you know it's
right. You have the makings of a happy relationship.*

*If the reflection you see is bad, when you realise in
your heart of hearts he doesn't see you how you want
to be seen, then walk away. Leave before he puts you
in agony, because for sure he will. Let him be the first*

to know he's just not worth it before you get anywhere near the level of needing revenge. Why waste your time? Go and search somewhere else for your best reflection.

Merry Christmas,

Suzie.

Suzie gulped before she carried on reading. She had written one other letter for the special Christmas edition and this was the one that really mattered. It was a risk, she knew, but she didn't know what else to do.

To whom it concerns

I saw my reflection. Just for a moment, in your eyes, on that dance floor under the glitter ball. And then it was gone. Ruined by my stupidity, by my selfishness, and by my self-importance.

I would do anything to see that reflection again. I know you are not a man on the verge of disappointing me. Quite the opposite. All you have done is give me confidence and self-esteem, while all I have done is be a big disappointment to you. Exactly what I have accused every man on the planet of being.

I realise now that we are all human and that we

all make mistakes. Maybe some mistakes do deserve to be punished, but now I realise everyone deserves the chance to put it right. And I want to put it right with you. Because I need to see that reflection again. And I need you to see your reflection in my eyes, because the way I see it, it's outstanding.

Please give me the chance to put it right. Please come back. I want the happily ever after and I want it with you, just like Harry and Sally.

You'll know where to find me.

Suzie

Chapter 29

New Year's Eve – 8.00 p.m.

Jackie poured a bottle of ouzo into the large bowl in front of her.

'When did you last go to Greece?' asked Suzie.

'It was with you, you muppet,' she replied. 'You remember, to celebrate my divorce. We lived on this stuff.'

'But that must be nearly ten years ago.'

'Yeah.'

'Won't it taste bad?'

'Probably. But how else do you get rid of the disgusting muck you bring back from holiday? I've got some Limoncello to put in it. That'll make it taste better.'

'I think I'll stick to wine,' said Suzie, pulling a face.

'Should you be drinking? You don't want to be pissed when he comes, do you?'

'When who comes?' asked Dave, coming over and dipping a plastic cup into Jackie's deadly cocktail.

'Drew,' said Jackie, reaching for the ginger ale.

Dave stopped mid-sip. 'The guy whose best mate you slept with?' he asked, totally aghast. 'I can't believe he's even talking to you.'

'He isn't yet,' said Suzie.

'But you've invited him tonight?' Dave pressed.

'Not exactly,' said Suzie, looking embarrassed.

Dave drained his plastic cup, coughed, and then gripped the edge of the kitchen counter as if to brace himself.

'So tell me, dear Suzie, how does he know to come if you haven't exactly asked him?'

'I wrote him a letter.'

'And you invited him in this letter?'

Suzie reached for a cup, dipped it in the punch, then downed it in one.

'No, I just hinted.' She stared at Dave defiantly.

'You hinted?'

'Yep.'

'Would you please tell me how you merely hinted asking someone to a New Year's Eve party?'

'I said that I wanted to live happily ever after, just like in the film *When Harry Met Sally*.'

'And that is a request for his company at tonight's party in what way?' asked Dave, his eyebrows shooting upwards.

'Oh Dave, for goodness' sake, have you no romantic bone in your body?' interrupted Jackie in frustration. 'Everyone knows that Harry and Sally get together on New Year's Eve.'

Dave stared at Jackie with a deeply furrowed brow.

'He won't get it,' he said finally. 'This is some kind of weird trick that you women dream up to get what you want and then you're pissed off when it doesn't happen. He's a man. He won't get it.'

'You're right,' said Suzie quietly. 'He is a man. He's a man who went to the trouble of trying to give me my hope back by recreating my teenage years. He put up a glitter ball, he played Rick Astley and drank weak Cinzano,' she said, almost crying now. 'If he wants to get it, he'll get it.' She grabbed a glass of punch and headed towards the door to the back garden to calm down.

9.00 p.m.

Suzie tried very hard not to keep looking up every time the door went, but it was impossible. Every time the cheerful chime of Rudolph the Red-Nosed Reindeer rang out from Dave's seasonal doorbell her heart leapt into her mouth. Time after time it fell back into her sparkly silver slingbacks as yet another batch of Jackie and Dave's relatives, friends and colleagues trooped in.

She had also realised as she surveyed the swelling numbers of the party that somehow in the last year she had crossed a threshold. Last year, the New Year's Eve party she had attended had been a strictly adults-only affair. Black tie, a band and tasteful black and silver balloons. This year she'd been thrust into the Wacky Warehouse World of New Year's Eve. Toddlers did their best to trip her up whilst chasing Bob the Builder balloons round and round the living room. Parents were dealing with their booze-drinking teenagers by getting pissed. On her way back from the bathroom upstairs she had caught a young boy and girl playing hide and seek under the coats on Jackie's bed. It felt like only yesterday when it would have been her on that bed at a party, getting groped no doubt by some drunken male. How had she ended up here – the lone single female at a family party on New Year's Eve? The spinster. She hurried downstairs to grab another drink and sit outside the front door until Drew arrived.

10.00 p.m.

'He's not coming!' shrieked Suzie.

'What?' yelled Jackie over the din of some unrecognisable music that the teenagers in attendance had put on.

'I said he's not coming,' Suzie repeated desperately.

Jackie grabbed both her shoulders.

'He'll come,' she said firmly.

'Prince Harry not here yet then?' shouted Dave over Jackie's shoulder.

'I was just telling her that he will come,' said Jackie. 'You tell her, Dave. He will come, won't he? You don't go to the trouble that he did and not give her a chance.'

'He's not coming,' said Dave. 'Get used to it.'

'What am I going to do?' wailed Suzie, burying her head in Jackie's shoulder. 'I've ruined everything.'

'Ignore him for a start,' said Jackie, glaring at Dave.

'I'm just giving her the blunt truth, sweetheart,' said Dave. 'Suzie believes in blunt truth, don't you?' he continued.

Suzie wailed her response.

'That man is a pure romantic, Dave Smith,' said Jackie. 'He will come. And when he does, take note, because you could learn a thing or two off him.'

'If he comes, he's soft as shit,' said Dave under his breath.

'Dave!' exploded Jackie. 'I will not have you swearing in front of the children. Now stop being such a twat.'

'He's not coming,' shouted Dave.

'He is,' shouted Jackie.

'He isn't!'

'Is!'

'Isn't!'

'You're a wanker,' declared Jackie.

'And you are a stupid cow,' replied Dave just as the track that they'd been shouting over finished and all went quiet.

The throng of kids turned to stare at the feuding couple whilst Suzie fled to get another drink and calm down outside.

11.00 p.m.

'He's coming!' shrieked Suzie, tapping Jackie furiously on the shoulder.

'What, where?' Jackie released her lips from a passionate smooch with her husband in the middle of the makeshift dance floor in the living room.

'He's coming,' Suzie grinned, embracing both Jackie and Dave in her slightly drunken excitement. 'But he's not going to get here until midnight, is he? Just like Harry. Harry turns up at midnight. I'm stupid. I've been watching the door all night and actually he'll turn up just as the clock strikes, like in the film.'

'Of course he will,' said Jackie, smiling. 'Won't he, Dave?'

Dave grinned back, the grin of a truly drunken man in the arms of his loved one.

'Of course he will,' he repeated, pulling his wife back towards him.

Just Past Midnight, New Year's Eve

Suzie stared out into the night until she couldn't see. Her vision went blurred and she realised she had steamed up the double glazing with her tears.

'He didn't come,' she muttered over and over to herself. She looked at the two glasses she had carefully filled with champagne and balanced on the window sill in preparation for celebration and realised how stupid she was. Of course he hadn't come. He was never going to come. She'd really disappointed him and she'd expected him to get over it just like that. She'd hoped he would understand that she'd made a mistake and forgive her. But she'd spent weeks telling her readers not to forgive but to punish, and punish hard. How could she expect Drew not to punish her? How could she even dream that not only would he forgive her but that they would both live happily ever after? She was stupid and deserved to be alone at the time of year when it hurt the most.

Eventually she decided she must tear her eyes away from the garden path, but she didn't think she could face what was going on behind her. She fully expected to be confronted by a sea of loved-up couples celebrating the new year with passion, fuelled by hope for the year to come and too many of Jackie's punches.

She turned around slowly and felt a curious sense of relief as she took in the only other occupants of the front room. A small swarm of children huddled in the dark watching the Cartoon Network on the TV, overactive, over-cheerful, over-colourful cartoon characters reflected on their exhausted faces.

She felt her heart suddenly soar at frightening speed.

Maybe her watch was wrong. Perhaps it wasn't midnight after all. Of course, that was it. She hadn't heard a hint of 'Auld Lang Syne' yet. She looked around desperately for a clock to confirm her assumption but there was none to be found. She bent over and grabbed the remote control out of a half-asleep toddler's hand and started flicking randomly between channels. She just needed to see Jools Holland and then everything would be alright. She'd know what time it was then.

Just as the sight of champagne-swigging, streamer-festooned celebrities filled the screen she felt a sharp pain in her left ankle and let out a magnificent scream. A boy of about seven stood in front of her.

'Give it back or I'll tell her to bite the other one,' he demanded, nodding at the cute little girl in a reindeer outfit with the sharp teeth.

Petrified, she dropped the remote control and limped away into the kitchen. Things were not going to plan. In fact, things must be way out of control if your first bodily contact of the new year was a toddler sinking her teeth into your leg.

She looked around desperately for Jackie. She needed to see at least one person who loved her, someone to make her feel minutely better than she did right at this moment. Jackie was nowhere to be seen in the kitchen so she made her way upstairs, thinking that she must finally be putting one of her brood to bed. The children's rooms were empty but she eventually found Jackie with Dave, scrambling under the pile of coats on their bed in a state of semi-undress.

Jackie peered up over a dodgy sheepskin when she heard the door open.

'Did he come?' she shrieked.

Dave's rosy cheeks appeared next to her in a flash and he looked at a downcast Suzie.

'Of course he bloody didn't,' he said. 'Now if anybody is going to come it's me, so can we drop all this romance malarkey and just get on with it?' He pulled Jackie back down.

Suzie felt her bottom lip start to tremble. She made a lunge for her red wool coat and fled, hearing Jackie shouting after her to come back. She didn't breathe until she was outside and had slammed the front door shut behind her. Then she collapsed onto Jackie and Dave's front doorstep at precisely eleven minutes past midnight on New Year's Eve and wept.

Chapter 30

She had no idea what time it was when she started to walk home. She couldn't bear to look at her watch again. In fact she couldn't look at her watch at all, because at some point she had taken it off and thrown it into the blackness in despair.

All she could hear was the steady tap of her shoes and the eerie sound that drizzle makes when it is being whipped around by the wind. Her hair was plastered to her face and she knew it must be cold but she couldn't feel a thing. Nothing.

She couldn't feel her feet, which was strange. Like she was floating on air. This would usually be the walk of pain, having had a night of full-on dancing in uncomfortable shoes, every step accompanied by a wince. Now she couldn't feel her body. She knew she wasn't numbed by alcohol as she had stopped drinking at eleven o'clock in order to be fully with it by midnight. But the weirdest, perhaps scariest thing was that she couldn't feel fear. Normally if she was walking the streets of Manchester alone after midnight she would be jumping at every shadow, convinced she was about to be attacked. But tonight she didn't care. No-one else was bothered whether she got home safely or not, so why should she care? This thought added further tears to mingle with the drizzle drenching her face.

As she turned the corner into her street she slowed down to a dawdle. She couldn't face the thought of her chilly, dark and empty flat and what arriving there alone would do to her already distraught mood. She couldn't bear to see the state she had left her bathroom in because she knew it was the perfect picture of the hope she'd felt at the start of the evening. Make-up, hair products, perfumes and moisturisers were strewn everywhere – the essential tools required to herald the start of a new relationship.

But most heartbreaking of all would be to see her

355

bedroom. Cleaned to within an inch of its life, fresh sheets, mood lighting and music at the ready, it was a room waiting for something significant to happen. Now it would be an unwelcome reminder of how alone she truly was.

Just yards from her front door she stopped in her tracks. That's all I need, she thought as she tugged unsuccessfully at her heel, caught firmly in a crack in the pavement. It would not budge so she was forced to step out of her shoe and feel the unpleasant sensation of grubby, wet pavement seep through her tights onto freezing toes. As she bent over and pulled hard at the shoe she became aware of heavy footsteps running towards her and finally her survival instincts started to kick in. This is it, she thought, panicking. This is the moment that I die. She yanked furiously at the shoe, mentally preparing where on the body of her attacker she should stab with her stiletto first.

Then the footsteps stopped and she could hear heavy breathing above her.

'Let me get that,' said a voice.

Just at that moment the shoe freed itself and Suzie stumbled back, falling onto the pavement.

'Leave me alone,' she shouted, brandishing the shoe.

'Leave me alone or you'll get this in the bollocks.'

'Charming,' said Drew, holding his hand out to help her up.

'Drew!' she yelped. She stared up at him as the filthy wet pavement seeped through her dress.

'Are you okay?' he asked, pulling her up. 'I didn't mean to frighten you.'

She continued to stare back at him, trying to process the stream of thoughts and emotions running through her head.

'What are you doing here?' she finally managed to ask.

'Well,' he said. 'After multiple viewings of *When Harry Met Sally* and consultations with several romance-obsessed females I finally worked out what you meant in your letter. I'm assuming you wanted me to come and meet you at midnight at Jackie's party, right?'

Suzie nodded silently, not trusting herself to speak.

'Only I don't know where Jackie lives, do I, you muppet?'

She stared back at Drew, dumbstruck. How could she have forgotten something as basic as that?

'So I thought I'd just wait for you here.'

There was an awkward silence until Suzie finally managed to speak.

'Why?' she asked shyly.

'Because you asked me to,' Drew replied.

'I know, but really why?' she asked again. Come on, she thought. Put me out of my misery. Tell me this is the start of us.

'Really why?' he asked, looking confused.

'Yeah, really why?'

'Is this one of those weird subtle things that I have to decipher, because I tell you what, we're going to need a translator.'

'Shall we start again?' she asked.

'Yes, please,' he replied.

'I'm so sorry,' she gushed, unable to stop the flow of tears. 'For what I did. I was so in the wrong. Can you forgive me?' She looked up at him pleadingly.

He didn't say anything for a moment, then he pulled her towards him.

'I'm not sure,' he said, looking into her eyes. 'I need to look at you first. Really look at you. I need to see what my reflection looks like.'

She gulped as she stared up into his eyes. Her friend Drew. Her soulmate Drew. She saw him clearly for the very first time – as the person she wanted to spend the rest of her life with.

'How does it look?' she asked finally, unable to bear the suspense.

'I like it,' he said, smiling. 'I like it very much. I think you take at least ten pounds off me.'

She threw her head back and laughed – the laugh of a woman who had achieved the greatest joy in life. To love and be loved.

'Just one more thing,' said Drew when she'd got herself back under control. 'If you ever make me watch *When Harry Met Sally* again it's over.'

'I don't need to watch it again,' she said. 'I've got my own happily ever after standing right in front of me. Well, almost happily ever after.' She put her arms around his neck and pulled him towards her for their first kiss, at precisely fifty-seven minutes past midnight on New Year's Eve.

Acknowledgements

Firstly I would like to say that this book was *not* inspired by the men in my life. Most of the men I know are brilliant. But there's always the odd one or two, isn't there?

Big thanks to my friend Helen for her down-to-earth wit which has helped me look funny in this book, and to Gemma, whose honest support is so treasured.

For technical advice I must thank Marc and Bruce on the football front, whilst Mum, Dad, Helen, Andrew, Gillian, Chris, David, and Gillian and Chris in New Zealand offer family sustenance that I simply could not cope without.

Many thanks must also go to Araminta Whitley and

Peta Nightingale at the LAW agency for their continued support. We've been there and back and up and down quite literally. I'm glad I've not been doing it alone. Jenny Geras, Selina Walker and the rest of the team at Arrow have welcomed me in and allowed me to share my thoughts as well as ask lots of questions. So much appreciated as well as all their hard work in getting me out there. Speaking of which, I must mention the book bloggers whose enthusiasm for books and willingness to share their joy with the world never fails to astound me, and I thank you all for the support you have given my novels.

Thanks and praise to The One Off, a design agency based in Derbyshire, who inspired the book cover. I have no doubt of the great contribution they have made to my success.

And finally to you readers. Thanks a million for making it possible for me to continue to write. A dream come true, for which I'm eternally grateful.

JOIN
TRACY BLOOM
ONLINE

www.tracybloom.com

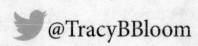 @TracyBBloom

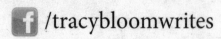 /tracybloomwrites